Chapter 1

"It's hard to come by jobs these days," said Benito, his wife and two kids at his side. With the construction business coming to a halt, he had been forced to roam the streets, looking for garbage of all kinds, just to turn over for a little cash. The fear of being picked up by the cops was constant. His brother had come to him with a job for his wife. He felt wrong about it, deep down...but now the situation was getting desperate. Benito knew they needed to make some money, or they would face having to live on the streets; and even worse, that would put them at higher risk for being deported back to Mexico. Their landlord had been sympathetic, but his patience was about to run out. Soon, action would be taken and the authorities involved. Benito just couldn't let that happen.

Benito and his wife Margarita lived in an old wood plank house that had been minimally restored after the flooding of Hurricane Katrina. The neighborhood was mostly black; punctuated by a few Vietnamese families who dabbled in the fishing business. Overall, despite its poverty, the neighborhood was a pleasant and relatively safe place to be; close to the beach and full of greenery. Benito had moved his family from Nogales, Mexico to Biloxi, Mississippi, to escape the growing threat of the Mexican drug gangs. He had worked on the post-Katrina reconstruction of the coast, when jobs had been downright easy to come by for a hard-working, skilled stucco worker like himself. But the short-lived boom had been just that: short-lived.

Right after the storm, there had been a number of exciting proposals, made by some of the most talented architects in the country. However, it soon became apparent that local politics weren't going to allow for much progress at all. It seemed the good of the few would once again prevail over the good of the majority. One of the main architects involved in the restoration project had quit out of sheer frustration; due to some of the beachfront residents who, in his words, wanted nothing more than to sit on their porches and watch their slaves do the work, while actively blocking any chance of achieving a progressive and modern urban planning for the reconstruction of the beachfront. Gone were the dreams of creating little communities with interesting buildings; making the area appealing to new investors, who would appreciate it for its natural beauty. Instead, ugly beach-front roads, shabby food chains, pawn shops and the many vacant concrete slabs were all back.

Benito's brother, Heraldo, had done well financially. He lived right off of St. Charles Avenue on a private street in New Orleans, in what could best be described as an antebellum mansion. In six short years, he had managed to become the number one supplier of narcotics in the greater New Orleans area, with franchises in the Northeast as well. In that short period of time, he had virtually eliminated the competition and had established himself as the only dealer of one of the largest Mexican cartels. All of this, while successfully remaining below the radar of an overburdened and depressed local police force; not that hard to do since New Orleans always managed to stay way up there in terms of daily murders, even with the decreased population due to the mass exodus caused by Katrina. But, Heraldo was a restless man and the comfortable, cushy life was getting to him. Now that he was the top fish, he no longer had to kill and intimidate to survive. He had a firm full of lawyers and an army full of thugs to do the dirty work for him.

It was early on a Monday morning in mid-July, already hot and muggy, when a team of five customs agents burst through Benito's front door. He was still asleep in bed when one of the agents grabbed him, turned him over roughly and slapped the handcuffs on him. Benito's first concern was for his wife and kids; who didn't appear to be anywhere around. Suddenly, his wife's scream sent instant chills up his spine. Two of the officers jerked him off the bed and dragged him to a small, windowless room in the center of the house. There before him was his wife on the floor; held down by a hefty white male cop. Two others were taking turns raping her. In a split second, Benito exploded into a violent fit of rage, only to be brought to his knees by a severe blow to his stomach, inflicted by a heavy metal pipe. Blood oozed from his mouth within seconds and he concentrated the little strength he had left on staying awake. One of the law men, whom the others called Johnny, was saying something about keeping her alive. He wanted to do her in the ass. "Save it for me," he said to the other man. Benito lay still, listening as his wife's screams turned to pitiful moans. After the men had all taken turns violating her, Benito squeezed his eyes shut as he listened to Johnny strangle her; with the garrote they had used to keep her from screaming. Benito was bleeding profusely from his mouth; no doubt the blow had ruptured some vital internal organ. One way or the other, he knew he was a dead man.

The man named Johnny held up his cell phone and took a couple of pictures of the scene. Then he took the handcuffs off of Benito. In the meantime, one of the men opened a large black bag, containing several gallons of gasoline, packages of nasal decongestant and a few drug-making utensils; all of which he dumped onto the floor. The men were done. The children had been chloroformed in their sleep and their parents were dead...or at least were about to be. One of the men quickly disconnected the gas range in the kitchen as they all left, leaving a candle burning in the room.

The driver smirked as he glanced into the rearview mirror, causing the others to turn and look. The car sped up the ramp of the interstate, leaving the casino area of Biloxi behind. A string of black smoke rose behind them; the result of yet another day in the lives of corrupt customs agents.

By the time the fire trucks made it to the burning shack, all that was left was a rough outline of the frame. The roof had collapsed and the remaining walls were ready to keel over. There wasn't much worth saving, but hoses were pulled out anyway and water sprayed on the debris, like flower petals on a coffin; a gesture for the living, but pointless to the dead. The incident made the local news. Not that much happened in the community and a fire always sold papers. "Crack house goes up in flames: four dead," it read. No details were given regarding what caused the fire, but the article pointed out the drug-making paraphernalia that had been found in the ashes. So, deductions were obvious. There was no mention of arson as the probable cause.

It was two days before Heraldo learned his brother had perished in a fire. Not from the authorities of course, since as a general rule, illegal aliens didn't leave addresses of next of kin on file. The letter came in the mail, with pictures. The warning was clear: get the fuck out or you're next. Heraldo hadn't been close to his brother; but still, his death was a shock. Benito had always been the square one; trying to do good for his little family and never getting involved in any kind of business that could endanger himself or his loved ones. Hot tears burned Heraldo's eyes. He felt a rage and powerlessness that he hadn't experienced since childhood; a rage that had last overtaken him when a local gang member back in Mexico had raped his sister and left her for dead. Thankfully, Heraldo had found her in time, on the side of a back road next to a garbage dump. Back then, revenge had been all that Heraldo cared about; and it had been swift and mercilessly brutal. When Heraldo had cornered the scum, the violence had come surprisingly easy to him. Heraldo had made the man pay for his sins, by eviscerating him with a box cutter and cutting off his genitals. He had felt nothing but euphoria as he had stuffed the genitals into the man's mouth. Little did he know, his actions that day would lead him into a life of crime and violence, from which there would be no turning back.

A good bit of Heraldo's current business was legit. He took great care to avoid any association with organized crime of any kind. He was quite savvy and no one could deny that he had the kind of charisma that made him the center of attention at any party, or anywhere else for that matter. Lately, he had made some substantial investments into the blooming Louisiana film industry, by financing several new projects depicting local people in their own elements. His film investments had started to pay off and he was beginning to think that he could soon give up his less desirable sources of income to become a full-ledged movie producer; not bad for a poor kid from Los Nogales.

But now...a giant hand from hell was pulling him back into the reality of his dark world. Once again, he would have to deal with his demons. His wife Maria walked into the room and instantly took notice of his tense expression.

"What's wrong?" she asked with concern. "What's going on?"

Heraldo answered without looking at her. "My brother is dead…his family is all dead; burned in their house in Biloxi."

Maria's mouth dropped open slightly. She didn't know how to respond. She had never seen Heraldo like this; cold and distant, an invisible wall separating him from her. She sensed that no words could appease him, so she walked slowly towards him. As she neared, he looked at her and she held out her arms, her eyes pleading with him to let her comfort him. He allowed her to take him in her arms. His body was tense, as if all of his muscles were firing at the same time. She felt powerless as she held him. Heraldo shut his eyes tightly and for the first time in his life, came close to openly shedding tears. But he didn't. He couldn't allow himself to be weak.

Heraldo knew he had lucked out with Maria. They had met at one of the producer's parties. She was an aspiring actress and had introduced herself to him. From that point on, the two had been an item. She was a beautiful woman: a light-skinned Creole with an hourglass figure and legs for miles. She made Heraldo the envy of every Latin male; every male for that matter. Their lovemaking had started out passionate and relentless and had never lessened. Heraldo, who had once been a ladies' man, was now truly in love for the first time in his life. He couldn't bear the thought of losing this extraordinary woman; another reason why he knew his next move had to be well-thought out.

Heraldo knew calling the cops was out of the question. He would have to find out what had happened at the scene from other sources. He thought furiously as he stood there in the arms of his wife, her hand slowly tracing his back. Finally, he slipped out of his trance.

"Maria, I think my brother and his family..." he paused as he eased her away from him and looked her in the eye, his hands on her shoulders. "I think they were all murdered. They say drugs were found on the premises. My brother didn't have anything to do with drugs." He sighed and furrowed his brow before going on. "I don't think the cops will do anything with this. They were illegal. I don't even think the cops know who my brother or his family are...well, were."

"What about a funeral?" Maria couldn't imagine not being able to have a funeral for her husband's family members. "I can have someone get in touch with the authorities and claim the bodies. We can have them transferred to a New Orleans' funeral home."

As expected, with the victims burned to a crisp, not much further had happened with the crime scene. The cause of death had been ruled accidental; caused by a fire that had resulted from the manufacturing of crystal meth. That wasn't uncommon in the area, so nothing warranted any further investigation. The funeral was private and unpublicized. Heraldo preferred it that way. The bodies were cremated and the ashes would be scattered at a later date back in Benito's birth place: Nogales, Mexico.

It was about ten in the morning when Gaspard Bourgeois, a private investigator in Gulfport, MS, got a phone call from Heraldo. Heraldo had used Bourgeois in the past and he had proven to be efficient and discreet. Bourgeois was about sixty, a retired contractor from New Orleans. He had become a private investigator after the real estate market had collapsed; a job he truly enjoyed and was luckily, really good at. Heraldo briefed the man on the situation and Bourgeois assured him that he would find out who the culprit was. Bourgeois liked working for Heraldo; he paid very well and his jobs were a cut above the usual cheating spouses he had to contend with.

The last job from Heraldo had paid twenty thousand dollars. He had chased down and apprehended some gambling addict in one of the local casinos. What had happened to the poor slob after he turned him in to Heraldo's men; Bourgeois didn't know for sure. But, that was none of his business, as long as he got paid.

The day was sunny and unusually dry. A front from the north had managed to make it all the way down. Although it wasn't exactly cold; a temperature in the low eighties matched with low humidity felt great to the hefty two hundred and thirty pound Bourgeois. Unfortunately, since his retirement, he had been putting on the pounds; eating out all the time just did that to people. He thought often about starting an exercise routine. What if he had to actually chase someone, or worse yet, what if he got into a fight? But those thoughts usually faded away as his appetite grew. Driving down the beach from Gulfport to Biloxi, he couldn't help but notice that even after almost eight years, many of the houses that had been leveled or gutted by the hurricane had not been rebuilt. Lots remained vacant; some with only the stony remnants of stairs or slabs nestled among overgrown grass and shrubs. It was hard to imagine what had been there before, as if it had all been erased and overtaken by nature's wrath; just like the bloody Mayans.

A solid ten miles away in the distance, Bourgeois could make out the silhouettes of the man-made monuments: the tall structures of the casinos. They looked as if they were rising from the sea. He knew he would be there in another twenty minutes or so.

Chapter 2

The house, or what was left of it, was still there; completely charred and virtually leveled. This fire had obviously burned fast, which wasn't surprising, considering the structure had been built entirely out of pine. Bourgeois was quite familiar with construction, from his previous job of remodeling old houses. He knew a house made of pine would burn just like gasoline, due to the creosote released over time. This was a house that had been built on top of just a few cement blocks. Most of the floor was also gone and as he looked around, he could barely make out the remnants of a refrigerator and gas range. From what he could see, there wasn't much there to learn. It looked to him like an accidental fire. Bourgeois started to make his way out of the debris when a voice startled him. He turned around to find an ancient-looking black woman. He couldn't quite make out what she was saying and wondered why, until he realized it was probably due to her complete lack of teeth. He smiled at her.

"Hi, my name his Bourgeois," he said.

The woman looked at him suspiciously. "You from the police?"

Bourgeois shook his head. "Na, do you know what happened here?"

A flash of sadness crossed her eyes as she nodded. "I know those people."

"What people?"

"The dead ones. I used to watch their kids sometimes. They was nice; they no crack heads like they all say."

Bourgeois felt sorry for the woman. She was obviously upset by their deaths. "Were you here when the house burned?"

She nodded. "Yep, I was feedin' my cats outside and smokin' a cigarette."

He pressed on. "Did you see anything weird that morning?"

She looked at him for a moment before answering. He couldn't tell what she was thinking. She finally spoke. "Well, there was a car that stopped there around the corner. Three men was in it. They were carrying some bags. They went in the house but I didn't see 'em come out."

"What did they look like?" he asked.

"White, short hair; kinda like army types. I never seen 'em before.

Bourgeois was intrigued. "Did the cops ask you about this?"

She shook her head. "Na."

Bourgeois thanked the old lady and left. This was certainly going to be more complicated than he had expected; three army-type white guys. That smelled of organization; not your run of the mill, drug-induced, pissed off murders. Bourgeois chewed his lip as he sat in the driver's seat of his car, thinking. Maybe someone else had seen something or better yet; he suddenly remembered the small convenience store over towards the interstate. He knew the time of the fire. If a camera had been rolling, maybe he could get an image of the car the men had been in. He knew it was a long shot, but decided it was worth trying.

A few minutes later, Bourgeois walked into the store. He headed straight for the clerk, an older Vietnamese or Chinese woman; he couldn't ever really tell the difference. She looked up as he approached.

"Excuse me," he said politely. "Do you remember the fire a few days ago?"

She looked him up and down. "Why do you want to know?"

Bourgeois nearly rolled his eyes. *Great*, he thought. *She's going to be one of those.* "Well, I'm investigating the fire ma'am." He flashed his private investigator's license to her, hoping it would open some doors of cooperation. "I was wondering if you have video surveillance outside of your store, you know...do you have cameras?"

She looked at him as if he had come straight from a psych ward. From past experience, he knew the next step. He quickly retrieved a hundred dollar bill and flashed it in her face. "I'll pay more if you have a videotape."

She glanced at the money and then back at him. "Let me get my son." She quickly went into the back door behind the counter and returned almost as quickly. The man who appeared was dressed in a white butcher's outfit, covered with blood. Once again, Bourgeois explained why he was there.

The man nodded. "Yes, we have the tape. We keep it for a week before we tape over it. We get robbed here at least once every six months."

The son led the investigator to the back room. Bourgeois was impressed with the level of organization. He had his tapes in bins with the days marked on top of each bin, split into am and pm hours; one tape for each twelve-hour period. Two hundred dollars later, Bourgeois had found what he wanted. It appeared to be a car speeding past the store at the right time. He thanked the man and his mother and started to head home. He had a lot of work to do. His stomach rumbled, reminding him that he was starving. So, before heading back west, he decided to stop at the buffet in the Grand Casino. Today was definitely not going to be his first day to lose weight.

Once home, he stuck the tape into his cassette reader, attached to his computer. He downloaded the scenes of the car going in and later out of the neighborhood. Heraldo had told him to spend whatever was necessary; he just wanted answers quickly. So Bourgeois decided not to mess with the video himself. He quickly made a few phone calls and within minutes, emailed the video file to a company in Virginia, with instructions to identify the vehicle and its occupants. He knew it would be a long shot, but it was worth a try. He also overnighted the physical tape to them, just in case they could sponge more data from it, than he was capable of, with only his run-of-the-mill cassette reader.

Back in New Orleans, Heraldo had summoned his lieutenants into his offices on Poydras Street. They needed to determine what their next move would be.

Heraldo spoke to the group of men as he paced behind his desk. "Looks like someone's going to muscle onto our territory soon. I guess they thought killing my brother would intimidate me enough to quit the business. But that right there shows us that whoever did this, doesn't know us." A few of the men nodded in agreement. Heraldo continued. "We have to almost certainly rule out the Mexicans. They'd love to see me dead, but they know any attempt against me or my organization would result in dire consequences." He stopped pacing, leaned down and planted his hands on his desk as he looked at each of his men. "War doesn't pay, not unless you're absolutely sure of winning." His jaw tightened. "I think this new threat is coming directly from South America, and I would bet, some hot shot Columbian is looking to expand his East Coast territories." Heraldo looked directly at one of his men. "George, can you investigate who in Columbia has ties to Florida, and also, who has the muscle to pull something like this off?"

George was in charge of importing their drugs directly from Mexico; some across the land border: mostly marijuana, but also some crystal meth, heroin and cocaine; through his fishing fleets based in Grand Isle, Louisiana. Some dedicated crews sailed to prearranged meeting points off the coast of Louisiana, where they collected floating buoys, tied up to submerged waterproof bags, containing the goods. The drugs were then extracted, and through a process perfected by his sailors, injected into the pre-cleaned bowels of large yellowfin tunas. Heraldo and his men, all sushi lovers, often snickered about the high they would get from eating fresh tuna. Once onboard, the fish were tagged and then sent to the processing plant in New Orleans; sometimes even under the eyes of the oblivious USDA inspectors. The guts were then discarded into a special bin, appropriately marked: "recycled".

George knew how to scrutinize an organization. He was a corporate lawyer and an engineer. He spoke Spanish fluently, although he had been born in Morgan City, Louisiana. He came from a five-generation family of shrimp fishermen. He was rich as well, due to a dark secret. Back in the seventies, some Vietnamese immigrants had moved to his part of the Bayou and his brother had been involved in selling them one of their larger fishing boats. Somehow, he had discovered they had a substantial amount of gold. Soon thereafter, the entire Vietnamese family had disappeared, boat and all. The story was, they had moved on to another part of the country, never to be seen or heard from again. But the other family members had their suspicions. Within weeks, George's brother began to purchase property and vehicles. He even started building the family a new house and funded the younger George's education. Many years later, George's brother; a heavy smoker and boozer, finally confessed to the deed on his death bed. He confirmed what had long been everyone's belief.

One day, soon after the boat purchase, Henry, George's brother, had run into the Vietnamese bunch while they were out fishing. Their boat was taking on water and before he could get close enough to do anything about it, they had drowned. That was Henry's story anyway. He said he then went to their shack and had taken their cash of gold that he had found stored under a board in the floor. The bodies of the Vietnamese were never found. In all likelihood, they had made a great meal for the local alligators. With no next of kin or ties to the community, the incident had never been investigated. Somehow, George Landry felt partially responsible, knowing that he owed part of his success in life to his brother. It was as if, in some ways, he had sold his soul to the devil in order to get to where he was. That guilt-by-association had driven him to the life he lived: a life on the fringes of society's morals, as if he were looking for the unavoidable consequences that would arise from his constantly skirting criminality. A man of his intelligence could have easily made a substantial living. As a lawyer and an engineer, he could have built a lucrative practice in both areas. But somehow that wasn't in the cards for him. Risk, excitement and the pursuit of extreme wealth was.

Heraldo's next topic of conversation was security. He told his men that there was no doubt; whoever was going after them would soon realize that intimidation would not work. "We have to be ahead of whatever move they have planned," he said sternly. "So, Antonio...you need to double security at all points. Watch for potential raids, change routes and stay vigilant. I think the shit's about to hit the fan." Antonio nodded firmly. He liked to be called Toni. He was the muscle; the only one of the crew that actually looked like a crime figure. A previously broken nose and some scars did quite a bit to reinforce that notion. With the meeting over, now came the hard part: waiting for things to happen.

Heraldo decided almost immediately that it was time for he and Maria to move out of their house; at least until things settled down. Back at home, Heraldo approached his wife.

"I may have to go out of town for a few days. Why don't you go see your friends in Los Angeles for a week or so?" Maria, as an aspiring actress, had lived in Los Angeles back in the years before she had met Heraldo. He didn't particularly like his wife's friends, but he knew she'd be safer with them than at a hotel. He definitely didn't want her to leave too much of a paper trail. He knew how thorough his enemies could be. His credo had always been: 'Never underestimate your enemy". Heraldo already knew he was going to tag her with some security, just in case.

Maria was surprised at the request. She knew about Heraldo's feelings towards her friends. "This is about your brother's death isn't it? You're worried they're coming after you."

Heraldo nodded. "Yes," he said. "I don't know what's going on and until I do, I think it's better you go."

Maria's face fell. "But I'll worry about you," she said quietly.

"Maria, I don't want to leave you. I don't. I know this is terrible, but please, do it for me. Nothing is going to happen to me. I'll move out to the boat for a few days. It needs to be run anyhow."

Maria looked at him carefully. "Okay," she said. "But I don't like it."

Heraldo was relieved she had agreed. "Good. I'll have the driver take you to the airport first thing tomorrow morning. Pack your things now and let's go to the boat tonight. I'll sleep better there with you, not that we'll do much sleeping." He grinned at her.

What Heraldo referred to as 'the boat', was actually a fifty-four-foot, state-of-the-art catamaran, equipped with all of the necessary bells and whistles. The interior of the yacht was a light mahogany, with upholstery made of subtle, full grain leather; custom-made in Italy. But what really made the sailboat so unusual was its super-light construction. The standard marine plywood, steel and fiberglass had been replaced by carbon fiber, Kevlar and epoxy resin. Even the wood surfaces were constructed of a hardened foam polymer covered in a thin wood veneer; also resin protected. This made the yacht lightning-fast for its size; able to sail at speeds close to twenty-five knots. The power plant was also quite unusual. A turbine-driven generator provided the driving force for two electric engines located in each individual hull. State-of-the-art batteries allowed it to function for several days without the need for a generator, and provided enough energy for propulsion, at a harbor speed, for several days. The propellers were retractable, allowing for minimum drag in sailing conditions. To top it all off, it even came equipped with an electricity-generating turbine that could be dropped into the water while sailing. This would allow the batteries to be recharged during extended wind-driven trips; making the vessel truly self-sufficient.

Within the hour, Heraldo and his wife left their house in a non-descript SUV, and headed towards the New Orleans Marina. Twenty minutes later, they arrived and boarded the vessel. The moorings were unfastened and the yacht silently glided out of the harbor. Its course was the middle of Lake Ponchatrain; about an hour or so away on battery power. Once there, Heraldo felt somewhat more secure, as any vessel approaching could be detected well in advance. They could also be dealt with quickly if needed. A radar-type bulb contained what could only be described as a modern version of a Gatling gun; capable of firing over a thousand rounds per minute. It boasted laser-guided surgical precision and was a weapon that would be the envy of any member of the Coast Guard. It could slice a small boat in half in no time at all...and already had in the past.

The sun set slowly on the warm July afternoon. A slight breeze from the west blew quite pleasantly as they set anchor. Heraldo, well aware of the weight on his shoulders, wanted this last night with his wife to be a memorable one. The ship came equipped with a full kitchen, rivaling some of the best in the world. It had grills capable of temperatures of three-thousand degrees, for the perfect searing of meats, and sous-vide ovens to preserve the consistency of the most delicate ingredients. This truly was a world-class chef's wet dream. It had to be, because both Heraldo and his wife were world-class connoisseurs. On the menu was an appetizer made of Maine oysters, sea urchins and langoustines; all served on the half-shell, accompanied by a bottle of Montrachet 2006; an excellent year, and some points of freshly baked black bread. It was the perfect aphrodisiacal start to an evening of passion.

The twilight was slowly replaced by a half moon; rising over the lake waters. In the distance, lights emanated from the tallest buildings in the city of New Orleans. Having finished their first course, Heraldo and Maria were slowly overcome by the beauty of it all. As their eyes met, neither could help blushing at the passion they both felt for each other in that moment. Slowly, Heraldo approached Maria and brushed his lips against hers. Soon, he could no longer resist her and his light touch became aroused into a deep kissing frenzy. She let herself fall backwards onto the bench she was seated on, revealing her long legs and her delicately laced undergarment. This was more than Heraldo could handle, and slowly lowering his hand between her legs, he removed the only barrier between his manhood and her. He proceeded in making passionate love to his wife. The apex of pleasure came fast for both of them, as if they were both conscious of the little time they could still share before Maria's departure for Los Angeles in the morning. They both knew there would be more of this before the night was over.

The staff onboard was always discreet. They knew from experience to leave the couple alone. With the euphemistic first course over, they began to clear the table and set up for the next course. Heraldo had planned the evening as a light and invigorating culinary event. With that in mind, the next course was a carpaccio of buffalo, with fresh baby arugula and some shavings of aged Parmesan; just enough to build up their strength, but not enough to load the stomach down. Heraldo could never understand the fascination most Americans had with heavy foods; why they always wanted to be filled to the point of gagging. Even as a poor boy in Mexico, he had appreciated the meals his mother had cooked and had enjoyed sitting at a table with his relatives, discussing and arguing, while slowly eating and taking the time to enjoy every bite. He guessed maybe Americans were the way they were because of the factory food that had replaced a mother's cooking in the role of feeding their kids. But he couldn't complain too much. Those same people were, after all, his best customers.

While sipping on a glass of 1996 Don Perignon, Heraldo looked at his wife. "I'll miss you. This is the first time you and I will be apart in a long time.

"I'll miss you too," Maria said softly, with a tear in her eye.

Heraldo quickly decided to lighten the mood. "Let's go finish this bottle with some dessert in the Jacuzzi." Grabbing his wife by the hand, Heraldo led her to the front of the boat and pressed a switch. In no time at all, the Jacuzzi filled up with warm water. After placing the bottle of Don in the refrigerated receptacle made for that purpose, he slowly undressed his wife, revealing her incredible body. She had small breasts, hanging perkily with slightly erect nipples. Her waist was slim and her stomach muscular, but not overly so. But what attracted Heraldo the most was her voluptuous derriere, as he was fond of saying: 'made for love'.

Chapter 3

It didn't take long for the folks in Virginia to come up with the identification on the vehicle; caught on tape at the small convenience store. It wasn't the license plate, which although readable, was not registered to anyone. It ended up being what was no doubt, an oversight on the part of the arsonists: a parking sticker registered to a Johnny Wilkins: customs agent at the Port of Pensacola, Florida.

Shit, thought Bourgeois. *What am I getting myself into? These are Federal agents.* Bourgeois quickly e-mailed Heraldo the very important tidbit and told him he would wait for further instructions. What Bourgeois didn't realize, was that the simple process of checking that parking identification had already started a chain of events that would greatly affect his life.

Although Heraldo received the email from Bourgeois, he was more interested in finishing a mouth-watering champagne sorbet, which was slowly melting between his wife's thighs. The e-mail automatically forwarded to his second in command: George Landry. Landry was an early riser and was about to call it a night when his phone beeped, alerting him to the email in question. Having been briefed on the situation, he proceeded to respond to Bourgeois with the following: *Go to Florida and dig up more on this guy. Try to find out who his contacts are and who he works with.*

Landry, who had already contacted some people in Miami regarding the situation, had been a bit surprised upon reading the email. Whoever they were, these guys had some balls and a long reach...all the way to customs in North Florida. There was no telling where their influence reached. He didn't hesitate as he reached for his phone to call Heraldo. The lights around the Jacuzzi slowly flashed; code for an emergency telephone call. Heraldo had just experienced the closest he could possibly come to total bliss. He was holding his wife, both of them naked in the water, slowly recovering from their mutual passion when he noticed the lights. He apologized to Maria and grabbing a large, fluffy towel as he stepped out of the Jacuzzi. He picked up his phone and immediately connected to George. He listened carefully as Landry updated him quickly.

"Be extra vigilant George," Heraldo told him. "These guys probably don't have contacts in New Orleans' Coast Guard, but you never know for sure. Let's slow down on import operations for now. That's probably a safe thing to do."

At almost the exact same moment, the wheels of a jet squealed as they touched down at the New Orleans airport; a flight from Miami. Onboard was Julio Cabral, a professional enforcer for the Luna's Cartel, based in

Miami, Florida. He answered to Ernesto Castillo in Cartagena, Columbia. The Lunas, short for Lunaticas, was an off-branch of Columbian rebels known as the FARC, who simply traded their Marxist revolutionary aspirations for more practical and lucrative narcotics' trafficking. Its leader, Ernesto Castillo, an industrialist and major producer of cement in that part of the world, had a penchant for violence and thrills that his legitimate business simply couldn't afford him. Contrary to a long line of dealers and producers before him, he went to great lengths to preserve his legitimate, rich man image; buying favors from politicians and government officials in a socially acceptable way, just like President Kennedy's father had done for his family. Castillo believed that the greatest failures of the famous traffickers of the past, such as Pablo Escobar, had been their need for the common man's love and admiration. Castillo couldn't have cared less.

Julio Cabral had a tight schedule in New Orleans. Some local toughs had arranged for his transportation to a bayou around Ponchatoulas, where a shrimp boat was going to ferry him to his mission: to kill Heraldo Sanches. The word had come earlier in the evening that Heraldo and his wife had boarded their boat in the Pontchartain Marina. It had been seen as a God-given opportunity to finish them off, somewhat discreetly on the water. A couple of fishing boats had been watching the Catamaran at a safe distance, pretending to be catching shrimp. It was close to eleven o'clock at night when Julio stepped into the small boat that was going to take him to his mission. At full throttle, it wouldn't take more than half an hour to reach their target.

In the large master suite, Heraldo resting on the king-sized bed with his wife, nestled on the starboard side of the Catamaran. Although he would have fallen asleep under normal circumstances, his body wouldn't let him. Something was off. A feeling of unease had crept over him and wouldn't budge. So, it came as no surprise when he heard the low-volume alarm sound off in the room. He quickly slipped into a pair of pants and headed for the command room at a jog. He was immediately shown the radar alarm system. A fast-running boat had been tracked for about five miles, coming towards them. It was definitely intentional, as all other vessels present were moving as expected; fishermen with their nets out, slow and steady, going in no particular directions. The radar showed the small boat's range as seven-thousand feet and closing. Heraldo gave quick orders to arm the defense system. The weapon was capable of a clean kill far beyond that distance. But, until they knew the intention of the speeding boat for sure, the weapon would remain silent.

Heraldo gave orders to retrieve all anchors and fire up the turbines. The slow whine became slowly audible; like a giant waking from his slumber. A flash of light appeared from the direction of the approaching boat and a self-propelled rocket was suddenly barreling for the Catamaran. Heraldo didn't waste a second. The two electric motors, used for propulsion, were activated instantly and, drawing a huge amount of reserve power from the batteries, they lifted the entire catamaran out of the water; the energy released providing enough acceleration to knock a man from his feet. Grabbing a hand rail, Heraldo pushed the auto-defense button on the weapon's monitor and the weapon's computer quickly locked in on the incoming missile and ordered an immediate Hell fire from its multi-barrel gun. Three thousand pellets later, the RPG exploded in midair about two-thousand feet from the Catamaran. Before the attackers could fire again, Heraldo changed the ammunition selection on the gun to the heavier explosive rounds and ordered the computer to fire one single salvo, directed towards the incoming vessel.

What followed was magnificent: a flash in the night that brought daylight to the surrounding waters. The mini-bomb had hit its intended target, resulting in a plasma ball of incinerated aluminum; its occupants reduced to basic mineral components. No bodies would ever be recovered from this scene. The few fishermen who had witnessed the explosion would later describe it as a sort of UFO crashing into the lake. But since no debris was ever found, their stories would be attributed to some kind of mass hysteria by people already known for their superstitious beliefs. It didn't take long for Heraldo to realize what had just taken place. He suddenly had no doubt that they were under attack by the same people who had killed his brother and his family. Whoever was behind this, was highly motivated and organized enough to reach into his own backyard and threaten him. He was certain that this was definitely not an amateur or local competitor wannabe.

Heraldo ordered his boat to cross the lake towards Slidell, Louisiana at full speed. Twenty five minutes later, they were pulling stealthily into an inlet; the turbines shut down to ensure minimum ambient noise, to avoid waking anyone in a surrounding upscale neighborhood with docks. Heraldo had bought a home there, under one of his shell companies set up for that purpose. This home, with a hundred-foot dock, was used as a safe house, just for an event such as this. Life experience had taught Heraldo to always be prepared. He expected the worst, not because he was a pessimist at heart, but simply because of his business. The worst always had a way of being pretty terminal. Maria had arrived in the command room shortly after the boat had slowed down before reaching the harbor. Heraldo explained to her what had taken place. He told her he was working on getting her out of there, to a safe place. On their way there, Heraldo had ensured that no other vessels had shown an inkling of following them, so for the time being, he knew they were safe.

Heraldo kept a small plane on standby at the private airport, close to downtown New Orleans. He sent a prearranged message for the plane to meet them at the airport in Slidell and received confirmation that it would be there in about one hour. So without further delay, Heraldo and Maria stepped into the large garage, adjacent to the house, and into a nondescript, late-model Ford Focus. At this time of the night, the town of Slidell was completely dead and the ride to the airport didn't take them long at all. The eastern horizon was slowly reddening as the sun crept up. The tiny airport was completely deserted at this early hour; no control tower, just a beacon and a runway in which lights could be turned on by approaching aircraft if needed. The two-engine Cessna landed without the use of any ground lights and started taxiing towards the small car.

The plan for Maria had changed, at least in appearance. She wouldn't take the commercial flight to Los Angeles, but would instead, fly there privately; the thought process being that they wouldn't be obligated to file a flight plan, so it would be more difficult to track. Also, there was no chance of Maria being seen at an airport, either departing or arriving. Heraldo gave her very specific instructions not to use her credit cards. He gave her a set of pre-paid cards and an unregistered cell phone; things he always kept for occasions just like this. They looked at each other and then hugged for a long time, both feeling a love for each other, deeper and stronger than ever before; to the point that tears now watered their eyes. It took all of Heraldo's mental strength to finally let go of his wife; to unselfishly let her fly away. But, it simply had to be done; they both knew that, for their own safety. The days ahead were going to be brutal and Heraldo needed to be focused on overcoming this crisis without having to worry about Maria. Slowly, she walked up the stairs of the little plane, turning her face back towards Heraldo. Her eye makeup had washed down her cheeks with her tears. That was the image that would be burned into Heraldo's memory for a long time to come. The cockpit door shut and slowly, the Cessna moved towards the end of the runway; its engines at a high roar. A couple of minutes later, the small plane lifted itself above the tall pines tree line, right at the same moment as the sun peeked over the horizon. The sun reflected off the back of the small craft, making it flicker, like a falling star in the newborn day. Heraldo watched for a few moments and then quickly left the small airport.

He headed for the interstate, back towards New Orleans. As he drove, he called Landry and once again updated him on the nights' latest events, minus Maria's departure. There wasn't much traffic on the way back and suddenly, Heraldo felt lonely. The events of the last few hours had reminded him of how fragile life could be; how little it took to change one's world. All of it had brought up the childhood memories of almost losing his sister…when he had first had to take matters into his own hands. The revenge he had taken back then had brought him to the attention of a gang: the rival gang to his sister's rapist. Those events had paved the road to his fall into the drug trade. The brutality and determination of his actions had earned him the respect of a then-notorious drug lord; who had quickly convinced Heraldo that it would be in his best interest to join their organization. Heraldo had accepted, knowing the consequences for murdering the rapist would mean that his family would be in danger. Protection for Heraldo's family had been a valid argument that couldn't easily be repudiated.

From that point on, Heraldo had risen quickly in the ranks of his newfound crime family; first, as an enforcer and then as a negotiator. But his real success had come in being able to organize a delivery of the product, with fewer intermediaries and multiple producers. Prices were kept low at the farmer's level, not by threats, which were the means of his predecessors, but by setting up a climate of competition among growers, who were given the tools and expertise to process the goods themselves; thus affording them higher profits. This giant co-op was spread throughout Central America and the remoteness and sheer number of its members made it impossible for any government to eradicate. Also, the motivation to do so simply wasn't there, since local economies benefited so much from it. What was surprising also, was the lack of use of the product by the growers and their families. They were simple people, with traditions and a strong cultural identity, where addiction was neither a luxury they could afford nor one they desired.

With the sun rising on his back, Heraldo could make out the rough outline of downtown New Orleans. His phone rang, snapping him out of his thoughts. It was George. "Good morning George. Anything new?"

George Landry quickly answered. "We found out who the attacker was. He came on a flight from Miami last night. He used the Boudreaux boys; locals out on the bayous in Pontchatoula, to carry out his plan. From what we can tell, they're no longer a threat. Heraldo had heard of the Boudreaux brothers before. They were a rough bunch who grew their own weed in the swamp. Every once in a while, they were stupid enough to venture into New Orleans to sell it. Up until now, they hadn't posed any real threat to his operation, and hadn't been worth the energy to pursue into their mosquito-infested world. But now...they would be dealt with appropriately.

Heraldo answered him quickly. "Meet me for breakfast at the Court of the Two Sisters in the Quarter in let's say...twenty minutes?"

After parking his car in a nearby hotel garage, Heraldo quickly walked to the restaurant, a tourist landmark; always busy, even during the week. He and George settled at a table in the back of one of the quieter rooms. After the waiter had brought them coffee, Heraldo started.

"I don't know who's behind this, but I bet our Colombian friends have something to do with this."

Over the past few years, production out of Colombia had been severely curtailed; not so much by enforcement, but simply by lack of demand. Central America had become solely capable of meeting the market's ever-increasing needs. Not to mention, distance had become a factor, as the farther one had to go, the greater the risk of mishap. It was about time they tried to reclaim their world domination on the trade.

George nodded in agreement. "You're right Heraldo. That's what I'm thinking: a hit man out of Miami. It's like we're back in the eighties. Also, the involvement of some paid-for customs' agents is definitely a bold move on their part. That must have cost them some serious money, not counting the fact that it was a stupid and unnecessarily risky move; thwarted with all sorts of pitfalls. We're dealing with an egomaniac here, someone with the power to not only bring themselves down, but us too. Our next move has to be carefully crafted. Our man in Pensacola has made visual contact with the agents and has them under surveillance." George lowered his voice and leaned in. "They go to this bar after work, so he plans to befriend them. We'll see how that goes."

Heraldo responded. "I'm assuming that we were under the Boudreaux brothers' surveillance before the attack, so counter that. Have some of our men catch up with them discreetly. The boat should be arriving back at the lake's marina by now, so that would be a good place to start."

George nodded. "Okay, yes sir." Right then, their food arrived. Both had ordered crawfish Eggs Benedict and they proceeded to devour their respective meals. The sleepless night and immense stress had definitely built up their appetites. Once finished, they each went their separate ways. Heraldo kept a safe room in an old house on Bourbon Street and walked the few blocks separating him from it. Located adjacent to one of the numerous New Orleans strip joints, it would be relatively quiet this early in the morning, and the only thing Heraldo needed now was some sleep to clear his head and regroup his thoughts. By the time Maria landed in Tuscan, Arizona for refueling of the plane, Heraldo was ready for bed. He quickly called her on his satellite phone. She sounded tired, but otherwise alright. She told him she had been able to sleep a little on the plane. Heraldo told her that they had a better idea who was behind the latest events and felt confident that they would soon be stopped. He hoped that news would help Maria relax. Heraldo had a fitful sleep, but thankfully felt rested and of clear mind when he woke up around two o'clock in the afternoon. His first call was to Bourgeois, the private investigator, currently in Pensacola.

"Hello there, Mr. Bourgeois," said Heraldo when the man answered.

"Good afternoon, sir," responded Bourgeois. "I have some interesting news. Last night I spent some time with our friends at a harbor bar and apparently, they're planning to retire soon. They did a considerable amount of bragging about it. Interestingly enough, they mentioned moving to Margarita Island in Venezuela where, according to them, they'll live in the lap of luxury, with whores and deep sea fishing. They said they had made some kind of investment that was about to pay big money and, combined with their pensions, it would be a sufficient amount for them not to ever have to work again."

Heraldo raised his eyebrows slightly in surprise. The going rate for knocking off people must have gone up. "Well, keep up the good work and let me know if anything new transpires. Thank you Mr. Bourgeois." Heraldo ended the call. Maria had landed in a small, local Palm Springs airport; a choice made for the sake of privacy. From that point, she was picked up by a limousine service that took her to a friend's home on Mulholland Drive, overlooking the city. She hadn't seen her friend in several years and was looking forward to spending some time with her; reminiscing about the early days of their acting careers and all of the crazy jobs they had each had, just to make it possible to 'live the life' as they had called it. Maria's friend, Celina, had been born in Colombia, but had moved to Miami at an early age with her brothers and sisters, a drunkard and criminally inclined father and no mother. She had basically raised her younger siblings by taking on jobs at the early age of sixteen. She had done quite well for herself on the account of her good looks and street smarts and had met Maria when Maria had vacationed to South Beach. They had hit it off instantly and so well, that both of them decided they would move to Los Angeles together to seriously pursue acting careers. Celina was now a working actress, having landed some parts on a few soap operas and even a couple of leading roles in two television movies. However, the scene had slowly mellowed, as she moved well into her thirties. Despite her good looks, roles were few and far between for actresses her age. Hollywood was still cruel to women who couldn't make the transition to more behind-the-scenes careers, such as writing, producing and directing. When Heraldo called Maria again, the car was just about to pull into her friend's driveway; a beautiful Mediterranean-style home, overlooking the valley, up on a hill. Maria reassured Heraldo of her present condition and the fact that she would be careful and keep a low profile. Yes, maybe they would even go on a trip to Napa Valley to visit the wine region she told him. Now that she was in Los Angeles, Maria's brush with death seemed far away and almost surreal, as if it had only been a bad dream. She was looking forward to some good times with her friend Celina. As soon as the car stopped in front of the house, Maria rushed to the door, which was already open. Loud shrieks of joy filled the air as the two women hugged each other hard, bouncing up and down together in anticipation of things to come. Maria looked Celina up and down with a huge smile.

"Looking good Chica!" Maria said lovingly.

"So do you!" answered Celina, in her sexy and slightly accented English.

Years before, the two women had terrorized many hearts of both sexes. Men would literally line up at their feet in lust and infatuation. Nowadays, Maria had found true love with Heraldo, while Celina was still playing the field. She didn't trust men, as a result of her father's history she supposed. She was obsessed with being in control of her relationships with men. That part of her life had left an empty space in her heart. Deep down,

she was a little jealous of Maria.

Chapter 4

After speaking with Maria, Heraldo called George to see if any progress had been made regarding the Boudreaux brothers. As expected, Landry had some good news. The Boudreauxs had been waiting at the marina and had been easily spotted, riding some over-the-top dually truck. A simple trap had been set, using a local call girl named Michelle, who had pretended to ask them for directions. While the boys had stopped to talk to her, two of Landry's men had taken control of the situation, so to speak, with the help of their semi-automatic handguns. The brothers had been driven to a warehouse, only a couple of blocks away from the New Orleans Court house; poetic justice applying. They were currently awaiting interrogation.

Landry informed Heraldo that he could come and pick him up now if he was ready. Heraldo, eager to get it over with, agreed quickly and got dressed for his short trip. Ten minutes later, a black limo with tinted glass, pulled up in front of the strip joint next door and Heraldo climbed in. Already, some of the strippers were hanging out by the door of the establishment, as if painting a portrait of the city's many sins. Less than five minutes later, Heraldo and George pulled into a nondescript warehouse, the doors automatically lowering after their entry. The Boudreaux brothers had been split up into different rooms. The warehouse itself had been used in the past as a butchering plant for a local fish company. The walls were sprayed with insulating foam and a musty smell lingered in the air. It was eerily quiet. No traffic noise could be heard and in return, neither could the screams and cries of the prisoners being held inside.

Heraldo didn't believe torture was an effective way of getting people to talk. In his business, torture was mainly used as means to a most unpleasant death. The more obvious the signs of trauma, the better warning for those who still had the benefit of living. In this case, there was no warning that needed to be passed along. Whomever was behind these two idiots, couldn't have cared less about their fate. In fact, they would probably even relish in their gruesome death. In cases like these, where specific information needed to be extracted, Heraldo relied on a cocktail drug made up of Oxytocin and Sodium Amytal; manufactured and procured by his team of scientists in Mexico. Drug dealing at his level, just like any other large manufacturing endeavor, required one to stay ahead of the game. To do so, required the full-time employment of some of the best brains in the field; continuously chasing the next best high. Heraldo walked into the first room. The tall swamp man had been tied up on a large, well-padded leather office chair. About ten minutes before, a small dose of the drug cocktail had been injected into his veins. He was now feeling no pain.

Heraldo smiled. "Hello Justin," he said. 'Justin Boudreaux' was his name, according to the Louisiana DMV. "We're not going to hurt you okay? All we want is a little information." Justin looked at him like a scared puppy.

Heraldo noticed immediately that the kid probably wasn't a day over twenty-two. This was going to be easy.

The kid nodded and Heraldo carried on. "If you cooperate, I promise; you'll walk away a free man. If you don't, we'll just start by killing your brother, and we'll make it slow and very painful. Then, we'll work on you. All I want to know is who hired you guys and what you're getting in exchange for doing this job?"

Justin had clearly gotten the point and became the face of cooperation. "Some guy came to us last week about doing a job. He said that we could get cheap drugs from him and he would pay us ten grand if we did what he said. He also gave us five pounds of meth as a down payment."

Heraldo smiled. "Good job Justin. Now, who was that guy? Where did he come from?"

Justin continued to cooperate. "He came from Florida sir. He said his name was Johnny. We told him that we really didn't want to mess with you 'cause we knew you would kill us, and we liked how things were going on, with you leavin' us alone and all. Then he told us that you were gonna be out of the picture soon...if you know what I mean. He also said that a man would be comin' from Miami to do that job, so we wouldn't have to get involved in it. He said once you were gone, his bosses were going to look at us to take over the New Orleans' operation."

Heraldo had to fight back a smirk. That was a con if he had ever heard one. No one in their right mind would trust these two retards to run anything on paved roads. For a split second, he felt a little bad for the kid. It seemed these boys had been taken for a ride. Heraldo had what he needed. Further interrogation of this swampbilly would just be a waste of time.

"You've done well Johnny. Go back to your family and tell them what we talked about. If these other people contact you again, let me know, okay? Here's my number on this card. I'll give you twenty grand if you can give me the name of the boss this Johnny guy worked for. Also, don't come back here into New Orleans or you won't be doing any talking next time...if you know what I mean." Justin agreed immediately, nodding his head so fiercely and with such wide eyes that he looked like a retarded bobble head.

After the interrogation, the two young men were shoved into a dark-windowed sedan and taken back to their vehicle. They scurried away quickly, like rats trying to escape daylight. Heraldo and Landry remained at the warehouse; pondering.

"You're right," said Landry. "This doesn't make any sense. We're missing a part of this puzzle, unless these guys were just temporary until more muscle came. But even that makes no sense. Why even involve them to begin with?"

The next day in Los Angeles, Maria and Celina prepared to go on a limousine trip to the wine region of California, in and around the Napa Valley. It would be a five-day junket and would encompass staying at some of the most prestigious wineries and hotels, while tasting some of the best foods and wine the region offered. This would be the perfect opportunity for them to get reacquainted in a fun-loving way, as well as a good excuse for a follow up trip to a top-rated spa. Just as the Romans had done, they would indulge, and then give up the products of their indulgence; but not as quickly and drastically as a short trip to the vomitorium. They would work off all of the food and wine with some sexy male trainers and undergo various cleansing insertions in the most neglected part of their anatomy. It was certainly good to be rich in the twenty-first century.

Maria made a phone call to Heraldo to inform him of her trip plans. He wished her the best and told her to enjoy her food and wine as if it was for the both of them. He laughed as he told her he would be living vicariously through her. Tears welled in Maria's eyes as her husband told her that he wished he could have come with her, but under the circumstances, he felt that this was the best possible place for her to be. He told her to be careful and that he loved her. She responded with the same, feeling a pinch of guilt in her heart. After the call ended, Heraldo felt a slight sense of uneasiness, but he couldn't quite put a finger on it. He quickly buried the negative thoughts and decided to do something positive and put his arms around the crisis at hand. The problem with this new situation, he decided, was that it had forced him to become reactive. He hated that. Unplanned responses usually led to uncontrollable and very often, disastrous consequences.

Heraldo was on his way towards Grand Isle, the most southern point of Louisiana's somewhat contiguous land mass. This part of the country enjoyed a subtropical climate, allowing for successful sugar cane plantations and the growth of citrus groves and palm trees. The issue here was more the absence of higher grounds and the continuous encroachment of the ocean on the few remaining peninsulas. As evidence of that, one could still see the remnants of old trees sticking up in what had once been fields; permanently submerged by the sea. Only a couple of years before, Heraldo had arranged for the purchase of an old shipyard; a casualty of the numerous hurricanes that had battered the area as of late. The owners, not willing to fight the elements any longer, had happily sold the remains of their operation; grasping at the chance to unload the uninsurable property. The yard and its structures had been battered, but the one thing Heraldo had been most interested in was the dry dock facility: still operational and watertight enough to be of use. Heraldo had purchased two large water pumps so that even during an average storm, the one-hundred-twenty-foot long by fifty-foot wide 'giant bath tub', as he liked to call it, would remain dry enough to work in.

The middle of the dry dock was currently the temporary home of what looked to be the Good Year Blimp, but was in fact entirely made up of reinforced concrete. At over one-hundred feet long and close to thirty-five feet at its widest point; the gigantic vessel floated on an array of steel bracing. On each side, it had what could only be described as giant mouth-like structures that tapered along its body towards its tail, where two large openings were located; somewhat similar in design to what one would see on a jet. These made up the propulsion systems; two large turbines powered by electric motors. This propulsion system could also be used as power generators, by simply anchoring the ship into any decent water flow, such as tidal currents or other naturally occurring streams of water. When put into its generative mode, the ship would protrude two giant umbrella-like structures to capture a greater volume of water and redirect it to its mouth-like openings. In optimal conditions, the contraption was capable of generating several thousand kilowatts per hour. Onboard, the submarine was equipped with two main sources of energy: advanced battery packs, able to store large quantities of energy in the mega-amp range, and several large liquid hydrogen tanks in which the hydrogen was safely stored through chemical bonding and released to power a fuel cell plant. A hydrolysis plant was also present to convert surplus electricity to hydrogen and oxygen; both for energy and living requirements. This ship was capable of extended stays underwater and although obviously not as powerful as a nuclear submarine, it would rival it in all of its other abilities...and only for a fraction of the cost.

Heraldo wanted to be able to go underwater for extended periods of time: months and even years if required. The surface of this submarine was coated entirely with an epoxy-like resin and made to resemble the appearance of a whale's skin, with all of its ridges and indentations. This would allow for smoother travel within the water and considerably less energy usage. The inside of the beast was divided into several sections. The engines and life support command room were located towards the end of the ship. Giant monitors covered the walls, adjusting to its curves. From this command post, one could watch the outside surroundings of the craft in high-definition resolution. It almost seemed as if the screens were windows to the outside underwater world. All the instrumentations one would expect to find on a submarine were there; all computerized and on display on smaller, centrally located monitors.

Two large captain's chairs, covered with thick, black grainy leather, stood as if on watch in front of the touch screen monitors. Each chair was outfitted with its own pair of joystick controllers, for complete control of the ship's propulsion and maneuvering. Voice recognition and command was also available to steer this sub. When it came to the living quarters, they rivaled some of the finest abodes in the world, done in what could best be described as Greco-Roman style architecture; featuring columns and granite and marble throughout the dining, living and two master bedrooms. The kitchen, of course, was state-of-the-art; with all of the equipment that a world class, top rated restaurant would require. Being a submarine, the extra weight was not an issue, and was even desirable, as it reduced the need for large ballasts and weight loading required for submersion. The crew quarters didn't leave anything to be desired either. The crew could enjoy a gym with the latest and most sophisticated equipment, the sailors had their own kitchen and bathrooms, dining and recreation areas and small individual bedrooms. However, what made this ship so unusual was the last large room which opened into the living room. Best described as a combination garden and greenhouse, it was the heart of the submarine, providing its residents with fresh vegetables, fruits and herbs; all grown within a semi-hydroponic system; combining soil, water and nutrient circulation. The area also came equipped with a chicken coop, disguised as a giant bird cage, so that fresh eggs would be available and leftover vegetables could be recycled.

Maria, having seen this set-up once, had made fun of Heraldo by nicknaming the greenhouse and chicken coop area, his 'Mexican hangout'. Heraldo had a special attachment to his chickens, from his childhood. For some reason, they made him feel safe. The ceiling of the greenhouse was covered entirely by thousands of small, high-tech lamps, capable of duplicating the required light spectrum and intensity needed by the plants, at a fraction of the energy requirements of a standard greenhouse system.

All of this was computer controlled and could be adjusted in every area, intensity and spectrum of light; to even out oxygen production. Heraldo had wanted to have a sufficient green mass, so to speak, to oxygenate the sub and to also filter out potentially toxic carbon oxides, making this mini-world one step closer to having its own self-sustaining eco-system, without having to rely on its chemical scrubbers. Two more compartments were present in this submarine. Although not as dramatic in appearance, they were still crucial to its functioning. A vault room was located in the belly of the ship; disguised as storage for ballast lead weights. It could detach from the rest of the sub. This room was actually loaded with several tons of pure gold cylinders, painted black.

Heraldo had been wise when he first started making large profits and he had invested them in a nationwide gold-buying operation; one where people could sell their gold jewelry for quick cash, leaving his business with huge profit margins. Rapidly, as the economy worsened, he had been able to purchase the yellow metal in vast quantities; over two hundred million dollars per year. He had easily set aside about one hundred million dollar's worth of gold per year, for this specific purpose, and had avoided arousing suspicion from the authorities. Now, he was sitting over literally...ten metric tons of twenty-four carat gold, worth close to one billion dollars. Heraldo was, by all accounts, a paranoid man. But as he was fond of saying: in his business, a healthy dose of paranoia made for staying alive. He had known too many who, because of the false security provided by their newfound wealth, had gotten careless and had ultimately ended up paying the price with their lives.

Heraldo didn't trust banks, and as a principle, never kept more money in them than was absolutely necessary for his business. His belief was that banks, and the people who ran them, were the ultimate thieves. They had managed to enslave an entire nation with their schemes and because they had grown so powerful, they had basically escaped any consequences for their plundering actions. Heraldo knew from experience that once a country was run by thugs, who kept the masses in poverty and ignorance and exploited them as a cheap labor force, that same country would ultimately join the fate of many empires of the past; in the doldrums of decline and mediocrity. He knew that the key to success was an enterprising mind and the ability to discover and create new things; to encourage new ways, not to subjugate them. Heraldo believed in progress and technology and that was why, even though he was not a formally-educated man, he involved himself in all of his technical projects, ensuring he understood the ins and outs of the most sophisticated systems he had at his disposal. His submarine held no secrets from him.

Heraldo had launched the project two years before and had brought people from all over the world to construct the unusual craft: a civil engineer from Holland, specializing in floating concrete structures and several technicians from China to handle the power plants and battery system. They had all been brought in to supplement his small local crew. The isolation of the area had kept onlookers to a minimum, and people in this part of the country were used to seeing large structures being built for the multitudes of oil and gas concerns in the Gulf. The total cost for the project so far, minus the gold ballasts, had been less than five million dollars; a drop in the bucket when it came to Heraldo's large fortune. As far as he was concerned, it was the best money he would ever spend. If everything worked according to schedule, his sub would be ready for sea trials in less than two weeks. However, due to the current circumstances, Heraldo had decided to speed up the final touches. He had announced substantial bonuses for every member of the crew, if they could finish the work within one week. Having spent the best part of two years of their lives on the project, most were quite happy to oblige and were anxious to return to their homelands.

After spending the morning consorting with his engineers and craftsmen, Heraldo finally headed back to New Orleans to meet with Landry at his favorite restaurant, near the International Airport in New Orleans. It was about six-thirty when Heraldo walked in to Osteria di Piero; the smells of northern Italian food immediately tantalizing his taste buds. Not having eaten anything since morning, he suddenly realized how hungry he was. Landry, in keeping with his old mob demeanor, had gotten a corner table in the back of the restaurant, his back against the wall.

Landry spoke as soon as Heraldo approached. "Nothing's happened since yesterday. We've been vigilant and I've put extra security on all the places we go, but to no avail. Either no one is watching us or if they are, they're extremely good at it. My feeling is, we need to get ready for their next move, maybe hit those guys in North Florida."

Heraldo shook his head. "No Landry. That would raise suspicion and attract unnecessary attention. We don't need another front with this going on. As much as I hate to admit it, all we can do now is wait and keep looking into Miami and our connections there. Until we know who's doing this to us, we can't act in an uncertain way, when we do know, then we cut off the head of the snake...if you know what I mean George."

The waiter came to the table right then and Heraldo, having decided on the wine, ordered them a bottle of Barbaresco: a beautiful red from a region in Italy, nestled between the northern Italian Riviera and Switzerland. The wine would go well with the chef's rendition of local andouilles sausage; a dish which included wild truffles and Langoustina: a small lobster-like crustacean from the Mediterranean Sea. It would all be served on a bed of baby arugula and fennel. Landry and Heraldo liked to take their time eating and savoring their wine. They kept their conversation to a minimum. Having been teased by the delicious appetizer, they both decided on the more substantial filet, served with a delicate green peppercorn sauce that would make the envy of any French master chef. They chose to accompany the dish by an even more substantial Amarone wine. After two hours of culinary bliss, they concluded their dining experience with an espresso and some grappa to help the digestive process. As always, di Pierro's had been the winning ticket and it was time to head back to their respective protected dens; hidden in the confines of the city.

The time alone gave Heraldo opportunity to reflect upon his life. It had been good to him in recent years and retirement from the drug trade was something he had contemplated many times. However, he knew, in order to do so, a change of venue would be necessary. Or, more appropriately, a complete disappearing act. In his business, you couldn't just quit without consequences, and although anybody could be replaced; replacement almost always came as a result of violent death. In a way, that was why Heraldo had put so much effort and resources into his sub. In his world, it was the closest thing to secure retirement that money could buy.

Chapter 5

Maria and Celina were thoroughly enjoying themselves at the luxurious spa, nestled amongst the vineyards of Napa Valley. The massage had just ended; a great way to unwind from their road trip and to build up an appetite. Celina had always had a crush on Maria, ever since the first time they had met in Miami. But although she had come close to expressing her feelings, she had always shied away from it in the most intimate of moments, for fear of being rejected. However, her crush on Maria didn't prevent Celina from pursuing men. She enjoyed the power she had over the opposite sex and was even well-known for some steamy sexual encounters with a few leading Hollywood actors. Celina was more than pleased to accept Maria's invitation to join her in the private marble Jacuzzi on the veranda right off of their room; to prolong the feeling of intense relaxation they were both experiencing after their massages.

The view from the glassed-in veranda was exquisite. The Napa vineyards stretched as far as the eye could see. The sun was slowly setting, covering the expanse of their view with a warm, soothing glow. Maria had slipped out of her resort logo-adorned robe, revealing her sumptuous body. She was slowly submerging herself into the warm, bubbling water of the Jacuzzi. Celina couldn't help but gasp at her beauty. She froze, mesmerized, as she watched Maria slide into the water.

Maria turned to her and smiled. "Come on in. The water feels great." Celina quickly slid out of her robe, dropping it to the floor and stepped into the warm water. Her whole body tingled as she submerged herself slowly. She drew her breath in silently as she thought of what sheer torture this was going to be. She bit her lower lip, willing herself to remain in control. Only seconds passed before Celina was unable to contain herself. She moved closer to Maria, with her budding lips, and gently kissed her on the mouth. Maria surprised herself by accepting the bold advance of her friend. Although she considered herself to be completely straight, she couldn't deny the feeling of erotic pleasure she instantly felt, as Celina's lips touched her own. She and Heraldo had once contemplated a sexual fantasy in which she would make love to another woman as Heraldo watched, but she had never had the courage to go through with it. She had feared she wouldn't enjoy it and had therefore feared rejection by her partner.

Maria sighed as Celina's lips worked their way down to her now erect nipples. She felt a surge of pleasure rising from between her thighs. It felt so incredibly good; so much so that she lifted herself up onto the tub's highest ledge to help fulfill Celina's intentions. She allowed Celina to make love to her in the most intimate ways. That night, Maria experienced what could only be best described as an earth-shattering orgasm. Screams of passion and tremors of pleasure emanated from every part of her body. As she slowly recovered from her ecstasy, Maria looked at Celina with a flushed, guilty smile; knowing full well that she had enjoyed a very selfish pleasure, taken from Celina's obvious passion for her. She knew she couldn't reciprocate and felt somewhat awkward. As if reading her mind, Celina kissed her on the lips and spoke gently.

"It's okay. I've wanted to do this to you for a long time, but I know this isn't your thing." She smiled at Maria as she spoke. Touched by Celina's honest words, Maria's eyes welled up with tears. She lifted her hand and gently stroked Celina's face with the back of her hand.

"I love you Celina. You're a great friend and I missed you so much," she whispered. Maria leaned forward slowly and kissed her on the lips, connecting with her for a long time. Their kiss grew passionately. Celina slowly lifted her friend out of the water and gently placed her on one of the bathrobes. She moved over her, completely covering her. Almost instantly, both women were in the grips of passion; Celina's orgasmic moans providing the soundtrack for their lovemaking, soon ascending into one long, passionate cry of pleasure. Both fully satiated, they rolled back into the tub, looking at each other with child-like grins.

That night, they both ate ravenously. The risotto with wild, local mushrooms, paired with a local sampling of the winery's best red wines were devoured completely. They experienced a renewal of their friendship, both knowing full well that their earlier passionate lovemaking would never be duplicated. In a way, both were relieved that they had experienced such intimate pleasure with each other. It had finally freed them from the slight tension that had always been with them, from the onset of their friendship so many years before. However, Maria felt a slight apprehension. The last thing she wanted to do was hurt Celina's feelings. In any case, Maria had a wonderful story to tell Heraldo. He would definitely get a rise out of this. He had met Celina on several occasions and had always thought of her as a very attractive woman. Celina knew he would probably even be a bit jealous, but she also knew he was secure enough in his manhood to be okay with it. Heraldo and Maria didn't keep any secrets from each other when it came to their sexual desires. In some ways, that's exactly what had always kept them so sexually tuned in and passionate towards each other.

Ernesto Castillo was meeting with his most trusted advisers and business associates in his immense skyscraper, overlooking the city of Cartagena. The view was breathtaking, built according to his personal specifications. The structure was, by far, the tallest in this part of the world; its style and flair rivaling the newer structures in the Orient and in the Middle East. Equipped with a helipad, Castillo never even had to set foot on the ground in the city, which by all accounts, was a wise move for a man of his stature. From this lair, Castillo controlled his empire and entertained his guests. From tropical gardens with grotto pools and giant aquariums with swimming mermaids, to frozen ski slopes; this building had it all. At a cost of just over a cool billion dollars, it had been constructed as a monument to a new Colombia; free of its past conflicts and finally entering an era of booming economic development and prosperity. But mostly, it was Castillo's play toy. Built to resemble a pyramid, it rose to nearly eight-hundred feet tall.

His bedroom was on the top floor, right above a modest, two-thousand square feet of living space, with a three-hundred and sixty degree view of the world. The window tint was electronically adjustable to complete darkness if he so desired and were of course bulletproof as well. Like a Pharaoh, but very much alive, he reigned supreme over the lower echelons. A sculpture of Osiris' eye adorned one of his bedroom walls, built out of pure gold, precious stones and spanning over twelve feet in length. It stood there, overlooking the world, as well as a gigantic bed where half a dozen white, toy-sized poodles lounged in various stages of relaxation.

"My dear friends," said Castillo. "We are entering the second phase of our operation in the United States. The fish has taken the bait and we will soon be ready to reel it in." A smile played on his lips as he continued. "Very soon, all of you will be rich beyond your wildest dreams. The reason I've summoned you all here today, is to personally give each and every one of you a check for fifty million dollars; a small deposit, in comparison to the balance forthcoming, but this is a token of my appreciation and a sign of my commitment to our cause. You can still walk away, right now. But once you cash these checks, you will be held accountable for your missions' success. Is everybody in agreement?" The quick nods from everyone in the group clearly showed that all were acquiescing. At this stage in the mission, all of them knew dissent was simply not an option.

"Good gentlemen. I would like you to meet our new business partner, Mr. Smith: a man that made our deal possible and will provide us with the necessary expertise to help retrieve the package. After you all get acquainted, we shall proceed to the garden salon, where you will all be served drinks and roasted meat."

Having chatted briefly over introductions; the group took the elevator to the dining area which overlooked a stunningly beautiful tropical garden. A large table had been set up for them, across the room from a large professional kitchen with roasting pits, containing various whole carcasses of sheep, pigs and cows. The scene was reminiscent of one of the paintings of town life by the Dutch Masters. The aromas coming from the kitchen area were mouth-watering, enough to make a carnivore out of the most committed vegan. The men's stomachs rumbled with expectation as they gawked at the culinary scene before them. They sat at the massive, intricately-carved wooden table, underneath the shadows of some trees and overlooking several small ponds. Their view included the mountains in the distance which surrounded the city. Soon after they were seated, a small army of extremely good looking waitresses; dressed up as Argentine cowgirls in short leather skirts, proceeded to serve them each their choice of beverage. Another group of waitresses then appeared with the first servings of meats and the food orgy had begun. Castillo was notoriously well-known for his incredible parties and this was going to be a memorable one. Once satiated, the men were offered more drinks as they retired to oversized leather sofas made out of animal hides, with the fur still present.

Upon entering the building, each guest had been handed a key to his own private suite, so they could each stay and enjoy some further relaxation after the meeting and sumptuous meal. However, as these special guests knew, the really interesting part of Castillo's parties usually came after the dinner. Several beautiful young women; a group that would make Hugh Heffner jealous, entered the area. They proceeded to mingle with whoever was free to do so. Needless to say, pretty much every man was available, with the exception of Mr. Smith, who had left shortly after the dinner due to an embassy engagement. Some of the men didn't waste any time at all, and acting like not-so-distant cave men's relatives, grabbed what was in their reach, immediately satisfying their primeval urges. Other more sophisticated gentlemen, simply disappeared to their suites with their companions for a night of more lasting pleasure. Castillo loved these organized parties and enjoyed watching the debauchery of his men in action. It reminded him of scenes from Roman times and caused him to feel like a Roman emperor. Soon enough, the few men left were no longer moving much, either from exhaustion, a drunken stupor or both. A crew of helpers discreetly assisted the men to their suites and administered the proper care if needed.

It was time for Castillo to signal the go ahead for the second phase of his plan. He reached for his phone and made a quick, long-distance call to California. It wouldn't be long before the wheels of the main part of his plan would start grinding and the long-awaited operation he had masterminded would reveal itself. Done for the day, he stepped into his private elevator and ascended to his bedroom where, under a barrage of scurrying dogs, he crawled into his bed and immediately fell asleep, thinking of the fifty billion dollars that would soon be his.

Chapter 6

It was a rainy Friday morning when Heraldo woke up in his small apartment on Bourbon Street. The sounds of hydraulic brakes, beeping noises and short, guttural screams filled the air: garbage collection on the streets of New Orleans. Today was an important day. One thousand pounds of pure cocaine powder was being delivered to his boats off of the coast of Louisiana. Four out of the fifteen boats in his fleet had been assigned the duty of collecting it. An additional amount of tuna, caught in recent hours, had been transferred to the four boats; to provide a sufficient amount of receptacles for the illicit substance. At roughly twenty pounds of cocaine per average-sized tuna, they would need fifty tunas; not always an easy catch these days. Heraldo had designed a somewhat ingenious device for what he called his 'drop pods'. Each fifty-five gallon barrel containing the cocaine paste, similar in consistency to the notorious and infamous McDonalds pink slime, was set to auto-submerge itself about ten feet under as soon as it was put into the water. A small transmitter wire floated on the surface of the water above each one. As soon as the Mexican delivery boats dropped them into the water, the Mexicans sent the drop coordinates in the form of a coded message. A computer program, designed specifically for that purpose, then computed the present location of the barrels based upon the ocean's currents at play. It wasn't a perfect science, but it usually allowed for no more than a one-square-mile search area, which wasn't bad at all. Once in the area, Heraldo's boats would activate a signal to which the antenna wire on the barrel would respond. Heraldo's boats had found the barrels, after continually pinging back and forth. Small, floating, orange tethers were released from each barrel to make them more visible in the last, crucial moments of searching. The barrels were then instantly connected to two hoses: one for suction and one for pressurization. Each barrel's contents were quickly extracted and replaced by salt water and air. The barrels were then released back into the ocean to once again auto-submerge to ten feet, where they would remain until collected by the Mexican boats at a later time. It was a quick operation that took less than five minutes. It was also difficult to notice from the air, since nothing of substance was ever visibly loaded onto the boats.

Once the drug paste was fully extracted, it was stored in a holding tank and subsequently injected into the cleaned-out stomachs of each tuna, making what Landry jokingly called "the best boudain in town"; referring to the Cajun sausage.

All pickups had gone smoothly, per the text message Heraldo had just received. The goods were sailing towards Grand Isle where the tuna would be unloaded and trucked to New Orleans. Heraldo had made arrangements for this shipment to go to dealers in the Northeast of the United States. A mere thousand pounds wasn't that difficult to conceal in five-pound tuna cans; barely a pallet. The cans would be shipped to a delicatessen in upstate New York for further distribution. Payments for the drugs would be made by third-party companies to the gold company; a purchase of gold that would never be delivered of course. The system had worked well so far, mainly because it was so basic and uncomplicated. Heraldo liked to keep things simple and without overhead. The less people involved, the less risk of discovery by the authorities, and the easier it was to cover their tracks in the event of a leak. Although his organization was quite vertical, no one at any level had direct contact with any other level. Levels of distribution were always separated by a buffer of innocent, third–party operators and communications were all handled by a few well-trusted men and some military-grade scrambling computer programs.

The nerve center of Heraldo's operation was in an office building located on Poydras Street in New Orleans, hidden in plain sight as a computer consulting company. That is where Heraldo was headed. Keeping an eye out for the unusual, as always, he drove into the parking garage of the building without incident and headed up to his office; or 'monitoring station', as he was fond of calling it. From the comfort of his expensive leather chair, he could check on the status of any of the shipments in real time. The delivery trucks had all been equipped with cameras and geo-positioning locators so as to be able to monitor any situation. Heraldo watched their locators as they approached their final destination in New Orleans.

The processing warehouse was monitored inside and out and was always on standby for the arrival of the goods. The ten-thousand pounds of tuna would be processed and canned in less than four hours. Then it would be delivered, not only to various legitimate wholesalers and retailers around town, but also shipped overnight to distributors all across the country. Even though there had been some concern about the safety of the tuna, due to the level of mercury content, it was a trade-off most fresh tuna lovers were willing to live with. Heraldo didn't spare words when it came to this concern. The concentration of methyl mercury found in large fish rarely came close to the levels found in ordinary processed foods such as corn syrup. However, the lobbyists for the processed food industry were so powerful, that any truthful information was quickly countered by its extremely powerful and well-funded propaganda machine. As in all things, moderation was the key, and tuna had certainly gained a huge amount of popularity among the affluent as a clean-tasting, savory source of high-quality protein which could be downright addictive for those who could afford it.

As the fish came in, they were eviscerated. The guts were sent to a designated room, where the intestinal tracts were separated and put into plastic containers. This was done by a small highly-skilled and specialized crew. They extracted the drug paste from the fish guts by what seemed to only be a simple washing process. A non-initiate would have never noticed the substance, instead being overwhelmed by the powerful fishy smell and sight of blood. Most would have only been focused on leaving the area as quickly as possible. On many occasions, Heraldo had given tours of the facility to personal guests as well as officials; all of whom had been completely oblivious to what was transpiring in this processing plant. Both Landry and Heraldo derived quite a vicarious thrill from doing so.

Out of caution, Heraldo had hired a private security firm in California to keep an eye on his wife. This wasn't something Maria had been fond of, but after some convincing from Heraldo, she had finally acquiesced. The security team had been instructed to stay in the background and not have any direct contact with her. Their job was to provide a buffer zone between any danger she might encounter and Maria herself. Once she and Celina had embarked upon their road trip, Maria had quickly forgotten all about the security team. She didn't even notice the large SUV that followed Celina's limo the entire way to the coast. Having enjoyed their time in the wine country, Maria and Celina had decided that some fresh ocean air and walks on the beach would be a nice way to complete their little adventure. After all, a little exercise would help burn off some of the calories from the sumptuous feasts they had consumed in the last couple of days; not to mention help clear their heads from the fog of a few too many wine tastings.

The same SUV had also been on the radar of the team of henchmen sent by Castillo. His men all had strong military backgrounds and had each made their living in recent years taking care of specific threats to Castillo's business concerns. From the assassination of prominent officials to the elimination of bothersome competitors; these men had done it all. They were a rag tag bunch of Caucasians, like a group one would encounter in the French Foreign Legion. The advantage of their ethnicity was that they could easily blend in; much better than a group of Hispanics possibly could, even in California. Castillo knew that once he put pressure on Heraldo, his reaction would be either fight or flight. If his knowledge of the man was correct, he was almost sure Heraldo would fight. However, Castillo also knew that a man like Heraldo would do anything to protect his wife.

Maria hadn't been very hard to track. Having studied her background, Castillo knew the trip to California was almost a given. It had also not been too hard to find Celina, and on the pretext of future work, his team had gathered an abundance of intelligence regarding her whereabouts in the coming days. Her limo had been tagged with a small geo-positioning locator. All they had to do was wait for the perfect opportunity to strike. The mercenaries had strict orders to capture Maria alive, without harm. She was going to be a valuable hostage. Castillo had known the operation would be a cake walk as long as they could control their surroundings. First, they had to eliminate the security team. Maria and Celina had chosen to take a scenic road to the coast of California and that had made the operation that much easier. The plan had been simple.

The limousine drove about thirty-five miles per hour along the curvy, mountainous road. Some of Castillo's men, riding in their stolen delivery truck, positioned themselves between the SUV and the limo. As a tight hairpin curve had come up, they had simply slowed down, as if to let the SUV pass. Once the SUV had pulled up beside them, the driver of the truck had quickly turned the wheel to the left, forcing the SUV off of the road. Before the driver of the SUV could even react, it had been given a final push into the ravine, by a heavy-duty dually pickup truck, full of Castillo's remaining mercenaries. The SUV had plunged into the ravine, stopped only by the rocks at the bottom of the large lake reservoir. It was doubtful the SUV would be found anytime soon. The limo driver and its occupants had been oblivious to the incident. They had already been out of sight, having made the hairpin turn seconds before. Without delay, both the delivery truck and dually sped up, quickly catching up with the limo. The dually passed, pulled in front of it quickly and slowed down, blocking the roadway and forcing the limo to a complete stop. The limo driver jumped out, obviously angry, and headed straight for the driver's side of the dually. At that moment, the delivery truck came to a stop behind the limo and three men jumped out, surrounding the limo with handguns drawn.

Before Maria or Celina could react, two of the men entered the back of the limo from each back door, while the third jumped into the driver's seat. The two men in the back instantly immobilized the two women, preventing them from escape. The third man quickly put the limo into drive. The dually had realigned itself with the road, but only after its driver had carefully pulled the trigger of his silenced handgun, landing a perfect shot into the limo chauffeur's forehead. Less than thirty seconds after the limo had been forced to a stop, the driver's body was thrown into the ravine and the limo was on its way again, followed by the trucks and their occupants. The operation had been a success, just as anticipated. A coded message was relayed to Castillo within moments: "the birds are in the nest". A couple of miles down the road, all three vehicles pulled onto what seemed to be a side road that climbed to a steep ridge. They drove about a quarter of a mile up and stopped.

The women, both gagged and with zip-ties around their wrists and ankles, were placed into padded crates inside the larger truck. They were too scared to resist. Two of Castillo's men doused the inside of the limo with the contents of a five-gallon can of gasoline, before climbing into the vehicles and heading back towards the main road. An ignition timer with a twenty-minute delay was thrown through the open sunroof of the dually as they sped away.

Maria was petrified, hunched over inside the four-by-four crate. The motion of the truck made her sick to her stomach and it took all the willpower she could muster to keep from throwing up. She knew doing so in such tight quarters would be highly unpleasant and she didn't want to die choking on her own vomit. She had instantly known what this was about. Heraldo's enemies had followed her all the way to California. She cringed at the thought. But why hadn't they killed her? They hadn't hesitated in disposing of Heraldo's brother and his family. As desperate as her situation was, she tried to find some comfort in the fact that they had not yet killed her, convincing herself that they must need her to remain alive.

The mercenaries' leader, Jacob, made a phone call to one of his associates, to coordinate a meeting point on the way to Moro Bay. Jacob didn't want to drive the stolen truck into the more urban areas where cameras could be on the watch. Thirty minutes later, a rented U-Haul van met up with them and the crates were transferred to the new vehicle. Once again, the other trucks were primed to burn with a twenty-minute delay. About half an hour later they reached their destination: a small harbor on the coast of California. There, they loaded the crates onto a very fast, twin-engine fishing boat before Jacob and two of his men also boarded. The rest would drive back to Los Angeles and catch a flight to Mexico City later in the day. The operation had been a complete success. Jacob, his crew and the crated women sped away to the mother ship, about thirty miles off the coast. Maria, as disoriented as she was from all of the movement, smelled the fresh air seeping through the holes of her crate. She closed her eyes for a moment. The air reminded her of being on the Santa Monica pier: much happier times. She knew they had left the coast and her chances of being rescued were fast diminishing. It didn't take long for the boat to reach its mother ship. The crates were opened and their occupants forced onto the larger vessel.

The mother ship was what could best be described as a 'super yacht'; over four-hundred feet in length. It had all of the accommodations found in any luxury hotel. Maria and Celina were quickly escorted to a large stateroom and freed of their restraints. However, one of the guards grimly told Maria not to try anything or they wouldn't hesitate to kill Celina on the spot. Then the guards left the two women alone, locking the stateroom securely behind them. Maria suddenly realized why they had kept Celina alive; to use her as a hostage to get Maria to cooperate. Once onboard, the large yacht picked up speed and headed south-southwest at thirty knots. The seas were calm, so the Mexican coast would be within reach before the day was over.

Earlier that day, the Puckett security computer system had issued a notice that it had been unable to locate vehicle four. No signal had been successfully delivered and all electronic attempts to communicate with the vehicle or its occupants had failed. Vehicle four had been assigned to some female actress earlier that week. Although system glitches were rare, they weren't unheard of. The man in charge at the time forwarded an emergency contact notice to the supervisor in charge. The supervisor was somewhat surprised and immediately attempted to call the vehicle's driver. Oddly enough, the phone showed up as non-responsive or disconnected. Drivers were never allowed to turn off their phones while on duty, so it became an immediate cause of concern. He quickly attempted to reach their client, Celina, and was met with the same result. The hairs on the back of his head stood on end. He had a bad feeling. He pulled up their last known location based on the vehicle's geo-positioning system. It showed up on a small mountain road off of the main road. He pulled up the area on his digital map and looked at the satellite view. Immediately, he came to the only possible conclusion: they had gone off the road into the water.

He called the State Police, advised them of the situation and quickly made arrangements for a helicopter pick-up to take him to the presumed location of the incident. An hour later, he walked up the side of the road overlooking the embankment from which the SUV had gone off. One could definitely make out some tire marks, some larger than expected for the vehicle in question. Somehow, he knew whatever had happened there, wasn't an accident. A police car pulled up. He introduced himself and shared his conclusion with the officer. Based on the larger tire marks, a notice was posted for a suspicious truck on the road. But because of the scarcity of patrol officers in the area, there was little chance it would lead to anything. The man boarded the helicopter and they took off. Immediately, the security man noticed a plume of smoke rising from a hill nearby. He realized quickly that it looked to be the remains of a limousine and he knew right then and there that it had to be their client's vehicle.

They landed and as he looked over the remains from a distance, there was some saving grace. There didn't appear to be anyone's remains in the charred car. Obviously, this had been a kidnapping. He immediately alerted the authorities. By sundown, the FBI had recovered all three of the destroyed vehicles, but no identification or leads were found. The trail went cold almost immediately. They couldn't determine conclusively which vehicle had been used in the final escape. Little did they know that the suspects and their victims were already outside the jurisdiction of the United States.

Chapter 7

Castillo was glowing. The "wife" was now in his custody and control and he could practically taste the victory. In a couple of days, he would have her transported from the yacht to his penthouse and would, at last, be ready to make his demands to Heraldo. His blood pressure was skyrocketing because of the excitement, but he didn't care. It was moments like this that made his life worth living; moments like this that made him feel god-like, with the power to control his fellow men and their destinies.

Heraldo received a call from the security company in California later that afternoon and was briefed on his wife's kidnapping. The fact that they hadn't killed her right then and there told him that there was more to this than just the simple elimination of a rival. No drug king pin would waste their time going to so much trouble, simply for elimination. Obviously, whoever was pulling the strings, had something else in mind. Heraldo was frustrated. He felt angry and more than anything, guilty, for having allowed Maria to go to California to begin with. He should have known better. But he was relieved that she was obviously still alive. Soon enough, he would know what this was all about. He promised himself that his revenge would be brutal. Little did he know.

Upon hitting a dead end, the California feds immediately turned their investigation to the victims. Celina was a well-known actress and although not wealthy by Hollywood standards, her net worth was around three million dollars; sufficient enough to possibly generate envy from people she might have had contact with. They were sure the kidnapping had the earmarks of a gang-related operation and that ransom demands would soon follow.

They soon discovered that Celina had a younger brother living in a guest house on her estate. He became their prime suspect and agents were sent to his place. After checking him out thoroughly, nothing indicated he had any involvement in his sister's kidnapping, so a broader search for suspects was initiated. Anyone known to Celina, from the gardeners to her well-known friends, were interrogated. A notice was sent out to the New Orleans' Bureau for the purpose of gathering information on the husband of the other kidnapped individual: Maria. When Heraldo got the phone call from the FBI, he wasn't surprised in the least. He had already known it was going to be yet another issue he was going to have to deal with, on top of everything else.

On the day of the kidnapping, he had contacted them in New Orleans; not because he expected them to help, but for the sake of appearances. He had been told someone would call him back. He was well-aware of how the American justice system relied on first impressions and he really didn't need the FBI poking around. Thankfully, Castillo felt the same way. A ransom note was mailed to Celina's brother, from a Mexican border town. It requested the sum of one million dollars be paid and told him to await further instructions. Once that document was in the FBI's possession, the investigation took on a different focus; reinforcing the fact that Celina was the primary kidnapping victim. Nevertheless, a routine background check of Heraldo was done, but the only significant facts uncovered, were his prominent role in the New Orleans community, the fact that he was a wealthy man and that he and his wife were very much in love, by all accounts. It came as a relief when the agent with whom Heraldo met, informed him of the requested ransom for Celina's release. Immediately, Heraldo volunteered to provide the funds required. But of course, the FBI couldn't support the action. The agent expressed his sympathy and told Heraldo they would keep him abreast of the situation as it unfolded.

Maria and Celina had cruised past the coast of Central America and were sailing off the territorial waters of Colombia. Besides being prisoners, the trip had been uneventful and quite comfortable. The crew members had been distant, yet polite, and the meals had been even better quality than your average cruise ship fare. Maria and Celina had passively settled into a routine, so they were startled when three men burst into their cabin, blindfolded them and took them away. Unbeknownst to them, their journey to Castillo's tower had begun. The helicopter ride was quite bumpy, and it was nearly as frightening as being in the crates, especially due to their unknown destination. Upon arrival and still blindfolded, both women were escorted to a large suite on the sixtieth floor, overlooking some mountains and the ocean far below. The main room had a large balcony, but the glass doors leading to it were locked securely. When their blindfolds were finally removed, all they could see was the ocean. Castillo, curious about his newest victims and full of trepidation to make their acquaintance, was waiting right there, sitting on a large, beige leather sofa.

"Welcome to my humble abode ladies. I hope the trip was to your liking." Looking at each other, Maria and Celina couldn't help but show their surprise.

Maria was the first to speak. "What do you want?" she asked in English.

Castillo smiled. "That's for you to find out...in due time. In the interim, I hope you ladies have a pleasant stay. We'll let you know what I expect you to do for me soon."

Celina, not nearly as polite as her friend, told Castillo the equivalent of "go fuck yourself" in perfect Spanish. As an emotional being, she was unable to stop herself. She lunged for him, but was quickly stopped in her tracks by one of the security men's high-voltage cattle probes. She hit the ground like a sack of potatoes, but quickly recovered enough to manage to give Castillo a dirty look.

Castillo raised his eyebrows at her, his eyes twinkling. "You're a feisty one, aren't you?" His eyes darkened and his voice became sultry. "I like that. Maybe you and I can do something about that extra energy later on." Celina was fuming, but knew better than to try to move at that point. "I'll leave you now ladies," said Castillo as he rose and walked out of the suite. His entourage scurried after him.

Heraldo knew that the ransom was just an excuse: a divergence. He expected that whoever was behind this elaborate charade would be in touch. Indeed, a package soon arrived, addressed to his name. The only thing it contained was a small, hard-drive type of device with some kind of computer interface. Simple instructions were included regarding how to connect it to a personal computer. Heraldo immediately proceeded to follow the instructions. After showing the standard booting screen and icons, the logo for the device appeared. It appeared to be some kind of elaborate decoding box, with the ability to jump in between internet providers from all over the world, based on a variable key. Words appeared on the screen and froze.

"Press this button at 5:00pm your time. Make sure all of your audio systems are functioning." That was only one hour away. Heraldo knew the wait would be agony, but at least he would get some answers to his many questions. He made a quick call to Bourgeois, his private investigator in Pensacola. Bourgeois had been casing the bar where the killers of Heraldo's brother had been hanging out after their work at the local customs office. They all seemed to be very friendly with a member of the National Guard from somewhere in Mississippi. However, Bourgeois hadn't been quite sure if the new guy was in on whatever they had been cooking up or not. But, he told Heraldo, from some of the conversations he had overheard already, it was most likely not the case. The men talked about nothing of interest except retiring overseas somewhere in Central America with money to spend. Bourgeois quickly communicated the latest information and apologized for not having more to offer. But Heraldo was a firm believer in being patient. He knew that sooner or later, something of value would transpire. But right then, it was time for the highly-anticipated phone call. After hanging up with Bourgeois, he clicked the mouse on the phone symbol in the middle of the screen. Immediately he heard a succession of tones and clicks and after about ten seconds, a voice spoke clearly.

"Good afternoon, Mr. Sanchez," said Castillo, his voice significantly altered by software. "You and I are going to be well-acquainted before all of this is over. I believe you and I share a mutual interest, if you know what I mean. I trust you understand what I'm driving at."

Heraldo answered simply. "Yes." The voice continued.

"No matter what you hear or see in the next couple of days, don't believe it. Act to protect our common interest. Go with the flow. Don't rock the boat." Before Heraldo could respond, the connection went dead.

Shit, thought Heraldo. *This doesn't help in the least. What can I do now?* His mind raced. *Maybe I should call Celina's brother to make sure he has the money.* But before Heraldo could think any further, his cell phone rang. He answered promptly when he saw it was the FBI.

"Mr. Heraldo Sanchez?"

"Yes, speaking," said Heraldo.

"Can you come to our offices right away? We have something of great importance we need to discuss."

"Yes, of course. Is there something wrong?" asked Heraldo in a 'not so assured' tone.

"When you get here, ask for agent Morris; see you soon." Heraldo was left with another dead phone line and his heart sunk. This didn't sound encouraging. Heraldo's mind raced with a thousand different scenarios. With great apprehension, he drove to the Federal Building, where he was immediately greeted by two agents who whisked him away to a small office on the tenth floor.

There, he was met by Agent Morris. After Heraldo was seated, the agent spoke. "Mr. Sanchez, we have bad news for you. Your wife has been killed by the kidnappers." Heraldo's heart dropped into his gut. He couldn't believe what he had heard. How could they do this? He had just spoken with the kidnapper. Before he could open his mouth, Agent Morris continued. "We received a video of your wife's execution; sent as a warning to show their determination, in case the ransom for Celina wasn't going to be paid. We would like for you to positively identify the person in the video as your wife. I know this is a horrible situation and we're sorry to be the bearer of bad news, but you can rest assured that we will spare no expense to catch these guys." Heraldo was distraught and he looked it. He just didn't understand.

He looked at the agent carefully. "Did you find her body?"

The agent shook his head. "No. We have reason to believe she was held captive in Mexico, so we don't know when or if we'll ever be able to recover your wife's remains." Heraldo simply nodded and looked towards the computer screen, waiting. Agent Morris pressed a key on his computer. A grainy picture of a woman appeared. She was kneeling down, her head on a stump. It seemed to look like Maria, from what Heraldo could tell.

After a few seconds, the agent paused the video and looked at Heraldo. "I understand if you don't want to watch the rest of this footage. It's quite brutal. Can you identify your wife from this?"

"Keep playing it," said Heraldo solemnly. The rest of the video was a gruesome rendition of a beheading, but the focus of the camera was so bad that all one could see was a human-like form; losing what appeared to possibly be its head. Heraldo felt a strange and rather bizarre emotion at that point. The words of the man on the computer rang in his head: *No matter what you hear or see in the next couple of days, don't believe it.* Heraldo desperately hoped the words were true. To the agents, Heraldo appeared lifeless. One of them put his hand on Heraldo's shoulder.

"We're so sorry sir," said the agent. Heraldo quickly regained his composure, but didn't show any signs of the hope he felt. Once he left, he immediately went back to his office. He jumped onto his computer and to his surprise, the call button on the screen had reappeared. He pressed it without hesitation.

"Well, well, well," said the distorted voice at the other end. "It didn't take you very long."

"Where is my wife?" asked Heraldo, trying to remain calm.

"She's perfectly fine. Oh, and a great actress I might add."

"I want to hear her voice," insisted Heraldo.

"Now now. In due time...in due time," said the voice. "But before I allow you two to communicate, there's something I want you to do for me. There's a place not too far from you that has something I want very badly. You'll get it for me, right?"

Heraldo wondered what the fuck the voice could possibly want from him. He had already taken everything he held dearest. Heraldo sighed inaudibly. "Okay," he said with resignation. "I will do what you ask, but you have to release my wife."

"I'm glad you're going to cooperate Heraldo. I will oblige. But first you will get something for me. Once this is done, your wife will be released. You have my word." The following words that Heraldo heard made up the most unexpected and surprising request he could possibly imagine. He was nothing short of flabbergasted.

"About an hour from where you are, there's an armory," Castillo began. "It's a U.S armory located close to a small town in Mississippi. Its perimeters are unguarded. There are some weapons stored there that I want you to get for me. To be specific; five small missiles, armed with nuclear warheads." Sensing Heraldo's bewilderment, Castillo paused before continuing. "Are you still with me?" Heraldo didn't quite know what to say but managed a sheepish 'yes'. His mind raced as the kidnapper continued. "I've been watching you for quite some time. You're not the average trafficker. You've also evaded my attempts to eliminate you, just as I thought you would. I'm confident that if there's one person capable and resourceful enough to carry out this operation, it's you. If you succeed, I will reward you not only with the safe return of your wife, but also with a substantial amount of money."

Finally, Heraldo managed to retrieve his train of thought. He couldn't hold back. "You're fucking insane man. Even if I could manage to pull this off, I'd spend the rest of my short life looking over my shoulder, waiting for a bullet to hit me in the back of the head or hell, even worse. It's one thing to fuck with the cops, even the feds, but the U.S. army? Those guys don't play by the rules man. They just kill you."

"Yes, you are correct," said Castillo calmly. "However, the blame for this, if you're careful, will not lie with you; but with the ultimate beneficiary of these weapons. I don't expect you will ever be caught. Now, you're going to receive an encoded transmission shortly, with the plans of the armory. It's a relatively small armory, heavily reinforced with concrete walls, dirt and state-of-the-art electronics. However, it's poorly staffed and far from substantial quick reinforcements: police or otherwise. I'll let you study this for a couple of days and then I'll call you back. I'll expect you to have a preliminary plan for me by then."

Heraldo didn't hesitate. "I want to talk to my wife. I need to know she's okay before I even consider doing any of this."

"Okay, I'm going to put her on the phone," Castillo agreed. "She's right here." There was a pause.

"Heraldo, I'm okay. They have me in another country; I'm not sure where." Heraldo wasn't sure it was really her due to the voice distortion software. He quickly thought of a test.

"Maria, what did you give me as a present on our first anniversary?" Maria answered without hesitation.

"I gave you an antique watch." Reassured, Heraldo quickly answered back. "I love you Maria." His heart nearly broke as she instantly began to sob. Castillo took the phone away and spoke immediately, catching Heraldo a bit off guard in the emotional moment.

"Now that you two love birds have been reacquainted...Mr. Sanchez, I will call you back in a couple of days for your completed homework. Good luck." The connection went dead. Heraldo sat in shock, unable to move. For the first time in his adult life, he felt completely out of control. Someone else was pulling the strings and he felt totally powerless. Maria wasn't dead. But he knew now there was a good chance he would die himself trying to save her.

Suddenly, a beep from his computer interrupted his thoughts. The file Castillo had promised to send had suddenly appeared. Heraldo opened it immediately. The armory was located about seventy miles from New Orleans in a very rural area; even by Mississippi standards. Heraldo guessed the armory had been established as part of the end of the cold war strategy of the military: to spread its nuclear weaponry among numerous, non-descript areas, rather than concentrating them at easily targetable military bases. The weapons in questions were tomahawk missiles, equipped with small, high-yield fusion nuclear devices, in the range of one hundred and fifty kilotons: large enough to level a mid-sized city. These suckers were seriously heavy in weight. From the information Heraldo was reading, they were each close to two thousand pounds; not exactly the kind of thing you would throw over your shoulder and run away with.

Per the information in front of Heraldo, the armory was heavily reinforced with one-foot thick concrete and vault-like steel doors; not to mention reinforced glass and cameras everywhere. It certainly wasn't the kind of place where one could walk in unannounced. Heraldo knew this mission would require some serious planning and manpower. Immediately, Heraldo had one major concern. Even if he could get the missiles out of the armory, could he transport them quickly enough to escape the onslaught of choppers that would no doubt be dispatched almost instantly, due to the close proximity of the armory to several military airports and bases?

In the best case scenario, Heraldo knew he would have twenty minutes, at the most, to make the nukes disappear. The more he thought about it, the more daunting the mission became. Another issue that came to mind was who to trust. It was one thing to live a life of crime, but quite another to face charges of treason. Landry was a solid member of his operation and had benefited greatly from their partnership. However, was he someone who would, in a sense, betray his country to save Heraldo's wife? That was the most immediate obstacle Heraldo faced. Heraldo had enough dirt on Landry to have him put away for good, but that also worked both ways. His only angle of approach, besides their friendship, was money. Heraldo wondered how much would it take. Heraldo pondered the conversation with his wife's kidnapper and the mention of a monetary reward. Considering the mission, he knew it would be an extraordinary amount of money. Within seconds, he called Landry in for a meeting.

Heraldo had to take a chance with Landry, so he was completely blunt with him. He explained the underlying reason for the recent events, sparing no details. Heraldo had decided to give Landry a choice: to stay out of this particular mission and continue their other business as usual, or join him and help rescue his wife. Landry surprised him.

"You and I go a long way back," Landry said without hesitation. "I'm about ready to retire anyway. Obviously, once you get this done, we'll no longer have a business anyway, not with the serious money you mentioned. It's a good thing you'll get paid well, especially once the proverbial shit hits the fan."

Heraldo was relieved to say the least. The next step was to get a feel for the area. It would be necessary to drive down in person to check it out. Being a 'home boy', so to speak, Landry decided he would use hidden cameras placed on an F-150 truck to take some pictures and videos of the armory. The truck would blend in perfectly in the local scene. The very next day, Landry drove to Mississippi to the location in question. The armory itself was about a mile from the interstate; not bad for a quick getaway. However, it was also next to a small town with a few traffic lights to pass through. Thankfully, they didn't appear to have any kind of surveillance cameras. Landry had decided it would be better for him to come alone. Routine police stops were common in these parts and a Mexican would have stood out like a sore thumb. Landry had pointed out that the last thing they needed was to attract attention before the mission. Heraldo had reluctantly agreed.

He knew that especially in the last few years, it had been harder and harder for brown-skinned individuals to freely move about in the rural parts of the U.S. without being watched, ostracized or even worse. In essence, Mexicans had become the new piñatas of North American society, scapegoats for all the ills that plagued the current economy. Heraldo had learned, from a very young age, to avoid confrontation with rednecks. He thanked his lucky stars that New Orleans was such a well-blended city of ethnicities and therefore, more accepting of people's differences.

Landry's reconnaissance operation went off without a hitch. He made several passes by the armory and took loads of pictures of it and the surrounding area; including police headquarters and all possible points of entry and exit. Hunger pains finally brought him on his way back to New Orleans.

Later that evening, Heraldo and Landry met over dinner at Ruth Chris Steak House. Keeping names and locations out of their conversation, Landry gave Heraldo a brief summary of the area. He concluded that, without a doubt, they would need an inside man for the job. There was simply no way anyone would be able to penetrate the armory by force and live to tell the tale. Landry also told Heraldo that they would need a pre-determined area close by, for both the planning and execution of the mission. It was decided that Landry would either purchase or lease some farm land, with a barn, under the pretext of needing some hunting grounds for the occasional weekend. Landry knew that shouldn't be too hard to accomplish considering the volume of 'for sale' signs he had noticed in the area. Realizing they would never be able to plan everything over a simple dinner, the men finally parted ways and Heraldo headed home to prepare for his phone meeting with the kidnapper the following morning.

As he pulled into the driveway of his beautiful home on St. Charles Avenue, Heraldo realized how much he missed his wife and their home life. He hadn't seen either in several days. Exhaustion overtook him as he stepped into the familiar safety of their home. When he finally went to bed, he slept deeply. The last few days had certainly taken their toll on him, but at least now he knew what he was up against. That knowledge alone made the recent events infinitely more bearable.

Chapter 8

Gaspard Bourgeois had once again gone to the bar in Pensacola to gather more intelligence. What he didn't realize was that one of the customs agents had become curious about him. So that night, on his way back to his hotel room from the bar, he had been followed. It had been easy enough for his pursuer to find out who he was. The next day, Bourgeois was headed back to Gulfport, when for no logical reason, he lost control of his vehicle on interstate ten. His vehicle crossed the median and hit an eighteen wheeler, head on. Little remained of the private investigator or the car.

When the kidnapper, Castillo, called early the next morning, Heraldo had been already up and about, exercising in his gym. He had hooked up his laptop to the encryption box and had quickly connected the feed.

"Good morning Mr. Sanchez," Castillo began. "I hope you are well rested. I can't wait to hear what you have to tell me." Heraldo quickly went over everything he and Landry had discussed.

Castillo seemed pleased so far. "I'm glad your friend Landry is cooperating. I can see how he would be an asset. You can tell him that I have reserved one hundred million American dollars for him, payable upon delivery of our goods. Of course, you will be receiving ten times that amount, under the same conditions. Furthermore, since I can see you are making progress, I have a pleasant surprise for you. We already have a man on the inside. He's military reserve and works at the armory about one weekend a month. He also lives in the area. I'm sending you his phone number and he will be notified that you or Mr. Landry will contact him soon. I'll be calling you soon after you meet with him." Castillo broke the connection and the line went dead. Heraldo sat there for a moment. Up until right then, the whole operation had been somewhat surreal. But now it had been brought down to earth.

"We're actually going to do this insanity," he mumbled to himself. Heraldo quickly called Landry and gave him the latest information, including the mole's phone number he had just received from the kidnapper. The man's name was Rusty Smith and Landry decided he would call him immediately to set up a meeting for the three of them. They decided to meet at five o'clock in the evening in Slidell, located about thirty minutes from New Orleans, at the boathouse where Heraldo and his wife had been dropped off earlier that same week.

Heraldo and Landry were sitting on the porch overlooking the dock and canal when they watched an old, blue Ford sedan pull into the house's parking area. A skinny, tall man stepped out of the car. They waved him up to the elevated deck where they were having drinks. After introductions, Landry offered the man some Member's Mark, straight up and they all sat around a mahogany wood table.

Rusty Smith had been the source of the information about the nukes. Even though he had not been officially informed about it in his capacity as a security guard, he had noticed a radiation monitoring device in one of the control rooms and had once seen what had appeared to be large missiles with radiation symbols, in storage in one of the ammunition vaults. That finding had confirmed his suspicions. In his earlier days, he had worked as a maintenance person at one of the nuclear plants. Therefore, he was very familiar with the equipment and its symbols. Mr. Smith seemed to be a nervous man. He was a chain smoker and obviously, quite a drinker by the way he was guzzling the whiskey. His drinking habits suited Heraldo and Landry just fine. The more information they could get out of the guy, the better. Smith continued to speak.

"My job there is to guard the front lobby; me and some other guy I don't know. The only time we're allowed anywhere else is when we get a shipment. Then we go downstairs with two more guards from the other side, and me and the other dude; we have to sit outside to help the truck back into the loading area. Landry's ears perked up.

"Tell us about the loading dock door," he insisted. Rusty shook his head.

"That motherfucker's a beast. It's actually a roll-down door; a heavy-duty one that unrolls from the top. Then there's another door that looks like some kind of reinforced garage door. It's made of what looks like maybe one-inch thick steel. Then each vault has its own steel door too. They also look like garage doors, but they come down from the inside."

Landry nodded before posing his next question. "What kind of walls do you have inside the armory?"

"It's all concrete walls," said Rusty Smith. They look like about one-foot thick; no cinder blocks or anything like that. The motherfucker is stout," the man said with a solemn nod.

"What about between the lobby upstairs and the rest of the building?" asked Landry.

"Same deal; all concrete with a metal door to access the rest of the armory, plus a regular door that goes to the bathroom in the lobby. There's also a small, reinforced glass window that overlooks the lobby. That's where the control room is with some of the monitoring equipment. It's also where the three other guards stand watch."

Landry's eyebrows raised in surprise. "You mean to tell me that this whole armory only has five people in it?"

Smith nodded. "Only five guards, yeah. But there's some office workers there some of the time too; six or seven. On the weekends, they have reserve stuff going on upstairs and the place is packed. They use the rooms upstairs for meetings and changing rooms and all that."

"Okay, good to know," nodded Landry. He smiled at Smith. "Now for the good stuff. What do you know about the security system?"

"Well every time I go there, I'm frisked and all of my stuff is checked. They send me to the changing room, where I'm given my equipment; same goes for anyone else entering the armory. The office workers are locked in their areas. The inside guards are the only ones that can wander around. As far as surveillance, they have cameras everywhere except the bathrooms and the outside of the building has some motion-triggered alarms. There's a perimeter fence that is kept shut when no one is scheduled to come in or out.

Heraldo interjected. "What kind of power supply do they have?"

Smith thought for a moment. "Well, they have a generator in the back of the armory. There's a propane tank buried in the ground. I know a truck comes to top it off every once in a while. Oh, and once a month, they fire it up to test the system. There's also a battery room, I remember when they trucked them in; big yellow things. But from what I heard, those aren't connected yet, cause of some kind of supplier manufacturing delay problem.

Landry spoke up next. "What about outside communications? Do you know anything about that?"

Smith nodded. "They got a satellite dish on the roof and all kinds of antennas. I know they're wired for the internet too, cause I was there when the phone company came for that."

"Is there any other kind of security besides the local cops?" asked Landry.

"No. They're pretty confident in their hardware man," Smith said with big eyes. "I would be too. Like I said, that motherfucking building is stout. Even if you made it into the lobby, there's no way you could penetrate the rest of the building without being wiped out. They got steel trap doors everywhere that can be opened from the control room. All they'd have to do is slip you a grenade and everyone in the lobby would be pickled."

Heraldo was pleased with what they had learned so far. "Alright, we have some good information to work with here. We'll be in touch as soon as we figure this out." Heraldo was getting worried about the guy making it home in one piece, given the rate of his boozing. Three glasses of Member's Mark would hit any man hard, even a hardcore alcoholic. He wasn't about to pour the guy another one. Heraldo stood up, shook the man's hand and helped him out to the steps downstairs. Disappointed, but feeling no pain, Smith obliged and made it to his car in a surprisingly short time. He sped away quickly; most likely to a local watering hole to finish himself off.

Heraldo looked at Landry. "We have some work to do, especially with the plans of the armory I got earlier. My question is: who else is monitoring the place? Even if we somehow make it in and incapacitate the guards in the control room; given the low level of manpower, I'm thinking they're being monitored by someone else...somewhere else. The minute we break in, they may hit us with such force that it would make D-Day look like a picnic. I'm not even sure if cutting all communication to the building would avoid that."

Heraldo sighed and looked at Landry. "So," he shrugged. "What the hell do we do?"

"Well," said Landry. "We sleep on it."

Neither of them had any desire to ride back to New Orleans at that time of the night, so they opted to stay there. Heraldo had a restless night. He dreamt that he was continuously trying to get to his wife, but every time he came close to her, she disappeared. Each time, he was given a new task to accomplish and although successful, the final outcome never changed. The reality, however, was a bit more complicated, as he realized upon awakening. The task at hand didn't seem solvable, at least not with the latest information he had gathered over the past few days. It was with this sobering thought that he met Landry downstairs in the kitchen. Both with a warm coffee mug in hand, they walked to the inside patio, air-conditioned and comfortable. Even this early in the morning, the muggy heat of late July would have been unbearable without air-conditioning.

"This is going to be tough," said Landry, once they had settled into comfortable chairs. "I think we need to buy some time with these people; the ones who have Maria." Landry looked at Heraldo who nodded slowly as he sipped his coffee. Landry continued. "I suggest we work on the storage and delivery of the missiles once we get them. I've been thinking about it all night. You know how we decided to get a place locally to plan and execute from?" Heraldo nodded again. "Well, I'm thinking that we're going to need to disguise these weapons somehow, really well. Everyone and their mother will be searching for them in no time."

"True," said Heraldo. "So, any idea?" Landry nodded, looking pleased with himself.

"Why don't we open a concrete forming plant? We could put the rockets in the frame of a concrete pile or caisson and truck them out of there at our convenience when things cool off." Heraldo nearly smiled, he was so impressed.

"Excellent idea Landry." Suddenly, Heraldo felt much more hopeful. "We can truck them all the way to my place in Grand Isle and load them up on a barge. They'll blend right in with all that kind of activity going on over there. Okay, go ahead and get us a place about five miles from the armory, on the West side of it towards Louisiana." Landry was fired up, happy that they at least seemed to have a solid solution to hiding and delivering the weapons. Without anything further to discuss, he left and headed to the small town. About an hour later, he stopped at a local realty company to inquire. He told them about his needs for some farm land, with a warehouse big enough to accommodate what he had in mind. He had rehearsed it in his mind. He was playing the role of a Louisiana contractor, looking for a piece of land to expand his concrete business. He gave a perfect rendition to the nosy real-estate agent. After looking at several properties in the area, they finally came to the perfect one. It was about fifty acres, off of a small country road with very little local traffic. It had a large metal barn that had seen better days, but a small ranch-style brick house that seemed to be in better condition. The property had been on the market for quite some time and the owners were eager to sell. They were from New Orleans; former 'weekenders' from back in better economic times. They, like many others, could no longer afford to maintain a second property in the country. Their dreams of country living and retirement had long faded away with the recession. One hundred and fifty grand later, the wheels were set into motion to make the property his. But it would take a few weeks, as nothing seemed to move fast around here, even when it came to money. Landry had insisted on an earlier closing date, but supposedly the seller's attorney wasn't available until then and they had insisted on using him for the sale, no one else. So, Landry didn't push too hard. The last thing he needed was to draw attention to himself.

However, in the meantime, the owners gave him permission to move in some of the equipment he would need for the operation. One thing Landry was glad to learn, was that a shitty economy meant that you could find pretty much anything you wanted for next to nothing, when it came to construction equipment. He got himself a couple of heavy-duty boom cranes, able to lift fifty tons without so much as a squeak, several concrete pumps, a stock of reinforced iron bars in various shapes and lengths, plenty of forming plywood and boards and even an old concrete mixing truck with several storage bins for the various aggregates needed in concrete making. Finally, he had all the makings of an old-fashioned concrete plant operation. He was planning to start production on forms as soon as possible. It was extremely important for the locals to see activity; trucks going in and out of the area, etc. The place had to look legit.

Heraldo's next phone conversation with Castillo took place about four days after meeting with their inside man, Rusty Smith. Once again, Heraldo immediately inquired about his wife and once again, Castillo allowed him to briefly communicate with her. Heraldo knew that his progress had been somewhat meager, since they still hadn't finalized a complete plan. However, he hoped their steady progress would keep the kidnapper sufficiently satisfied for the time being. Castillo was no fool. He quickly summarized Heraldo's oral report and without further comment, said one thing: "Next time I call, you will have a plan."

A couple of uneventful weeks had passed and Landry and Heraldo were meeting once again; this time on the Catamaran. They hoped that inspiration would somehow strike. But all that came to them was perspiration. The weather had actually managed to become hotter, even on the lake. What had felt like a soothing breeze before was now more like a blow dryer set on high heat.

"Man, I don't believe I've ever felt this hot on the water," Landry said, wiping his brow yet again. "You know, as much as I hate to say it; only a hurricane could cool us off now." Suddenly, it was like the boom of the sailboat had hit Heraldo in the face.

"That's it!" he yelled as he jumped up. "We need a hurricane and a damn strong one. That's the only thing that would keep the soldiers at bay, knock down all the communications and give us enough time to do what we need to do."

Chapter 9

Back in Cartagena, Maria and Celina were indeed enjoying the lap of luxury, even as prisoners. Castillo had given them access to some of the amenities of the building, including the spas, pools and exercise rooms. However, they were on a set schedule since they weren't allowed contact with anyone but the servants. It didn't take long for Celina to figure out where she was. Although she didn't have a direct view of the city, she remembered enough from her childhood to notice the help was Colombian and most likely from around Cartagena. On several occasions, she had attempted to speak with one of the maids around them the most often, but she didn't get anywhere. The maid had obviously been given instructions to keep their conversations to her duties and nothing else.

Over the course of the past few weeks, Castillo had made several attempts to woo Celina into having dinner with him, but she had consistently refused his advances. It wasn't because she found him physically repulsive. In fact, he was quite attractive and could even be charming if one were able to forget that he would kill anyone that got in his way. She simply couldn't stand the thought of spending social time with her own kidnapper.

On many occasions, Maria and Celina discussed escaping, but simply didn't see how it could be done. They were under constant surveillance during waking hours and assumed they were probably monitored while they slept as well. Soon, the conversation turned to Castillo's interest in Celina. Maybe getting closer to him would be a way to explore new avenues for escape, so when Castillo asked Celina to join him for dinner once again, to his surprise and delight, she reluctantly accepted. She was, after all, a very good actress. She knew she'd be able to milk the situation for what it was worth. Castillo had gone out of his way to seduce her. A table had been set up on a balcony of the building overlooking the city, amidst a beautiful garden and fountains. A string quartet played in the background, hidden by some palms and a harpist with a siren's tail stood on a Roman-style seat on a large pedestal. Once Castillo and Celina sat down at the table, the harp filled the air with romantic harmonies. With the glow of the city in the background and the soft lights from the various torches in the garden, the scene had a surreal feeling. Celina was mesmerized. The entire scene could have been a caricature of Heaven itself, or the playground of some Greek gods. Celina, who always had a penchant for the dramatic, couldn't help but be impressed. She even began to relax, helped along of course by the Beluga caviar and Cristal Champagne.

By the time they completed their meal, she was very aroused, as much as she hated to admit it. Something about the man did indeed turn her on. That wasn't surprising though, considering she had been known for her flings with dangerous types. When they finished, it didn't take much coercing at all on the part of Castillo, to woo her to his suite. The private elevator's brief ascent to his bedroom was just long enough for a passionate embrace. Castillo lifted Celina, placing her legs around him and carried her to his bed. Her short skirt had slid up above her hips, revealing her long slender legs which she had wrapped tightly around his waist. It didn't take Castillo long before he briskly pulled her lace panties past her feet, and slid his manhood inside of her like the Satyr he was. Celina couldn't help but cry out, not from pain, but from incredible pleasure. She couldn't remember having had such a powerful feeling of release and contentment. Celina and Castillo barely stopped for the rest of the night; their passion fueled even more by the judicious use of cocaine. Both were experts and knew how to use it without falling into the boredom of addiction. After several hours, Celina was completely spent and finally asked Castillo if she could go back to her room. She explained it was for Maria. She didn't want her to worry. Reluctantly, Castillo let her go, thinking how nice it was that this operation had indeed had some unexpected fringe benefits after all.

Castillo had his choice of women, of course. He could bed just about any woman he wanted, but never did he feel quite equal in his relationships. However, this one was different. She had something special. It wasn't just physical; it was something else. She was like a female version of himself; strong and willful. Both were almost non-existent traits in most of the beauty-queen types he usually slept with. Suddenly, more than anything, he didn't want to lose her.

Maria had worried a bit when she woke up around two in the morning and Celina hadn't returned. She barely slept after that and was relieved when she heard Celina come in a little while later. Maria peered up at her as she walked towards her. Celina looked like she had been through a wind tunnel. Her hair was all over the place and her makeup had all but disappeared. One good look at her and Maria knew that nothing contrived had taken place in all that time. Celina had obviously partied hard and her face now wore a grinning smile, mixed with a bit of guilt. Maria relaxed and smiled.

"Looks like you need some sleep," she told her. "I'll talk to you in the morning. I'm glad you're okay." Celina nodded, leaned down and hugged her and made a beeline for her bathroom. She was relieved Maria had been easy on her. She took a long, hot shower and within minutes, was snuggled in her bed, hoping she'd be able to wind down enough to get some rest. When she finally fell asleep, she dreamed about her dead father; specifically about his funeral, after he had been shot multiple times in a drug-related bust.

Two weeks before, back in California, her brother had worked hard to raise the one-million-dollar ransom the kidnappers had required. Celina, though successful, was also a newcomer to fame and wealth and had surrounded herself with all of the trappings and expectations of being a popular actress. When it came down to cashing in, it became obvious to her brother, Emilio, that even her jewelry wouldn't fetch anywhere close to the price she had paid for it. Without Celina's consent, he couldn't sell or mortgage the house, so therefore he had only been able to raise four hundred thousand dollars. The FBI had advised against paying the ransom and had also informed him that since the money was to be delivered to Mexico, they had no jurisdiction and therefore no control over the situation. They had also told him that cooperation with the Mexican Federal Police, for such a relatively low profile event, would be difficult. In other words, Emilio would have to deal with all of this on his own.

No further notices from the kidnappers had surfaced by mail or otherwise, and the FBI had run out of options. After a week of closely monitoring Celina's house, they had decided to put the case on the back burner. Emilio was left sitting at home with nearly half the cash requested, but no one to transact with. The fact that the kidnappers had not resurfaced was not that unusual. People disappeared all the time in Mexico and when it came to the criminal-types, everyone had to watch their backs.

Castillo had banked on that fact and had no intention of keeping up the ransom charade any longer than necessary. The diversion had worked and that's all that mattered. For all intents and purposes, Celina would be considered missing and presumed dead, and that suited him just fine since her returning to Los Angeles was now out of the question...for more reasons than one. So when he was woken the next morning by his beloved poodles, the first thing he did was initiate a request for contact with Heraldo. About an hour later, they were on the phone.

"I have good news for you," said Heraldo. "I think we found a way to get in there without starting World War Three. But it's going to require some patience. Landry and I have discussed this thoroughly and we're both convinced that it's being monitored from the outside. There's no way this armory would be left to fend for itself in an emergency; not with two major military bases within fifty miles.

However, let's go back a few years when hurricane Katrina hit. All communications in the area were down, including cell towers and there was no electricity and virtually no passable roads due to debris. I'm certain that during the storm itself, the high winds rendered helicopter rescues impossible."

Castillo quickly interjected. "You mean to tell me, you want to wait for a hurricane to strike to do this?" The kidnapper didn't seem too happy with the idea.

Heraldo braced himself for Castillo's reaction. "I'm afraid so. During a normal time, we would have twenty minutes at the most before military reinforcements would make it to the armory. That's simply not enough time for us to remove several tons of weaponry and then secure it all at our location down the road."

Castillo wasn't happy. But he also didn't want to send anyone on a fool's mission, by any means. Deep down, he knew that he really didn't have a choice. He sighed. "Fine, you have thirty days from today. You better pray to the gods of winds and storms my friend. You will need them."

Heraldo didn't like to leave anything to chance or to the gods, but he didn't have much choice. In the absence of a precise mission date, all they could do was concentrate on preparation; plenty to focus on considering the task at hand. From that day forward, Heraldo became one of The Weather Channel's most devoted fans. He watched gulf water temperatures from the myriads of buoys in the gulf, through various government websites. Anyone living in the area could attest that things were looking favorable for a hurricane. It had been a very hot summer and the water temperatures were all measuring in record-high ranges. The energy for the storms to develop was there, lurking in the ocean water. The only thing needed was the right depression to work its way into the gulf and use up the massive quantity of heat stored there in the water. Heraldo knew it was possible but they wouldn't have much time to prepare.

Landry had closed the purchase of the farm property and the new concrete plant was in full swing. Wood forms had been erected in the shape of giant Y's. The core of each one contained a three-foot-wide metal pipe, in the same "Y" shape, surrounded with enough space for a filling of six solid inches of concrete all the way around. Anyone who asked what they were for was told they were the building blocks for a sea wall being built in Grand Isle. The cores of the Y's would be filled on location, if so desired, allowing for ground transport of the lighter structures. Once the Y's were completed, they would be trucked to Heraldo's marine yard, loaded onto barges and distributed to their final locations. Each tractor trailer truck would be able to carry up to four of the giant blocks, without exceeding the maximum load weight for the roads. Landry had purchased two large forestry tree movers, both with monster-sized tires and a couple of heavy-duty trailers for them to tow. The plan was to use those to transport the nukes from the armory to the concrete plant. Landry had also purchased a couple of small, gas-powered loaders to help lift the heavy weaponry onto the trailers. He was anxious to ship some finished Y's, not just to justify his activities to the locals, but to test the routes to their final destination. An operation as sensitive as this one would certainly have loose ends no matter what, so it was essential for Landry to control every aspect that he possibly could.

The gods had proven favorable to Heraldo. One week after he announced his plan to Castillo, in mid-August, a storm was making its way into the Gulf of the Yucatan Peninsula. It had been somewhat impeded by the land mass, but had retained enough of its wind speed to quickly strengthen once again in the warm Gulf waters. Still days away from any land, the probable cone of uncertainty brought it anywhere from Galveston, Texas to Panama City, Florida. For Heraldo and Landry, it was time for action. Over the next couple of days, equipment and men slowly made their way to the farm in Mississippi. A total of six men had been chosen for this operation; all of them veterans of the drug trade's roughest and most dangerous assignments. Most of them had seen combat within a vast array of foreign and domestic military organizations and were familiar with demolition and head-to-head urban warfare. But what distinguished them the most from anyone else, was their complete dedication to their employers. All of them knew civilian life simply wouldn't work for them. They had lived by the power of their guts and guns and couldn't even conceive of any other way of life; especially considering the large sums of money they had made as private soldiers. Each of them was more than happy to work on this high-stakes mission. Heraldo had simply provided more excitement for their lives, as well as the camaraderie that only combat can bring. So the men were immensely grateful to their employer.

One by one, in separate vehicles, they each arrived at the farm. The traffic out of New Orleans was already getting heavier, even though no official storm warnings had been issued. When all six men arrived, they all found their way to a single, large room which had been furnished with six beds. It had its own bathroom and kitchen area as well. Landry had arranged for several shipments of fully automatic weapons from New Orleans, along with six shoulder-type rocket launchers and plenty of ammunition. Landry had spoken with Smith, the renegade guardsman, to make sure he would be on duty during the coming storm. Thankfully, he confirmed that he would be, since preference was given to locals for guard duty during hurricanes. Landry had also rounded up several unusual pieces of equipment, including a radio jammer that would make it impossible for any broadcast to take place within a four-hundred-foot radius. It wasn't just a brute force device that simply overpowered all other signals with a stronger one. It automatically picked up all signals and send out an opposite wave pattern of the same, in essence, neutralizing them and making it appear as if no signals were present at all. Landry had also obtained some high-power explosives and detonators; twenty pounds of Thermate and the pièce de résistance: a miniature sewer line robot. Rusty Smith would drop the robot into the toilet plumbing to do its thing.

Chapter 10

A couple of days later, Heraldo headed towards the concrete plant. The storm was approaching rapidly and mandatory evacuations of the coastal regions and New Orleans itself had been ordered. The trip, which should have only taken an hour, was already in its third hour and Heraldo couldn't help but realize it could very well be the last time he would ever see the city and his home. Although the dikes and equipment, used to pump the water out of the city, had been updated, no one in their right mind believed that they would save the city from a full hit of a category four or five storm. That level of storm would cause total devastation. The walls and dikes just wouldn't be effective enough to sustain that type of onslaught of the elements. But regardless of New Orleans' survival, once the operation was underway, there would be no turning back anyway. It was with this sense of closure that Heraldo finally made it to the interstate exit which would take him to the concrete plant. Oddly enough, it was the first open exit since he had left the city. Because New Orleans was such an isolated city, with only two major transportation routes in and out of it, all interstate traffic had been directed one-way only; out and away from the city. Even on the smaller road off of the interstate, traffic remained bumper to bumper as people hunted for gas stations that still had fuel. They were few and far between. Heraldo knew this was going to be a mess, regardless of the outcome.

As he pulled into the farm, he could see that the rest of the team was already there; sitting on the porch having a barbecue. As he parked and got out of the car, Landry walked down the porch steps and headed towards him. Landry had invited some of the locals who worked at the plant for good measure. As far as they were concerned, the six members of the assault team were just workers from Landry's other plant in Grand Isle. The subterfuge seemed to be working.

"Welcome to the party for Hurricane Gordon," said Landry with a slight smile as he approached Heraldo. "I thought we'd have a small get together for everyone before the storm gets here." Heraldo was introduced as the Grand Isle Plant Manager and both he and Landry mingled, just enough to give credibility to the event. A few hours and several cases of cheap beer later, the locals were sent on their way and preparations for the operation were underway. Per the most recent weather reports, the storm wasn't expected to hit the coast of Louisiana until late the following afternoon, with strong winds beginning as early as midnight. Both Heraldo and Landry decided to have everyone get to bed early. Everyone would need to be up by two in the morning to ensure everything was prepared by noon, just to be safe. They knew the next day would be a long one and everyone needed to be well-rested. Having consumed some serious amounts of brew, the men were relieved to follow the orders of an early bedtime and headed for their room. Landry and Heraldo took a quick tour of the property while it was still daylight, quickly checking out the various pieces of equipment, particularly the generators, as there was no doubt that the grid power would be gone by daybreak.

Landry entered the bedroom of the six men at precisely two o'clock and flipped on the lights. Within minutes, the men were getting dressed as Heraldo's cook prepared breakfast in the main kitchen. Half an hour later, they were all seated at the wooden table in the dining room. It was a massive table; carved out of a six-foot wide cypress tree, the surface of which had been covered with a transparent epoxy resin to beautifully display the grain of the wood. Heraldo and Landry sat opposite each other at the narrow ends of the table, presiding over their men like warlords of a long-gone era. Heraldo was taken by the moment as he looked around at the men. He held up his hand for silence so he could speak. The men obliged instantly.

"All of you have been with us for quite a while and have seen both rough times and good times." Heraldo looked at each man gravely. "Today is the day that will mark the end of our partnership, if we are successful. I will personally have enough money to retire and plan to do so. I want each of you to have the same option, so I'm pleased to announce that upon completion of this mission, each one of you will receive an additional bonus of ten million dollars." Short gasps and mumblings of gratitude filled the air. Heraldo held up his hand again for silence as he continued. "It is imperative that we succeed men. Because failure here will, without a doubt, result in nothing short of death. So be extra vigilant. We only have one shot at this, gentlemen. Good luck to you all. Let's eat!"

At around three in the morning, the men had all finished their breakfasts of eggs, steaks and breads, along with plenty of coffee. The television had been tuned to The Weather Channel and they all watched the progress of the storm. It was located about one hundred miles south-southeast of New Orleans and was moving towards the Crescent City at about seven miles per hour. The winds were sustained at one hundred and thirty miles per hour and the weather professionals were predicting that the storm would intensify even more over the next few hours. If nothing changed, the eye of the storm would be on top of them and the armory, at around nine that evening. It was certainly going to be a long day. Landry looked around at all of the men as he spoke.

"Okay, I want all of you to go to your assigned vehicles and start them up, drive them around and check them out. Make sure everything works perfectly and continue checking them until the sun comes up. Let me know if there are any issues. Landry and Heraldo followed the men outside into the early morning darkness and immediately felt the already steady, warm and moist breeze coming in from the Gulf. The rain hadn't started, but clouds completely obscured the half moon from time to time. The air was thick with moisture and already about eighty degrees; warm enough to cause someone to sweat just standing still. Following Landry into the warehouse, Heraldo felt a sense of excitement he hadn't experienced in a long time. Somehow, even with the dangers at hand, he was looking forward to this operation and the changes it would bring to his life if it was successful. Even with the possibility of death lurking, it was truly exhilarating.

The lights inside the warehouse were turned on and the many Y frames stood tall in front of them, some already encased in concrete and some still waiting. The cement, gravel and sand bins had been topped off, ready to spew their contents into the mixer at a moment's notice. The wind rattled the old tin metal sheets that made up the roof of the warehouse. There was no doubt they would be some of the first casualties of this storm. Landry had a small reinforced concrete structure built inside of the warehouse. Inside were two small, twenty-five kilowatt diesel generators and one large diesel fuel tank. One of the generators would be sufficient to supply all of their electrical needs. The other was for back-up.

Landry walked towards one of the hollow Y's, already covered with concrete. "This metal pipe is actually much thinner than it looks," he explained to Heraldo. "It's composed of two metal pipes; one about two inches smaller than the other. In its walls, we poured melted lead which was a bitch. Then we welded the ends shut so it looks like a thick two-inch-walled pipe. This will considerably reduce the radiation signature of its contents. We may need these to get past any road checks."

Heraldo was impressed with Landry's detailed planning, but then again, being deceitful was his way of life. After all, he was a narcotics trafficker and this was part of his skill set. Outside of the warehouse, the massive diesel engines of the tree movers had started up; their loud rumbling filling the air. It almost sounded like one of those big-foot truck events at a state fair. The good thing was; no one outside of the direct area would hear any of it, due to the low frequency roar of the steadily increasing wind as it blew through the many tree branches. It was well after five in the morning and daylight was slowly starting to penetrate through the thick, low clouds.

All of the equipment had proven functional; each performing as expected, once fully warmed up. It was time to retreat to the house and wait for the storm to progress. Rain showers were hitting the area and the men rushed inside to the comfort of the dry, air-conditioned house. Large, heavy raindrops smacked the windows and the lights flickered. Heraldo suspected that it wouldn't be long before the grid power went out. In these heavily wooded parts, loose branches wreaked havoc with power transformers. It was quite often that power companies would shut down entire zones of the grid as a preventive measure against transformers shorting out. The lights flickered again and sure enough, suddenly went out. They were engulfed in almost total darkness, except for the faint attempt of the daylight making its way through the windows. Landry threw on his raincoat and ran out to the warehouse where he manually disengaged the grid switch and turned on one of the generators. Once he was satisfied with its speed and operating temperature, he switched on the main power breaker. Immediately, the machine whined into action and lights came on everywhere. They were now officially on their own, separated from all of the conveniences provided by modern civilization. They would most likely be on their own for a long time to come.

The men gathered around the large, flat-screen television in the living room. Thanks to a satellite feed, they were able to watch the local channels of New Orleans, with the usual reporters outside, dramatically braving the elements. Wind gusts were already peaking at over seventy miles per hour and the storm was still over forty miles away. Because of the relatively slow speed of this hurricane, over ten inches of water had already fallen over the city of New Orleans, rendering most roadways impassable despite the unimpeded and massive pumping effort. A major cause of concern was now the great Mississippi River. It was rapidly swelling from the tidal surge. This sudden influx of so much rain in such a short amount of time only compounded an already heavy river flow; due to unusually heavy rains up north during the last several weeks. Discussions had already been underway within the Army Corps of Engineers, on whether or not to open the various locks located upstream. However, the consensus was soon reached that it was too late. Opening the locks would only expand the disaster area. By the sound of it, New Orleans had already been written off as the first casualty of this storm.

Heraldo and Landry looked at each other with the same expression of awe. This was going to be a day of reckoning on the disaster scale, no doubt. It would almost certainly surpass the damage caused by Katrina. By ten o'clock that morning, the news feed from New Orleans went dead, along with all of the local radar activity. Wind speeds had exceeded one-hundred and seventy miles per hour at the eye wall. The area immediately south of New Orleans was now an open field of water, pushing its way into the city by overflowing what had once been the banks of the Mississippi River. Towards the belly of town, the flow of the water was practically that of white-water rapids.

The fact that there was no reporting of any kind out of the city, including The Weather Channel, became the news of the moment. A high-flying weather plane was dispatched to gather data as the eye of the storm grazed the west side of the city. Several drones had been dropped into the eye and were taking real-time video of the scene. What was supposed to be the city of New Orleans, was only recognizable due to a view of some gutted structures that had once been downtown office buildings. Landmarks such as the Superdome were no longer intact and in some cases, not even recognizable. The only intact structures were the bridges that had once spanned the width of the Mississippi River. Now it looked as if the bridges were just decorative objects in the middle of an ocean. They were surrounded by water as far as the eye could see. The only saving grace was the fact that there had been plenty of warning time. Most people had managed to get out of the city and besides the usual crazies and homebodies who always refused to leave; human casualties were expected to be very low...at least that's what everyone hoped.

Having submerged the whole city of New Orleans, the storm barreled straight towards the farm and the armory nearby. It was over Lake Ponchartrain and by the best estimates, the wind speeds had dropped to around one-hundred and sixty miles per hour, not enough to really matter.

Heraldo looked at Landry with a serious expression. "I guess we won't be going back to New Orleans anytime soon. Thank God I had the catamaran moved to Florida a couple of days ago. I guess all of our places in New Orleans are gone and I doubt anyone will ever rebuild after this. It just wouldn't make sense now that all of the old buildings are gone."

Heraldo also had the submarine, completed only a week before, moved to a safe, deep-water location until the storm passed. It was a good opportunity for the crew to test all of its features, while escaping the storm at the same time.

"Looks like the eye wall should hit us at about five this afternoon," said Landry. "That will be our window for action. Per my calculations, we should have about a forty-minute window of little or no wind during that time. Let's take a break until half an hour before," he told men. "Everyone be ready to go by four-thirty."

The wind had picked up substantially, with the branches of trees blowing almost horizontally, their leaves and needles completely shed and debris flying everywhere. Heraldo had made sure all of the equipment was anchored securely with chains to the concrete slab in the middle of one of the fields. It was all getting battered now, but it was tough, tree logging equipment, built for abuse. Landry knew it would all be fine and could take a lot of punishment from falling branches and rolling logs.

Most of the men had gone back to their beds to rest until round-up time. Heraldo and Landry had tested their two-way radios with Rusty Smith; on duty at the armory until further notice. Per the latest information they had received from him, the armory was being guarded by four men in the control room, plus himself and one other man whom he had only met once before, up front in the lobby. Their orders were to hold down the fort until after the storm. They had been warned it could be thirty hours or more before anyone would be able to relieve them. Just like at Landry's place, the power had gone out earlier that morning and the armory was running on generators. Smith hadn't had a problem bringing his backpack inside later that morning, using the excuse that he didn't want to leave anything in his car during the storm. No one even bothered to search it because they were all preoccupied with the hurricane; watching the news and talking about it. It was almost better than the Super Bowl, especially being safe and sound inside such a secure place.

It was approaching five o'clock in the evening and even though the wind speed hadn't seemed to decrease yet, all of the men were sitting in the living room with Heraldo and Landry, geared up and ready to go.

Landry looked the men over before he spoke. "In a few minutes, the storm will slow down to almost nothing as we enter the eye of it. You'll have ten minutes to reach the armory. Someone will be there to let you in. You've been briefed on your respective jobs. If there are any questions, now is the time to ask. Remember, once we get going, speed will be of the essence. You don't want to be caught in this storm as the eye passes over and it starts up again."

The men didn't say anything. They appeared serious, eager and focused. Landry was pleased. "Good, let's get the show on the road."

Chapter 11

As they stepped out of the farmhouse, they were immediately greeted by the brutal force of the wind. It was difficult to even stand and even harder to breath when facing into it. By the looks of things outside, the place had taken quite a battering. There were tree limbs everywhere, including the field adjacent to the house. Hundreds of pine trees looked like twigs, having had nearly all of their needles and branches ripped away. Some large oak trees had also been tumbled, giving their surroundings a naked, desolate and apocalyptic feel.

The wind suddenly slowed down and the men rushed to their tractors, unhooked the safety chains and quickly gunned their engines on their way to the small country road. Immediately, they ran into problems as trees of various sizes littered the black top. Thankfully, the tree movers were able to part a path through the debris in short order. Fifteen minutes later, they had all arrived at their intended destination. On the way, Landry had given the signal to Smith to proceed with his plumbing operation. Smith had grabbed his bag and gone to the bathroom in the lobby, telling the other guard he needed to take a dump. The other man had just looked at him and shrugged.

Once in the bathroom, he proceeded to quickly remove the toilet. He inserted the robot into the four-inch sewer pipe. From the schematics Heraldo had received from Castillo, they were able to program the robot to make its way to the other bathroom in the secured area where the control room was located. The robotic sewer inspector came with its own tether and a small video screen, so that Smith could actually watch its progress in the armory's plumbing. Smith watched as the device quickly worked its way into a larger pipe. It entered the secured area; quickly found another four inch pipe and climbed into it. About thirty seconds later, it worked its way up to the bottom of the toilet. Having arrived at its destination, it quickly extended a flexible hollow pipe through the elbow trap of the toilet and slowly emerged from the standing water. In its belly, the robot had a small pressurized container which released its gaseous contents: a powerful, paralyzing nerve gas agent. The odorless fumes quickly spread into the area. Within minutes, the men in the control room simply stopped moving; completely paralyzed.

By the time Smith came out of the bathroom wearing his breathing mask, no one was moving, including the other guard in the lobby. With his mask securely in place, Smith quickly reached the door and opened it. Soon it would be safe to breathe the air again. Landry and the men quickly made their way into the lobby of the armory. The jammer had been turned on earlier and all remaining communication cabling had been disabled from the outside. The control room door was quickly cut open and the guards were injected with a powerful sedative. Access to the armory was now theirs.

Smith quickly opened the loading doors on the lower level and a trailer backed up to them. During this short amount of time, one of the men stood guard by Landry's pickup truck for any potential intruders. The street where the armory was located was completely deserted. The locals had all gone to various safe areas, including the local cops. The vault door was opened without delay. For some reason, it hadn't even been locked and Landry looked at its contents in awe. He knew they had hit the mother-load. He had expected to see a full tomahawk missile all along, but what he saw were six crates, each containing a separate nuclear warhead. No propulsion systems, so these were going to be much easier to load up. As planned, they decided to leave one warhead in the vault and put the other crates quickly on the trailer. Five minutes later, the trailer was on its way back to the farmhouse with one of the pickup trucks and a tree mover leading the way.

From time to time, they stopped and loaded the trailer with fallen branches, as cover for their cargo. They shut the vault door, but not before Landry placed a large bag, containing Thermate, and a small trigger device on top of the last crate; the timer set for twenty minutes. Smith watched the men as they went about their various tasks and didn't notice one of them sticking a needle into his neck until it was too late. He was unable to react in time and like the other guards, was sound asleep within seconds.

Having completed their tasks, the rest of the men rushed to leave and headed back to the farm at full throttle. The wind was already picking up again when the last vehicle made its way into the farm's driveway. They had just enough time to unload the crates into the concrete building inside the barn, which looking like it had taken a beating, even though Landry had spent a considerable amount of time and money reinforcing it prior to the storm. It had been twenty minutes since Landry had set the device in the vault.

Suddenly, a massive flash of light, followed shortly thereafter by a shockwave, brought everyone to attention. Landry was surprised and instantly knew the Thermate had somehow managed to partially trigger the device rather than simply burning it, causing it to go nuclear; but thankfully, not all the way. He knew they wouldn't have been standing there otherwise. He decided the new development may work in their favor. The Thermate had apparently brought temperatures within the room high enough to ignite the conventional explosive devices inside the warhead and at the same time affect its safety mechanism. It wasn't the full yield this bomb was capable of but had been sufficient to cause a partial fission chain reaction as powerful as the equivalent of one thousand tons of TNT. There wouldn't be anything left of the armory; all of it vaporized and everything within a half-mile would be completely destroyed. They all looked at each other knowing full well what would come next and they all hit the ground simultaneously.

The blast from the bomb had actually been surprisingly mild. The furious storm winds had returned and the blast appeared somewhat lost in Nature's fury. Also, the area where the farm was located stood protected from the east by several hills that, without a doubt, deflected some of the bomb's energy. What happened next was even more surprising. The winds seemed to die down a bit, as if the eye had returned to their location. The explosion had somehow affected the eye wall, expanding it horizontally and making it bigger and wobbly. It was only a temporary effect however. Quickly, the storm's large, spinning momentum reclaimed control and absorbed the new energy released by the bomb. In no time, the hurricane was back on its north-easterly track and even managed to regain some wind speeds as it exceeded over one hundred and thirty miles per hour. This unheard of event didn't go unnoticed by the meteorologists at The Weather Channel; baffled by the fact that a hurricane had actually managed to gain intensity over land.

Heraldo had been correct in his assumption that the armory was being monitored from a remote location. All facilities of its kind were indeed watched by a dedicated central command located inside of the Pentagon in Washington, DC. When they lost all signals from the Mississippi armory at the peak of the storm, they weren't overly alarmed. Other locations on the coast, close to the direct path of the storm, were offline as well. A notice to make contact was given to the surrounding military bases to send reconnaissance teams as soon as it was safe to do so. The New Orleans' disaster took precedent over all other missions and relief teams from Florida and Texas were quickly being prepared. It would be quite a while before anyone physically showed up at the armory location.

Landry and his men had all made it back to the farmhouse and were riding out the remaining hours of the storm with booze and food while attempting to catch the satellite signal on television. Heraldo was anxious to complete the processing of the nukes, but knew that any outside work at the moment, especially in the barn or what was left of it, was still too dangerous. The wind finally subsided around eleven o'clock and the men reluctantly made their way outside to start their final work.

The crates were opened and their cylindrical contents revealed. Each device weighed close to two hundred pounds and required four men to carry it. Because the actual warheads were much shorter than expected, Landry decided to put them all in one Y form. After gently lifting one of the Y's legs, they slipped the first nuke into its hollow core, letting it slide in on cut, two inch PVC piping, which allowed it to roll towards the center of the Y. When all five nukes were inside, they lowered in a spray rod and injected expanding foam, similar to what would be found in any hardware store. The foam encapsulated the bombs in soft, but strong protection for the coming transport. An added benefit to the foam-based material was its propensity to absorb the heavier particles emitted by radioactive material, while the lead in the outer casing did the same for the lighter gamma particle radiation. The legs of the Y were long enough to accommodate two bombs each, so they had no problem fitting all five of them into a single Y. Upon completing the foaming operation, they plugged all three ends with lead disks and steel plates, which they welded to the inside of each pipe opening. Three inches of concrete was then added and the form was sealed at the three ends. By morning, it would all be dry and hardened, ready to be taken out of its forms. It only took about an hour to complete. They all enjoyed more beer while they watched the pile of crates, debris and trash burn on the outdoor concrete slab. It had been a long day indeed and by one o'clock in the morning, too tired to worry about anything else, all of the men headed to their respective beds to get some sleep. All was silent except for the low frequency sound of the diesel generator and the heavy snoring coming from the men's bedroom.

The next day came in clearly; the clouds of the storm gone. It was a beautiful summer day, minus the leaves on the trees and the chirping of birds. Heraldo was the first to wake and headed out to the porch, coffee in hand. The darkness hadn't revealed the extent of the devastation. But now it was painfully clear. Trees were down everywhere, but what was most striking was the change in color. Everything looked brown. The storm had literally washed all greenery out of existence, making the land appear apocalyptic. Landry joined him and they both looked at each other, their expressions speaking for them. *Now what?* That was the question. The storm had surpassed the worst estimates of devastation, so they needed to rethink their next steps. It would obviously be impossible to drive the nukes to Grand Isle, or what was left of Grand Isle, which was most likely nothing at all.

The storm had driven itself all the way into Tennessee by that morning, leaving a fifty-mile wide path of destruction. It had been more intense than Katrina, but thankfully, not quite as large. Helicopters from military bases in northwest Florida had reached New Orleans and were scouting the area for survivors, though there wouldn't be very many. Most of the homes there had been leveled by the combined force of wind and water. After nearly five hundred years, the French Quarter no longer existed. The Mississippi had overcome most of the protective earth dykes and was now flowing freely over what had once been the city, making itself at home in its new Delta and rendering any hope of rebirth hopeless; too costly and unrealistic. The great city of New Orleans, granted a reprieve after Hurricane Katrina, was officially defunct.

However, as dramatic as the loss of an entire American city was, it was going to be overshadowed by a much more insidious and hidden threat. During the course of the night, several warning systems had activated around a few nuclear plants, scattered around the path of the storm. The reaction of the military had been swift, but no sources of radiation could be confirmed as emanating from any of the plants. None of the plants had sustained any significant damage from the hurricane and officials were puzzled to say the least, unable to figure out exactly what had happened. The press had picked up on the news and was already running with the story, showing footage of the Fukushima nuclear disaster and speculating about a cover up.

At the Pentagon, efforts were underway to reconnect with the armory in southern Mississippi. They should have been able to communicate by satellite or radio, but all were non-responsive. A reconnaissance team had been scrambled for an update as soon as it became available, which had not been until mid-morning. Priority had been given to the city of New Orleans with every available asset in the area committed to it. When the recon team finally arrived in the small town, according to the GPS coordinates anyway, they knew immediately that something had happened; something that had nothing to do with damage from the storm. Where the armory would have been, was instead a crater of molten, smoking earth. Its surroundings had been completely flattened as if peeled off by a giant razor. Nothing stood for a solid five hundred meters in any direction. Empty concrete slabs and brick piles scattered here and there were all that was left of the town. The information and moving pictures of it were instantaneously relayed to the monitoring station at the Pentagon. Within seconds, the proverbial shit hit the fan. From the damage, it was blatantly obvious that some kind of nuclear explosion had taken place, but they knew the armory didn't contain sufficient ammunition to justify that level of devastation. To the commander of the unit, it became clear that the radiation alarms, activated throughout several states, had just been the result of the storm carrying the radioactivity generated by the explosion; not related to any nuclear plant malfunction. He relayed the information and in turn, the new information was immediately relayed to the highest level of military command and the President of the United States. When President John Russell received his briefing on the subject, a look of dumbfounded stupefaction covered his face.

"How could this even be possible? How could we have such dangerous weaponry stored within a disaster-prone area, unprotected?!"

Immediately, one of the generals interjected. "Mr. President, we don't know yet exactly what's happened. It's premature to assume that this was a direct result of the storm. It could have been an accident...or something worse.

"Is that supposed to make us feel better Tom? Really?" replied President Russell.

"No, of course not Mr. President," said the General, shaking his head quickly. "We're investigating and moving assets into the area. It will take some time. As you would expect, the roads are littered with debris and in some cases, completely blocked. But I'll have a report for you before the day is over sir."

The President nodded. "Okay, what about the radiation? I heard reports that it's all the way up into Tennessee."

One of the other men present at the meeting cut in. "Mr. President, we've already started our emergency deployment of the nuclear disaster team. It's logical at this point to assume that a good bit of the explosion's radioactivity is being carried by the hurricane and is being dropped by the rains the storm has generated on its northerly path. Thankfully, this storm isn't too wide and the areas affected by it are, for the most part, rural. But we can expect life threatening conditions all the way into Tennessee, with pockets of intense radiation here and there, tapering down significantly by the time this storm reaches us later today."

The President went on somewhat sarcastically. "So that should be comforting Mister...?

"Richard Stanford sir...from the Nuclear Regulatory Commission. I have a P.H.D. in nuclear physics, Mr. President."

The President seemed satisfied. "Okay, you have until three this afternoon to come up with some facts people. The American public needs to be informed and we need to call for evacuations ASAP. Notify all appropriate branches of local government once you've determined the exact areas that are affected. We'll meet again at three; understood?"

Everyone in the room acquiesced and as the President stood up and left the Oval office, so did the rest of them. President Russell had a lot to ponder. How could he explain this crisis to his fellow countrymen? He had no doubt that heads would roll. Once they resolved the crisis, he knew someone would have to pay and he sure as hell hoped it wasn't going to be him.

Chapter 12

The radiation corridor from the preliminary findings had proven most intense within the first fifty or so miles from the explosion, following the direction of the storm. Heavier particles had settled down along with the rain which had fallen in the extended area. FEMA was now the primary caretaker in the emergency and plans were devised as how to best deal with this new crisis. The actual site of the explosion was quarantined, which proved to be an easy task considering roads were already blocked with storm debris. Orders were issued to not remove any of the debris within a ten-mile radius.

The residents within the zone would simply have to fend for themselves until aid arrived. An emergency announcement was made on the local weather radio, requesting everyone to stay indoors until further notice. It was unspecific as to the nature of the problem. Because of the assumed low population remaining within the blast zone, it would be quite a while before rescue operations would be assigned to the area. Most of the help was being directed towards medium-sized towns located to the northwest. That was where most of the higher-level radiation seemed to be settling.

Evacuations and decontaminations were already underway. Quarantine areas were quickly being set up according to exposure levels and first aid given mostly in the form of salt tablets, showers and clothing. By noon, the media had finally caught on and speculation was rampant as to what had happened to cause the nukes to blow up. Fox News ran with a possible terrorist plot story which was countered by CNN, who attempted to discredit them by stating that this kind of action in rural Mississippi was at best improbable. CNN's stand was that no terrorist in their right mind would venture into Mississippi to blow up anything. The focus quickly switched over to the military's storage of nuclear weapons and the dangers of something like this happening in a highly-populated area. The usual, talking-head generals were interviewed and the public was reassured that this couldn't happen again and that nuclear armories were nowhere near populated areas.

President Russell went on the air that afternoon. After explaining the events that had happened, he blamed the explosion on the storm and assured the American public that they were fully investigating all of the nuclear weapon sites and would be reevaluating their risk, vis-à-vis the surrounding populations. The blame had been elegantly shifted to the military without any apparent ill effect on his political career.

Landry and Heraldo watched the news and the President's address. The fact that their area was within the perimeter of the quarantined area worried them somewhat. Landry quickly activated some radiation detectors he had purchased for testing purposes and they checked various locations within their surroundings. There was some mild background radiation on the gravel outside, about three times what one would expect, but certainly not a threat to their health. They also tested the concrete structure holding the nukes and those results were even lower than outside, at only about twice the normal level. So, the area was safe but until the quarantine was lifted, traveling anywhere wasn't going to be easy. They were fine at the farm for the time being, but the quicker Heraldo could get his men out of there the better. They decided that he and Landry would take a quick ride to scout out possible exit routes.

Driving west in Landry's truck, away from the epicenter of the explosion and towards Louisiana, they didn't encounter much of a human presence at all. The roads were littered with fallen branches and they had to cut their way through with a chain saw several times. When they finally reached the main highway, it was pretty much clear of debris; not because it had been already cleaned up, but simply because it was far enough away from any large trees that had fallen. They saw a couple of vehicles and kept driving towards the Pearl River; the dividing line between Mississippi and Louisiana. When they finally approached the border, they saw what appeared to be a road block set up at a truck weigh station. Landry slowed down. Already too close to turn around without raising suspicion, he slowly approached the local cop car and the standing officer. Rolling down his window, Landry looked at the cop and asked him what was going on. The young policeman told him that he was under orders not to let anyone in or out, except for officials and emergency vehicles. Landry told him he was on his way back to Louisiana after having spent the night in his cabin not far from there and wanted to know when he could go back home. The officer responded by telling him to check the news for changes and said he didn't have any more information. Landry thanked him and turned around.

"So much for that," he said to Heraldo. "Time to regroup and come up with another plan."

"Guess so," Heraldo sighed. "Now what? It looks like we're going to be stuck here for quite a while. Let's go back." Heraldo wasn't at all happy with the new turn of events. They were, for all practical purposes, now trapped like rats in a maze; driving around and going nowhere.

Back at the farm, Landry decided to load up two of the concrete forms onto one of the flatbed trailers. After hooking it up to a tractor, they backed up the trailer into the warehouse and slowly loaded their cargo, placing the one containing the nukes closer to the front. The concrete structures had dried nicely and their final product looked as professional and elegant as could be. Landry had installed a satellite internet dish before the storm so they could keep up with the events. He was online searching out any information possible about when they would be allowed to leave the area. By the looks of things, it would be several days before any information became available. The only positive thing they could hang their hopes on was the fact that they had been spared the brunt of the radiation, making it reasonable to assume that they could expect the perimeters of the quarantine area to be substantially reduced, thus allowing them access to freedom sooner rather than later.

Heraldo wasn't keen on playing the waiting game though and was searching local area maps for possible exit points that would likely be unguarded. A small side road appeared to be a possible route, but that also meant dealing with a considerable amount of storm debris. They needed to get out before any troops moved into the area. That was a concern he immediately shared with Landry.

Landry understood and agreed, but was hesitant on whether or not they could even do it. "Okay Heraldo. But you do realize we'll be in for quite a journey if we make it out of here? First of all, forget about refueling anytime soon. Wherever it is you want to go, count on there not being any fuel available within a five-hundred mile radius; I guarantee it. Second, there's bound to be several road blocks and check points, even outside the area. We can probably make it past them with some bogus paperwork. But if they set up any sophisticated radiation equipment, we might be detectable." Even with the possible issues they may have to face, the two men agreed it was best to take their chances and leave as soon as possible.

A couple of hours later they all left the property, after having stored or buried most of the combat equipment they had used for the retrieval of the nukes. The plan was for Landry and Heraldo to drive one of the tree movers a couple of miles ahead of the tractor trailer and its cargo, to make sure all was clear and safe. With the bug-like machine leading the way, they moved northwest at about twenty miles per hour along the small country road. They soon passed the ten-mile mark, from the epicenter of the explosion, without encountering anyone. The few residents in the area were obviously keeping to themselves. Though they were relieved at not having encountered anyone, they both knew it didn't mean they were home free by any means. Just like the checkpoint they had discovered on their scouting expedition, there were bound to be more along the way. Two hours later, they finally emerged from the small country road to find a four-lane highway. They ditched the tree mover on the side of the road and joined the others in one of the tailing vehicles. They were finally moving freely, at highway speeds, heading west with Landry's F-150 in the lead. Soon, their cell phones all had full service. It was nice to be back to the land of the living. Landry suggested they go to Morgan City and Heraldo agreed, knowing that Landry was from the area and knew his way around the bayous well.

"Let's avoid the interstates and major highways. We can take the small, less traveled roads and use the less sophisticated truck weigh stations," Landry suggested. Everyone agreed it was the best plan.

After another two hours of driving, they finally made it to the Louisiana border, just above Baton Rouge. Landry took over the eighteen-wheeler and all went without a hitch, especially since they were a solid five thousand pounds lighter than the maximum weight limit for the road. Landry's suspicions regarding fuel had been correct though. No service stations had any gas or diesel available. They were glad they had loaded up on fuel, via two large, portable tanks. The trip to Landry's place, close to Morgan City, took them close to ten hours. All of the men were both physically and emotionally exhausted. As accustomed as they were to risk and danger, this operation had been the most stressful any of them had ever experienced by far. However, Heraldo wouldn't fully rest until the weapons were out of the country, safe and ready to be traded for his wife.

The small town of Morgan City had been spared the brunt of the hurricane and only had minor damage. They quickly found a joint for a late bite to eat when they arrived. The truck was parked at Landry's place and the men were sent on their separate ways, with their fat bonus checks and some cash to spare. Their part in the operation was over and they would each, no doubt, scatter across the world after collecting their funds at various offshore banks. Landry and Heraldo were enjoying a simple meal of boiled gulf shrimp, beer and fried catfish. Even though this particular fare wasn't their cup of tea, it was nice to eat some fresh foods after having lived off of canned and frozen food over the previous couple of days. As they ate, they both came as close to relaxing as they could, given the circumstances.

The next day, they both scrambled to find a barge equipped with a crane. Landry's old connections came in handy and he was lucky to find an old floating pontoon, sturdy enough to accommodate the weight of the concrete Y's. Prices had gone up, as they always did after a hurricane. But Landry didn't flinch. He enjoyed giving back to the local economy anyway. The tractor and its trailer were driven to a dock where its cargo was swiftly unloaded onto the barge. They rode with the tug boat to a meeting point, ten miles off of the coast of Louisiana.

The seas were still quite rough from the storm and Heraldo didn't exactly enjoy the ride. Landry, having been raised a shrimper, was able to take the ocean's motion much better than his business partner, therefore avoiding the numerous trips to the bathroom. The concrete structures had been well-fastened to the barge via several large chains, but were still being tossed around quite a bit. Waves crashed over the barge constantly, which thankfully was unsinkable, due to its numerous floating pontoons. The original plan had been for Heraldo's catamaran to take over the towing once they reached it south of Atchafalaya Bay. But given the state of the ocean, they quickly decided that wouldn't be feasible, as it would no doubt result in severe damage to the large yacht. The catamaran was still over ten miles away and for the sake of appearances, Heraldo decided they would ride in the hard hull inflatable tender rather than meet up with the tug boat with the cat. As far as the tug captain was concerned, they were delivering emergency anchor loads to an oil rig further in the gulf. He had been told that another tug would be coming from the derrick to carry on the towing.

When the small skiff arrived, both of the men boarded the inflatable quickly and sent the captain on his way, leaving the pontoon barge adrift. There wasn't much wind, despite the six-foot swells, so controlling the barge drift wasn't an issue. Heraldo had dispatched a message for the submarine to join up with them, but that would take some time.

An hour later, they were all onboard the catamaran with a rope and large bungee cord tied to the pontoon. That made a little towing possible, at least until the submarine arrived. With each swell, the rope expanded, absorbing the energy from the water and preventing the mass of the barge from pulling too hard on the relatively fragile catamaran. It was by no means an ideal set up, but it would get them by. Heraldo and Landry were in the main stateroom on the yacht, discussing their future activities.

"I don't want the cat to tow this for very long," said Heraldo. "Not just because of the risk of damage, but mainly because this looks really odd, especially to anyone flying over. This set-up isn't something anyone would expect to see, not in this industrial part of the gulf. Someone's bound to notice and start asking questions."

"I agree," responded Landry. "However, this doesn't solve our problem. The sub will also attract attention."

Heraldo interjected. "Only if we travel on the surface. But I have an idea. I think the forms are stable and secure enough on the platform. What if we sink the whole deal and tow it underwater?"

Landry pondered for a moment. "That might just work. But we'd have to balance it just right. We don't want the load to sink us all. I think if we put some kind of valves on the pontoons to let the water in just enough to balance it correctly, it will slowly sink to the depth we want on its own. We can rig up a couple of self-inflatable water recovery floats. In fact, we have a few in the sub. So when the time comes, the whole structure can be brought back to the surface."

Without further delay, Landry and one of the men got geared up and went swimming towards the floating pontoon. Each had brought some tools in a small dingy and a few tap valves as well. Climbing up onto the pontoons proved to be somewhat hazardous, as they were going in and out of the water. It was more like a wild rodeo than a quick fix. It was hard to drill the holes for the taps while being jerked around so much. Somehow, an hour later they had managed to let some water into the air tanks of the pontoon and the whole thing was barely floating. It had been a difficult balancing act, requiring both divers to work in unison, letting the same amount of air out at the same time, so as not to tip the barge too early in the process. When the whole thing did in fact tip though, it took all of their strength to escape harm. One of the valves had caught a loose part of one of the chains and had gotten ripped off its tank. The contraption was sinking slowly to the bottom of the ocean, as Heraldo watched in shock and despair. They had come so far without any mishaps. Failing now just wasn't an option. Landry quickly made it back to the cat.

"Don't worry," Landry told Heraldo. "I think this was an iffy idea to begin with. It's not too deep here, no more than fifty feet, so diving won't be an issue. What I want to do is attach floating devices to the form and tow it. That will be much simpler and I'm sure much safer and faster for the submarine."

With that being said, they quickly dropped a small anchor and float so as not to lose the location of the sight. All they could do was wait for the submarine to arrive with the equipment necessary for this final rescue operation.

Chapter 13

Back in Washington at the Pentagon, General Al Paten was put in charge of the investigation into the presumed accident at the armory site in Mississippi. Something had happened there that was, by all accounts, simply unexplainable. What was also unexplainable was how none of the backup safety communication measures had been operational during the storm. They had lost all contact with the site, even before the event occurred. He needed answers to all of these questions and being only one year from retirement, the pressure was on him; greater than any combat situation he had ever been faced with.

He was viewing the latest footage of the site with a team of nuclear warfare experts. Things just didn't add up. Six nukes and not even enough energy released to account for one, not even one tenth of one.

"We obviously had a partial explosion here," said one of the scientists. "Something these weapons are specifically designed not to experience unless programmed to do so. Even if you blew them up by conventional means, all you would have is what is known as a 'dirty bomb'; no nuclear energy release to speak of, just nasty radiological isotopes. All I can think of is that a bomb was made to detonate using its internal charges and somehow partially malfunctioned."

"What about radiation?" asked General Paten. "Can we be sure that all the weapons are accounted for, given what we found on the site?"

"Well, that is a problem," the scientist acknowledged. "Under normal circumstances, we could approximately match the levels of released uranium and plutonium at the site, with what was supposed to be in the weapons; given a simple non-nuclear explosion. We've worked that scenario and are pretty competent when it comes to reverse engineering the original amount of nuclear material and its composition. However, because in this case, some of the material went into nuclear fission; it complicates that equation a good bit and will take us some time to make accurate measurements. Another considerable obstacle is the fact that when the devices exploded, most of the materials were dispersed into the atmosphere which, as we all know, was quite active at the time. Hurricane Gordon actually somewhat absorbed the debris cloud and helped further spread its deadly contents. So...and this is my professional opinion, we might not reach a conclusive, decisive answer to your question: was there more than one weapon involved in the explosion?"

Fucking great thought General Paten. *Now I can't refute or confirm the first question that I know President Russell will ask me later on today.* "Alright," said Paten. "I want top priority on this issue. You have full authority and will be working with Homeland Security or...let me rephrase; you'll be telling them what to do. It's about time these guys earn their keep."

General Paten was old school and looked at the relatively newly-created entity as just another way for the government to blow money; money that could have been used more efficiently by the professionals in his department.

"Now gentlemen, let's all get back to work and don't hesitate to call me the minute you have anything new to report. I mean it, day or night. You have my cell number. Thank you." Paten went back to his office and immediately barked orders to plan for the deployment of the military to cordon off area. If some of the nukes had been taken, he was sure as hell going to get them back, if it was the last thing he ever did. Later that day, he met with President Russell and preempted the discussion by immediately telling him what had transpired in his meeting with the nuclear scientists. He asked the President for his approval to use the military to conduct the operation, stressing the fact that he didn't want to use local forces, for fear that going public this soon would be of adverse consequences and could seriously impede his investigation.

The President was not pleased. "You mean to tell me that you're not sure these nukes were taken, but you want me to authorize you to use military power in a domestic civilian area; in essence, bypassing any and all local state authorities?"

Paten cleared his throat. "Yes, Mr. President. It's the best way to do this in my opinion. I'm sure something can be worked out as to the legality of it all. If I'm correct, the security of our nation is on the line."

"I'll tell you what General. I can recommend that the local reserve be put at your disposal and under your command, given the nature of the emergency and the technical expertise required. Just make sure your commanders can pass the mustard on the nuclear issue. This is a rather delicate situation. Let's not allow it to become the next Washington scandal." With that said, President Russell dismissed his guest and went to work. His first phone call was to the governor of the State of Mississippi, an ultra right-wing Republican and as expected, it would be interesting.

"Governor Slate, this is President Russell. I'm calling you first to express my condolences on the catastrophic effects of the hurricane in your state. I've been working with FEMA and other government organizations to speed up the relief process in your area. One issue I want to address is the nuclear emergency that is ongoing. I've been made aware of the gravity of the situation in some of the towns in the southern part of Mississippi and I'd like your cooperation with the military, as to decontamination and the processing of the civilian population involved. General Paten has been assigned this task and would really appreciate the help of some local forces, to be put at his disposal, for the containment of the affected areas. I understand one major military base was severely affected by the nuclear fallout and we've made arrangements for military relief in that area. But we need your support for a state-wide military effort."

The governor scoffed. "You mean to tell me Mr. President, that you want to invade my state with the army and take control?"

The President responded quickly. "No, not at all. We just want your help in this matter. People are suffering right now and the quicker we can get them the proper treatment, the better their chances of making it. I can go public with this, but I wanted to give you the opportunity to take the lead in this area and request assistance from us publicly."

"Can I think about it? asked the governor.

"You have until tomorrow morning at ten my time. I'll be doing a live television appearance at ten thirty and I'd like this matter to be resolved by then.

"Thank you," said the governor. "Goodbye, sir." The President sighed as he hung up the phone. *Well that went better than expected*, he thought. *That guy may be a contrarian, but he's also a politician. I don't think he'll fight me on this one.*

Not wasting a moment, President Russell phoned Paten, already onboard a military jet to Gulfport, Mississippi.

The President spoke immediately. "Well General, I have good news for you. I think our friend, Governor Slate, will cooperate. But I'm giving him until tomorrow to respond, just for the sake of politics."

"Yes, that is good news Mr. President. The quicker I can get this place under my control, the better. Time is of the essence."

It had been three days since Hurricane Gordon had hit the coast of Louisiana and General Paten was giving last orders for full military containment of the explosion site. A cordon of approximately ten miles had been drawn around ground zero, with checkpoints manned by the National Guard, under his supervision. Nuclear testing equipment was on the way to checkpoints to scan all outgoing traffic, not that there would be much. The wounded and severely exposed were being taken out by helicopter to quarantined hospitals in Alabama. Partly due to the low population density and the fact that most residents had gone to shelters, very few people died from the blast of the explosion itself, but the radiation contamination was a very real threat to the survivors.

General Paten had dispatched a team of scientists to map out the immediate surroundings of ground zero, in an attempt to reverse engineer the event. The goal would be to determine if the explosion involved more nuclear material than in a single bomb. The actual size of the explosion was quickly determined at around one kiloton to TNT equivalent. This information itself was confirmation that the bomb had accidentally released some nuclear energy. The device in question offered the ability to set the size of the explosion, however that particular size just wasn't a realistic option as the primary fission blast alone would have exceeded that amount. Even greater explosions could be obtained by varying the amount of fusion material in the secondary phase of the explosion. What they concluded was that there had been a partial primary fission explosion; most likely due to improper timing of some of the conventional explosives, used to increase the plutonium and uranium densities past their critical masses. This somewhat lopsided explosion had resulted in a rather incomplete use of the fissionable material, thus only releasing part of its potential energy. All they needed to do was figure out how much of the original material there had been in the six bombs combined, minus the material used up. That would give them the total amount of uranium and plutonium that should have been released in the surrounding areas. This would have been a rather simple determination had the blast occurred deep within the ground. However, because this had been, for all practical purposes, a surface blast; where elements had been released high up into the atmosphere and even grabbed by the vortex of the storm, a quantitative determination would be a challenge and would have to be modeled by supercomputers. It would take a significant amount of time.

General Paten had requested to be briefed and had specifically ordered the scientists to look for a greater than one scenario, meaning to immediately notify him if they felt confident that enough nuclear material had been released to account for more than one bomb. This would by no means solve the problem, but it would definitely be a sign that it was unlikely that the other nukes had been taken.

In the meantime, a search of the area was done by low-flying, active radiation detectors, just in case the weapons had been taken and were still in the area. The detectors worked by sending a high-energy beam into their targets and then listened for the telltale signs of bomb-grade nuclear material, which would respond in a very unique signature when stimulated; like a dog responds to his master's words and only to his master's words.

General Paten did however assume; that if foul play had indeed happened, the bombs were most likely long gone. It had been three days and the area was still leaking people and was full of small country roads leading out, with hardly any residents to witness anything. Also, the warheads were small; only weighing a little over three hundred pounds each including their crates, small enough to fit in the average pickup truck. A team of military investigators was sent to question the surviving residents who had stayed in their homes, to determine if they had seen anything unusual during the storm. So far, as expected, there had been no reports of suspicious activity. Most residents had boarded themselves into their homes; too afraid to venture out during the hurricane. However, one man had seen a tree mover on the road, but he told them that during Katrina, most of the initial road clearing had been done by local farmers. He was sure that's probably what that was. But his story was noted and transferred back to headquarters in Gulfport.

Paten couldn't stop thinking of the worst case scenario; that nukes had been stolen. So he continued to try to put himself in these guy's heads if they existed. They would have had to brave the elements as well as the fallen debris to retrieve the nukes, so when he saw the report about the forestry equipment, something told him to check it out further. He immediately informed the troops to notify him every time a tree mover came into sight, with coordinates. The old Massey tree mover, sitting on the side of the road about thirty miles from ground zero, was located by one of his commanders a few hours later on his way out to a checkpoint. Immediately, the equipment was taken by truck to a warehouse and checked for radioactivity. It showed a level that was actually somewhat higher than expected for the area it had been discovered in. Obviously it had been used closer to the epicenter than where it was found. That in itself wasn't too suspicious. But the fact that no owners of the equipment could be found immediately raised some eyebrows. The identification numbers on the machine appeared to have been removed years earlier and it appeared to be over fifteen years old, so ownership would be nearly impossible to determine.

A scenario played in Paten's mind...these guys must have gotten out west of the storm, using that piece of equipment to work their way out of the hurricane-impacted area. He knew that opened up all kinds of exit possibilities. They could easily be in California already, planning to blow up Los Angeles for all he knew.

Chapter 14

When the submarine finally showed up, it was in the early hours of the night and no time was wasted. The submersible was equipped with a loading bay area on its belly, so they winched the Y form containing the nukes, inside of the submarine rather than towing it. A couple of divers were sent to unfasten the concrete structure from the sunken barge, by cutting the chains. It was dangerous work due to the remaining buoyancy of the barge. Once freed, the barge and the remaining concrete Y slowly rose back to the surface. Landry ordered the small tender boat out, with instructions to sink it. The bay doors of the submarine were shut and the Y was set aside on the loading platform. Landry didn't want the nukes to remain in their concrete enclosures; for fear that moisture could damage them. So, he ordered them cut out. About an hour later, all five nukes were sitting in a storage room at the very bottom of the sub, surrounded by the black-painted gold ballast rods, which provided a rather expensive, but quite effective insulation vault for the moderately radioactive weapons. It was time to leave the area. The sun was starting to rise and the sitting catamaran could easily attract unnecessary attention from the Coast Guard Patrols.

While Landry remained on the catamaran, Heraldo quickly boarded the submarine, which had partially surfaced, and immediately ordered both the sub and the cat to sail south at cruising speed, to get out of US patrolled waters. Heraldo finally retired to his state room where, after a long, warm shower in the luxurious marble bathroom, he went straight for his large king-sized bed and fell deeply asleep. He hadn't slept that well since before his wife had been kidnapped. When he woke ten hours later, about one hundred miles from the coast of Louisiana, they were still in an area riddled with oil platforms and service boats. The catamaran had been leading the way, sending a consistent low-frequency beacon signal, so the submarine could follow easily without having to rely on active sonar detection for its journey through the man-made obstacle course. The last thing they needed was to hit one of the underwater structures. Landry himself was exhausted as well, but had only slept about five hours. The motion of the boat, still in rough waters, woke him up several times. It was the middle of the afternoon when Landry saw what appeared to be a Coast Guard vessel, heading straight for them. Not wasting any time, he signaled the sub through the beacon system. Although it would be unlikely that the submarine would be detected at the depth it was running at, the plan was for it to go silent and still for an event such as this. Heraldo had been awake for about an hour and was standing in the control room watching the monitors; watching the blinking dot of the approaching Coast Guard vessel.

General Paten was ever more convinced that someone had made off with an undetermined number of nukes. The evidence wasn't proven scientifically, but his gut instincts were usually right on the money. In his line of work, when something could go really wrong, it usually did. Local scans by the helicopters hadn't revealed anything of interest. So, it was more than likely that the nukes had breached the containment zone and were on their way to their intended destination, wherever that was. His next step was quick and decisive. He would have to go nationwide with the search. A general alert was sent out for all law enforcement agencies to be extra vigilant and for searches to be initiated on all suspicious vehicles. This applied to all branches of civilian transport including maritime. The Coast

Guard vessel had been given the same instructions and became part of the active search.

Captain Borman, an experienced mariner, had set his sights on the yacht heading due south. It looked quite modern and somewhat out of character with what he usually saw in this area of large, iron, industrial floating structures. This could be interesting. About fifteen minutes later, he and four armed men were heading for the catamaran on a hard-bottom inflatable that had been lowered from their vessel. Landry was watching the whole scene, readying for the encounter.

"Permission to come onboard," called out one of the Coast Guardsmen. Landry, in his best bayou drawl, responded.

"Absolutely. Welcome aboard Captain."

"The Captain eyed him carefully. "With your permission, we need to inspect your boat. It's just a routine check, nothing to worry about."

Landry smiled and nodded. "Okay, no problem sir. All we got is some whiskey, but you're welcome to it," he said jokingly. Captain Borman decided Landry looked like a local; probably one of those rich Cajuns that had been lucky enough to have oil discovered on his land. He suddenly thought it doubtful that they would find anything there besides the usual guns and booze.

Landry stepped aside and watched the sailors do their work. Immediately, his attention was drawn towards one of the pieces of equipment they were using. He had seen one like it before; a sophisticated, portable radiation detector. This was impressive. They were already looking for the nukes. Oddly enough, only a cursory search went on. It became obvious that all they were interested in was the readings on their radiation counter. They didn't even flinch at the gun cabinet in the state room and hanging gun racks in the pilot room. This fiberglass boat was an easy detection environment and the Captain obviously didn't want to impose upon them any more than necessary. So, about fifteen minutes later, they were back onboard their inflatable and heading back to their mother ship. Landry let out a huge lungful of air that he had been unaware he was holding. He thought of the five years that had just been shaved off of his life. He knew things would need to get less stressful soon or he wouldn't even be around to enjoy his newfound wealth.

In Bogota, Castillo wasn't too comfortable. He hadn't received any news from Heraldo since Hurricane Gordon had hit the coast. The events of the last few days including the nuclear crisis in Mississippi, pointed to the fact that the operation had indeed taken place. The question was: had it been successful or had Heraldo's men just perished in the blast? Castillo had sent Heraldo a coded message, requesting an update, but that had been over three days ago. Castillo was starting to worry a bit. He sent another message, this time urging Heraldo to communicate as soon as possible.

After all, he still held Heraldo's wife hostage and was sure to stress that fact in his message.

Heraldo had been careful not to communicate with anyone post-hurricane. He was waiting to get far enough away from the United States to safely use his satellite communication system. On one hand, he was sure all signals would be monitored with extreme diligence in the affected areas and he didn't want to take the risk of attracting attention to himself. On the other hand, he was worried about his wife and the risks that his lack of communication posed for her. Soon after he received the news that the visit from the Coast Guard had been uneventful and that they had left the area, heading for the mainland at cruising speed, he ordered the floatable satellite antenna released from the sub and soon thereafter had connected to the phone message system. He initiated a call to Castillo. It didn't take long for the signal to go through and Heraldo spoke immediately.

"We've succeeded in gathering what you wanted." Castillo almost couldn't contain his excitement.

"That's just beautiful my friend. I was beginning to worry you had perished. I take it you're safe now and ready for the exchange?"

"Yes, we are ready, but I request the exchange take place at sea. We have reason to believe our secrecy has been compromised," said Heraldo grimly. He was referring to the news from Landry about the radiation detectors used by the Coast Guard.

Castillo paused, considering the revelation. "Okay, I agree. That might be better indeed. If you can deliver the goods to some point off the Cuban coast, we'll do our best to accommodate you."

Heraldo, not wanting to lose any power in the exchange, replied quickly and decisively. "I'll meet you off of the southwest coast of Cuba, just out of their territorial waters."

After a short pause, Castillo acquiesced. "Fine. You may have your wish. Can you be there in two days?"

"Yes," replied Heraldo and continued without pause. "What about my wife and the money?"

"Your wife is fine. As for the money, one billion dollars is a considerable amount. To raise that much cash might be difficult." Heraldo interjected quickly.

"I'll take gold if you don't mind." Heraldo knew a little more of the yellow metal would be easier to store and since he wasn't planning on using the money anytime soon, gold was a better investment for sure and a useful ballast for the submarine in addition to that. As an added bonus, it would be more valuable than ever, once the world heard of their little escapade.

"Gold it shall be," replied Castillo. Heraldo was eager to end the call. Even with the encryption system, he knew he could never be too careful.

"I will call you back in two days," said Heraldo. Goodbye."

Castillo smirked as the connection went dead. He didn't intend to fulfill his part of the deal at all and a plan immediately surfaced in his devious mind. Castillo had long nurtured good relations with the Cubans. His drug trade had benefited from the cover that the Island of Cuba provided to him, so close to the coast of the United States. Payoff of top officials had been routine, to facilitate his smuggling activities. Just like Hugo Chavez, he also enjoyed a privileged stature as one of the many benefactors of the island.

He decided quickly that he would enlist his connections in the army to capture the weapons. The payoff to them would no doubt be much less than the money he had promised to Heraldo.

Shit for that much dough, I could buy the whole fucking Cuban army, thought Castillo. In his mind, the change of venue for the weapons' delivery had been a Godsend; a sign that he was one step closer to maximizing his profit. *I need to let my little Persian friends know the deal is about to take place,* thought Castillo. *Maybe Cuba wouldn't be a bad location for them to take possession of the lot. I could literally kill two birds with one stone.* The thought of bringing the nukes to Colombia had made him a little nervous anyway. The last thing he needed was for the Americans to have an excuse to be able to dispose of him on his own soil.

Chapter 15

Later that day, Castillo met with his Iranian trading partners. As usual, it would be a long, tedious and draining endeavor. The delivery of the fifty billion promised, of which Castillo had already received close to one billion, was frothing with logistical problems. It was a complex deal to funnel such a large sum of money, involving the set-up of third parties as well.

Originally, Castillo had insisted on wire transfers. But due to recent political developments, he knew that would be impossible. Western banks wouldn't deal with any of the financial activities of that country and assets had been frozen until further notice. Talks then shifted to possible oil contracts, but that had also proved to be impossible. Embargos had been set up and smuggling that much traceable oil was out of the question. That only left one plausible solution. It wouldn't be the simplest by any means, but if he could work out the details, it could prove to be a huge windfall for him.

The Chinese would purchase oil, the payment of which would be reinvested via mining contracts in China. Castillo's company would hold a large, but still minority interest in those mining contracts. The exported rare earth minerals would generate the payoffs Castillo was due and then some. The only foreseeable problem with this solution was that he would basically have to give the fox the keys to the hen house and trust the fox not to go in and eat the hens. These would be Chinese contracts after all, notorious for being unenforceable. Castillo knew he had to make it work, and the only way he could do so was to retain control over some of the nukes, releasing them one by one, as he received compensation from the Chinese mining operations.

After a solid ten hours of arguments and discussions with his Chinese contacts, a semi-agreement was reached. It gave the proceeds of fifty-percent of the oil sales to China, back to Castillo's company, in the form of mineral contracts. They also agreed upon a fifteen-percent rate of return on the money owed, to incentivize a quick repayment schedule. The agreement would be translated to Chinese and endorsed by the proper authorities there. It all looked good on paper, but Castillo's only real leverage was possession of the weapons. There was no doubt the Chinese would go along with the oil part of the agreement. They, like the rest of the world, were starving for cheap, crude oil. The Persians gave Castillo a two week deadline as to ratification of the contract by all other parties involved. This gave

Castillo a little time to figure out how he would capture and hold the nukes; the next step on his agenda.

Heraldo and Landry, each in their respective vessel, headed for the west coast of Cuba; two days away given the present wind conditions. Finally in the open seas, the catamaran had erected its sails, using the wind for power. Even though the turbines were relatively unobtrusive, sailing on the wind alone was almost a religious experience; nothing but the sound of the hull breaking the wave tips, as it moved along at about ten knots per hour. As an added benefit, sailing made the ride much more comfortable; quickly dissipating any hint of sea sickness among Landry and the members of the crew.

Heraldo's world was somewhat different. The submarine was extremely quiet when in motion. It derived its power from two large hydrogen fuel cells; generating electricity for the motors of the two main propellers. Computers regulated the sub's speed, matching the catamaran by locking onto its beacon and therefore, practically driving itself. Any new or out of the ordinary conditions were relayed to Heraldo immediately via the sexy, feminine voice of the onboard computer.

Heraldo took the opportunity to catch up on some well-deserved sleep. It had been a rough week; not so much because of their actions, but mainly due to the immense emotional and mental stress of avoiding detection, as they made their way out of the explosion site and out of US waters. Heraldo was feeling some excitement now; allowing himself to finally think of the reunion with his wife. However, he still wasn't quite sure about the logistics of the entire operation. Castillo didn't seem like the type of man who would hand over payment freely. The deal they had discussed now seemed somewhat unrealistic. Heraldo knew he had to be extremely cautious in this last phase. In his mind, saving his wife was a main priority; the money secondary. If worse came to worse, he would be happy to just get Maria back.

Landry and Heraldo communicated briefly every twelve hours or so on their way to the bay of Corrientes, south of the western-most part of Cuba. Heraldo kept abreast of the latest news from the short bursts of condensed video signal that the catamaran's satellite dish captured and sent to the sub. The news had broken that there had been a possible theft of nuclear weapons at the armory. One of the local guardsmen had overheard a snippet of some conversation: "we can't find the nukes" and had blabbed about it on a popular social media site. His posting had gone viral and almost instantly, everyone and their mother were aware that the army was looking for missing nuclear weapons. The citizens of the United States were in a state of mass panic.

The New York Stock Exchange had to be closed for fear of meltdown and people were leaving major metropolitan areas such as New York, Los Angeles and Washington D.C., for fear of being atomically roasted. Within a matter of hours, security checkpoints to detect radiation had popped up in every single major city in the country. The President had appeared on television to reassure the masses that exploding one of the devices in a large city would be very unlikely. He explained that those in charge were scanning every vehicle on the ground and in the air and that they had other ways of detecting the weapons as well.

Gold was at a new all-time high and Heraldo couldn't help but pat himself on the back for having collecting so much over the last few years. No doubt, the economic impact of people's fear was much greater than any physical impact rendered by five exploding nukes, even if they did all target highly-populated areas. People easily forgot the vast resources of a large, wealthy country like the United States. Some nations, like Japan, always had nuclear phobias; apparent in their popular culture by radiation-born monsters such as Godzilla. Americans also feared nuclear annihilation, but more so out of ignorance, rather than firsthand experience. Heraldo was just glad to be out of the United States. It had been a good ride for him, but just like all good things; it had to come to an end.

The submarine had been cruising at a depth of about three-hundred meters; deep enough to render detection difficult, while still maintaining solid, low-intensity communication with the catamaran. They were about fifty miles north-northwest of the western-most part of Cuba: a flat and unpopulated area of the island. As a natural pathway for many hurricanes, the area had never been developed. Therefore, despite its beautiful sandy beaches, it remained well off the beaten path of most tourists, with the exception of a few adventuring sailors.

Once out of American waters, Landry ordered the name and port of call of the catamaran to be changed to Montreal, Canada. Even though they were quite far away from the United States, the presence of the US Coast Guard remained a concern around the northern part of the island. Coast Guard vessels were present right outside of the Cuban territorial waters, acting as deterrents for any fleeing islanders. American boats were prime targets and Landry didn't want to draw any unnecessary attention. He knew flying the Canadian flag was the best way to go virtually unnoticed. Landry spoke fluent French and could easily fool any American as to his lineage. He had been one of the lucky few, back in the bayou, who had held onto his language and traditions; thanks to the refusal of his parents to submit to the heavy influence of the Anglos and their culture. As a lawyer in Louisiana, he was also familiar with the Napoleonic code, as it still applied in that state. He had spent several years at the Sorbonne in Paris, studying French law and perfecting his language skills.

Even though they came from totally different backgrounds, Heraldo and Landry shared the similar struggle of being minority in America; a struggle not to be assimilated and dissipated into the blob that represented modern American culture or the lack thereof. Out of this complex background, came their similar love of culturally-rich food and mutual disdain for the grub that had become the staple of most Americans. Heraldo often poked fun at American fast food chains; stating that they alone were responsible for more premature deaths than all of the illegal drug dealers in the world combined. Heraldo was disgusted that no one seemed to ever be able to improve the health of Americans when it came to food; as if eating crap like a fucking hog was an inalienable right. Those who opposed the horrible eating habits of Americans were quickly and firmly pushed aside and ostracized; even president's wives.

The submarine settled to the west of the bay of Corrientes, at a depth of about four-hundred meters. It waited there, recharging its batteries and hydrogen tanks. One positive aspect about that locale was the intense underwater currents, joining the Caribbean Sea and the Gulf of Mexico. The sub had a range of about four-thousand miles when it had full tanks of hydrogen and fully-charged batteries, so the relatively short trip from Louisiana had hardly made a dent in its reserves. But it was better to be prepared for the unexpected since charging-mode was only possible if it could anchor to the bottom of the ocean. If the sub needed to run in deep waters where anchoring was impossible, having full reserves would be optimal. Heraldo wasn't exactly sure how deep he could take his submarine. Theoretically, a maximum depth of four-thousand meters should be possible, although as most submariners, he was unwilling to try that level of crushing pressure unless he absolutely had to. He was happy with the much shallower depth of four-hundred meters that they had decided upon. It was also within the range of the small, two-person submersible, stored in the belly of the sub. Heraldo sealed himself inside of it to join Landry on the surface. The quick trip to the sky-filled world was over in less than ten minutes. Heraldo watched in awe as the small vessel rose from pitch darkness to the beautiful sunshine-filled day of the Caribbean Sea. It took him a few minutes to adjust to the motion of the ocean once he reached the surface. Even with the dark sunglasses he had smartly had the presence of mind to wear, the bright sunlight was overwhelming. All of his senses were awakened as he stepped out of the confined space of the mini-sub. From the area between the two keels, where the sub had been berthed, Landry reached out for Heraldo and pulled him onboard the catamaran.

"Welcome onboard my friend," said Captain Landry with a smile.

"I must admit it's nice to be back on the surface," said Heraldo as he boarded with Landry's help. "As comfortable as the sub is, it can be a bit claustrophobic." Thankful to be on the surface again, Heraldo looked out over the sea. The Caribbean water was strikingly beautiful, reflecting the perfect blue sky above them; quite a change from the murky waters of the Mississippi Delta. The ocean was calm, adding even more of a festive feel to the whole situation.

"Where are the Margaritas?" asked Heraldo jokingly.

"I knew you would ask that," said Landry with a chuckle. "Actually, I've prepared some fresh ones on the top deck if you will oblige me." Heraldo was happy to do so. Both men quickly climbed the steps towards the large control and lounge area of the ship. It boasted a three hundred and sixty degree view of the sea.

Once settled into their comfortable captain's chairs, sipping their excellent Margaritas, Heraldo spoke.

"The more I think about this exchange, the less I trust this guy." Landry raised his eyebrows and nodded slowly as Heraldo continued. He had felt the same. "I have a feeling that once he thinks he has our cargo, he'll forget about Maria and the money and maybe even us for that matter."

"You're right Heraldo," said Landry quickly. "The same thoughts have crossed my mind and I've been thinking about a solution." Landry leaned forward. "Here's what I think we should do. These people don't know about the sub. Once we give them our location, they'll be on top of us like white on rice. Obviously, they'll assume we have the nukes onboard the catamaran. I think we should tell them that we've dropped all five nukes into the ocean, in five separate locations, and that we'll retrieve them once we've received Maria and the payment.

Chapter 16

Castillo had flown to Cuba in his private jet. He was greeted by one of Raul Castro's generals at La Coloma: a small airport located less than an hour from the southwest coast of Cuba. He and the General, along with several men, quickly drove to the port where Castillo's yacht waited for them. General Martinez had arranged for several outdated and run-down patrol boats, of the southern part of the island's security flotilla, to be on maneuvers in the area. It was more for show than anything, to keep the United States' wandering Coast Guard vessels far enough away from them, so they could take care of business.

A few years back, General Martinez had been introduced to Castillo by Castro himself, as liaison for a possible cooperative project between his company and the Cuban government. Castillo had invested in and had provided the technical expertise for several large hotel developments within

Cuba. With Raul Castro currently in power, the shift towards Chinese-style socialism had been initiated. Castillo was anxious to beat out his competitors in the large oil field located off the coast of the island. One ace he possessed was the fact that no one in Cuba wanted the Americans to benefit from this new venture. Venezuela was a player, but Castro didn't really trust Chavez to pull it together, for fear of the chaos that his style of management would bring to this part of the world. Castro knew the real benefits could be derived from new partners, such as one of Castillo's Brazilian oil exploration companies; rapidly overtaking deep sea oil exploration in that part of the world. It was certainly a fast-changing world and Castillo was dead set on becoming top dog in this new era: the rapid economic expansion of Latin America.

Castillo's yacht took up most of the space in the small, protected coastal harbor of Coloma. It stood out as an anachronism among the old and rundown buildings surrounding the harbor. Onboard, Maria and Celina had been assigned their usual cabin, but had been free to move around the yacht. It was anchored with no place for them to really swim too. Celina and Castillo had continued their torrid, teenager-like romance and that had provided Maria some additional freedoms. She had been able to watch the news and even talk to the help; enough to figure out what had happened. She had a pretty good guess as to what her husband's involvement had been. Sadly, she also fully understood that the events which had taken place in her native New Orleans would keep her from ever returning. Since the yacht's arrival, its tender helicopter had been sent out on reconnaissance missions to locate Heraldo's catamaran. It soon located it, not too long after Castillo landed on the island.

Landry and Heraldo were still relaxing on the top deck lounge when the computerized radar alarm sounded and a rapid description of the approaching helicopter was given.

Landry peered up into the sky as the two men quickly made their way to the radar. "It looks like our friend has found us." Heraldo focused on the close-up images of the flying object on the screen.

"Definitely not Cuban; way too new and pretty," Heraldo said.

"Can you make out any identification?" asked Landry.

Heraldo nodded. "Yes, it looks like a tender helicopter for a yacht." Heraldo read the information from the computer. "According to this data bank, it appears to be a Colombian owner; registered in Gibraltar. This has to be our guy." Heraldo looked up at Landry as he spoke. "My guess is; he must be lurking along the coast of Cuba somewhere, ready to pounce on us." The helicopter made a couple of passes and as quickly as it had appeared, faded into the wide, blue sky.

Castillo and General Martinez had boarded Castillo's yacht; busy planning their next move. 'Overwhelming force' was Castillo's plan. Four of the frigates would be sent to intercept the catamaran while the yacht stayed back a few miles and directed the operation. Castillo had gotten wind of the fate of his hit man sent to New Orleans, so he was well-aware of the defensive capacity of Heraldo's catamaran. But with overwhelming force and his power of having the hostages, he believed he could prevail due to having the definitive psychological advantage. It was time to contact Heraldo. Heraldo picked up the expected transmission signal quickly.

"Good afternoon," said Castillo. "I'm glad you made it safely to my part of the world. It's time to exchange our goods, but I knew you would want to speak with your wife, so I've taken the liberty to have her on the phone." Maria had been brought to the stateroom and was handed a phone. She spoke immediately and anxiously.

"I'm alright Heraldo. Is everything okay?" Heraldo involuntarily drew in his breath at the sound of her voice. He hadn't heard it since the hurricane and was instantly reminded of the frailty of her situation. He needed to keep things cool and under control, even though a large part of him, feeling angry and frustrated, just wanted to charge in and rescue her. Mustering his greatest inner strength, he quickly spoke. "Yes my darling. Everything will be okay. It's almost over."

Taking the phone from Maria, Castillo spoke quickly. "I need you to sail to the following coordinates. I will be waiting there with your wife and we will then proceed with the exchange. The location Castillo had chosen was around ten miles off of the Cuban coast, right in between La Furnia and the island of Cayos de San Felipe. It would take the catamaran about four hours to get there based on present wind conditions. Heraldo immediately sent instructions to the sub, via his computer keyboard, for it to standby and follow them there.

"Alright," said Heraldo. "We are raising our sails and heading your way. Over and out."

What had started as a pleasant afternoon was quickly turning into a survival mission. Heraldo and Landry had no illusions. They knew this would be a hard fight. During the entire trip, they brainstormed and discussed ideas and scenarios for the events soon to follow.

It was nighttime when they finally arrived at their meeting point. Castillo's large yacht was clearly visible in the distance and reminded Heraldo of a cruise ship; all lit up and party-like. Smaller lights were also visible, scattered all around them; some on land and some at sea. Heraldo knew the area probably hadn't seen that much activity since before Castro's takeover. The phone rang and Heraldo quickly answered Castillo's call.

"Welcome to Cuba my friend. I don't want to proceed with the exchange in the darkness. Load up your tender boat with the goods. You will bring them to me tomorrow morning at nine o'clock. In the meantime, please come join me so we can discuss our business arrangement further, over a meal and some wine. I'm sure you are dying to see your wife again, are you not?"

Heraldo was somewhat surprised at his request and immediately informed Landry of it. Not quite knowing what to say, Heraldo responded simply. "Okay," and hung up the phone. He looked at Landry, who was shaking his head.

"I smell a rat here," said Landry quickly. "He wants you onboard his boat so that he can control you while the catamaran is taken over somehow. Look," Landry said, pointing at the radar. "There are several boats around us. They look like Cuban military, with some heavy guns topside."

Heraldo peered at the screen, his brow furrowed. "Probably," he responded. "But it looks like we don't have a choice." He looked at Landry as he thought for a moment. Finally he spoke. "Here's what I want you to do..."

After discussing a plan of action with Landry, Heraldo launched the hard-bottom inflatable tender and headed full speed towards Castillo's yacht. The ship was even more impressive up close, greatly overshadowing his small motorboat. A steep ramp was lowered from its deck as he approached and Heraldo quickly climbed up onto the vessel. He was immediately searched by two armed men and then escorted to the upper deck area. His eyes scanned the deck and suddenly stopped as the blood drained from his face. There stood Maria, right there looking at him, smiling with tears in her eyes. His heart nearly stopped as they simultaneously lunged for each other. Forgetting all restraint and everything around them, he kissed her like never before. The feeling of her safely wrapped up in his arms was the most exhilarating thing he had ever experienced. She seemed unharmed and he was beyond relieved.

Castillo stood at her side and smirked at the two of them, thoroughly enjoying the full control he had over the situation. He winked at Celina as their eyes met for a brief moment.

"Why don't we go sit down?" Castillo finally said. "I'm sure everyone has built up quite an appetite."

Heraldo, quickly brought back to reality by Castillo's words, reached for his wife's hand and followed Castillo to the table. As directed, they each took their seats around the oval jade table, set perfectly with crystal glasses and fine china.

"I'm glad we are finally meeting in the flesh Señor Heraldo," said Castillo with a smile. "As I knew you would, you have completed your mission in splendid fashion; better than any of my paramilitary teams could have possibly done. I guess what people have said about you is true; you are quite a resourceful man. Rest assured, you will be rewarded for your hard work." Heraldo rewarded the man with his best grateful smile, but instantly had the distinct feeling he was being buttered up for the kill, like a cannibal would do to their victim before cooking and eating them. Heraldo knew that all he could do was go along and seize whatever opportunity came along to regain the upper hand.

As surrealistic as the scene of them eating together was, he gave Castillo credit for putting on such a sumptuous feast of various tastings of exotic fishes, expertly prepared with tropical fruits, vegetables juices and extracts. The meal was a sensual pleasure for the eyes as much as for the palate. One could easily forget the rather unusual circumstances of the meal and simply delight in the feast. However, Heraldo was constantly reminded of the need for action as he watched Maria sipping on her drink across from him. His mind raced with ideas of how to escape their predicament. Heraldo had boarded the yacht with what had appeared to be a cell phone in his shirt pocket. It hadn't raised any interest from the guards during the cursory search. The small camera and precision locator gave Landry an exact position of Heraldo, in relation to the rest of the large boat. Landry sat in the control room of the catamaran watching and listening to the dinner party from his computer, slowly putting together a detailed plan of the ship. After completing their sumptuous feast, Castillo invited his guests to join him on the back of the yacht, to sit and enjoy the warm summer breeze while he smoked his obligatory Cuban cigar. Throughout the meal, Castillo had purposely omitted any reference to the business at hand. This abruptly changes with the next words out of his mouth.

Castillo looked at Heraldo. "As I'm sure you are aware Señor Heraldo, I have surrounded your boat with the naval might of our Cuban friends. I will soon give the order for them to board your vessel and retrieve what is mine.

I expect you to cooperate and give orders to your men to surrender without a fight. If you do so, I will allow you and your wife to live, free to go back to your yacht and enjoy what will no doubt be the beginning of a beautiful holiday."

Heraldo and Maria quickly exchanged glances. Maria looked frightened but Heraldo's stern stare suddenly gave her reason to hope. Heraldo, eager to stall for more time, spoke quickly.

"What about the money you promised? Not so much for myself, but for my men. They are expecting payment and will not take kindly to this change of plan." Castillo, in full control, simply shrugged his shoulders and smirked.

"Well, that's simply not my problem Señor Heraldo." He looked like a cat that had eaten the canary; very proud of his accomplishment.

Under any other circumstances, Heraldo might have punched the grin right off of the motherfucker's face, but he restrained himself. They were still free to move about the yacht and he didn't want to risk losing that privilege. He was well aware of Landry's presence via the camera.

Landry was fully suited up and had finished loading the mini-sub with enough gear for two additional people. The small vessel was just large enough for two average-sized humans and some cargo, so it would be a very tight fit for the three of them. Landry was thankful Maria was petite and limber. Landry dove slowly, using the electrical power of the two small wing engines. Making a vertical descent to about five-hundred feet, deep enough to ensure invisibility from the vessels surrounding him, he rotated the engines to their horizontal positions and slowly headed for the large ship about a mile away. The deep water navigation of the mini-sub was mainly via sight and depth-finder. There was also sonar onboard, but it couldn't be activated due to risk of detection. Landry also avoided using his depth finder for the same reason. He prayed no one close by was equipped with underwater detection equipment. At least he didn't have to worry about that with the Cubans. Even if they had once had it, their equipment was most likely non-functional by now.

However, the large yacht was broadcasting a faint signal, from which his computerized, onboard detectors showed to be the typical telltale signature of active sonar. Using it as a beacon, Landry slowly approached the area where the yacht was anchored. Lucky for him, the sonar they were using was somewhat directional, pointing about a hundred and fifty degrees ahead of the ship. Landry easily circumnavigated the sensitive zone and stayed clear of detection. The noises of the large ship were even more audible without his equipment and the onboard generators dominating the wide range of sounds. Landry wondered how the whales ever slept with all of the noise.

Once underneath the ship, Landry slowly raised the mini-sub and magnetically locked himself to the hull silently, right below where he thought Heraldo had last been; the back, uncovered area where the occupants onboard had enjoyed their after dinner drinks. Landry slowly released the mini-sub's antenna to the surface and was finally able to see the latest visual broadcasts of Heraldo's camera. Those onboard were all still sitting in the large comfortable chairs and just talking from the looks of it. He signaled Heraldo's phone via a short vibration, inaudible to anyone around him. It was Heraldo's signal that everything was in position, ready for the next phase of the plan. Landry squeezed himself into the small decompression compartment and after locking the hatch to the main cabin area, slowly let the water in, readying for the dive. Once fully submerged, he opened the hatch to the ocean world and uncoiled himself from inside the small chamber. They had planned it well. Landry would release a flare on the opposite side of the boat from where he wanted them to jump off; allowing for a long enough distraction. Heraldo felt the vibration and knew it was time. He slowly moved closer to his wife, using his facial expression to let her know something was up. He grabbed her hands as if to kiss her. When his mouth came close to her ear, he whispered.

"Get ready to jump with me." Maria squeezed his hands in agreement and moved her lips to kiss him. As expected, Castillo was watching them and couldn't help but interject that his yacht had plenty of rooms to accommodate them if they so desired. They ignored his comments, truly enjoying their kiss, as Heraldo kept one eye open slightly...waiting.

Suddenly, a swooshing sound came from the starboard side of the ship, causing everyone but Heraldo and Maria to turn. Heraldo smiled and whispered, "Now!"

Both jumped up, Heraldo holding Maria's hand firmly as they raced for the opposite side of the boat. About four seconds later, as everyone else jumped up from their seats and rapidly moved towards the noise, a firework-like explosion illuminated the sky nearly a hundred feet in the air and close enough to give everyone temporary blindness. The flare had been large and bright enough to light up the entire sky, but the intense light didn't last more than a couple of seconds. Heraldo had lifted Maria up over the guard rail and had thrown her into the sea about six feet below. He quickly followed her. The flash of light had been so intense that Castillo hadn't recovered his sight enough to notice his missing guests, Celina was at his side. Several of Castillo's men surfaced from inside the ship, to find out what had just happened.

Landry was waiting. He reached Maria quickly and outfitted her with the portable oxygen tank, mask and breathing apparatus within a matter of seconds. Heraldo grabbed his set and put them on just as quickly. Within ten seconds flat, all three were underwater, making their way underneath the ship towards the mini-sub's single blinking red LED light, as fast as they possibly could. Landry went in first, reversing the process he underwent earlier so that Maria could go second without having to man most of the decompression operation. With all three onboard, Maria slid her way back to the decompression chamber, pressing against Heraldo. She kept the hatch open so that she could communicate with them. It had been less than three minutes since they had jumped into the water. They all knew that Castillo would know by now that they were gone. There wasn't a moment to spare.

Landry quickly released the mini-sub's magnetic hold from the ship's hull and directly descended to two hundred feet, right to the bottom of the ocean in this area. With full power to the electric motor pods, the mini-sub moved at about eight knots, certainly not enough speed to escape the flotilla that Castillo controlled on the surface, but enough to put some distance between them and the yacht and to avoid detection by hugging the rocky rapidly sinking bottom as closely as possible.

Castillo's hair suddenly stood on end, his scalp tingling. They were gone. The whole scene had been a set up for his benefit and deceit. What he couldn't figure out was the seemingly desperate appearance of their escape. It was much too far to swim to shore and the catamaran wouldn't be an option, as he immediately gave the order for it to be commandeered. Certainly Heraldo would know he would do that. The yacht's tender was put into the water and an extensive man-hunt ensued for Heraldo and Maria. Using powerful searchlights, they covered the entire area around the ship and headed towards the catamaran. The Cuban patrol boats joined in like dogs on the trail of a fox. Castillo wanted the catamaran to be taken without the use of heavy weaponry. Its composite hull wouldn't stand for any kind of heavy machine-gun assault.

Onboard the catamaran, the second in command knew this wasn't a fight he could win. True, he could probably take out a couple of the smaller boats, but in the end his fate would be sealed. It broke his heart to have to abandon this beautiful ship, but he knew his chances of survival were, at best, a terminal stay in a Cuban prison. That made his final decision somewhat easier. He knew the plan. He was to climb into the catamaran's emergency pod: a small, heavily reinforced egg-shaped structure; easily accessed via a hatch in the command room. Before doing so, he would flood all of the compartments, the entire ship, with the remains of diesel fuel in the tanks, about a thousand gallons: plenty for one giant, glorious bonfire.

Chapter 17

Castillo had decided to take the lead towards the catamaran. Onboard his yacht's speedy tender, equipped with twin, three-hundred horsepower engines, he raced towards the cat with the Cuban flotilla following closely behind. About a hundred yards from the cat, he picked up the hand-held control to the speaker system and yelled out for all of its occupants to surrender and show themselves on the deck. This was the sign the second in command had been waiting for. The only other people on the cat, two deckhands, had already joined him. With one finally glance around at the beautiful control room of the catamaran, he switched on all of the valves and pumps, releasing the diesel fuel into the twin hulls. Then, just as quickly, he activated the short timers on four incendiary devices located in the hulls. The powerful aroma of diesel quickly spread.

"Goodbye old friend," he whispered to himself. In an instant, all three men were in the small pod. The powerful aroma of the diesel didn't go unnoticed by Castillo, who instinctively knew what was about to take place. He screamed for a full reverse of his small, speedy boat.

As the cat's small egg-shaped vessel dropped into the depths of the ocean, taking the three crewmembers to safety, the first incendiary device kicked in. The starboard hull quickly became engulfed in thick black smoke, soon followed by the other side. Thirty seconds later, what had once been one of the most beautiful sailboats in the world, was no more. It was only a large plume of fire and thick, black smoke. Several explosions screeched into the air, rocking the vessels in the water nearby; the force of which leveled the upper structure of the ship, no doubt the result of all of the ammunition onboard. The flotilla of small ships surrounding the burning remains stood their ground, as if witnessing some tribal sea-fearing funeral. Castillo was livid. What in the fuck had happened here? There had to have been another ship, but he had been assured that no one had been seen leaving the catamaran prior to the night's events. Just as no one had seen Heraldo and his wife after they had slipped away.

Once in the pod, the second in command of the catamaran had released its hold on the yacht and slowly, the egg-shaped vessel had sunk to the deep, dark depths of the ocean. Although it had very little autonomous moving capacity, it could either dive or stay on the surface with the command of a switch. The purpose of its existence was to be able to escape the surface in the case of a major weather event. It also came equipped with its own oxygen generator and air quality scrubbers. It could provide a life-sustaining environment for a period of up to seven days, just on power from its miniature hydrogen fuel cells. The plan was for them to descend to the bottom of the ocean and be picked up by either the mini-sub or the mother-sub.

Onboard the mini-sub, Heraldo, Landry and Maria headed for the location of the mother-sub. It was waiting for them about five miles out, on the ocean floor. Hugging the bottom closely, they raced at maximum speed, in awe of the incredible wonders of the ocean. Caught in their headlights were a number of small squid-like creatures, scattering away like herds of sheep. Larger shadows loomed in the distance, shark-like creatures or possibly whales. It was difficult to tell, but their presence was obvious. The bottom was silt-like and large plumes of powdery substances were kicked up every once in a while, as they made directional adjustments to their propulsion pods. Heraldo couldn't help thinking about how the ocean floor appeared as if someone had flooded the moon: desolate, cold and inhospitable to humans. They had dropped to nearly sixteen-hundred feet and were close to the mini-sub's safe maximum pressure capacity.

The small vessel was being guided by a complex sound wave, emanating from the mother-sub. The wave mimicked the sound of whales, with a complex built-in algorithm that allowed for slow, but effective communications within the depths of the ocean. It was the only way for them to locate each other, as trajectories at this depth obviously couldn't rely on GPS and compass headings were subject to distortions. Knowing all of that somehow made the whole experience even more claustrophobic than it already was. Maria, claustrophobic anyway, was having a particularly hard time and Heraldo knew from experience that a panic attack, in this very confined environment, would be rather unpleasant. The water temperature at this depth was icy cold, and despite the craft's top-of-the-line insulation and cabin heater, sixty degrees Fahrenheit was the current temperature and was the warmest it would get. Maria was shivering, even though she had been given a large beach towel. She hadn't ever expected to be experiencing anything like this, not in the Caribbean in the middle of summer. She felt as if she were on a different planet.

Castillo watched the remnants of the catamaran burn away and continued to watch as it finally started to sink. Soon, it was only small areas of floating debris; a pale reminder of the splendor that had once been the beautiful sailboat. Castillo had no prisoners and no weapons of mass destruction. The evening's events had turned out to be a total fiasco and Castillo barked at his men to take him back to his yacht. He clenched his teeth as he stared back at the floating remains of the cat. "I'm going to find these motherfuckers if it's the last thing I do," he snarled. Castillo could have kicked himself for not taking more precautions. He had grossly underestimated Heraldo and his men, even though they had proven to be more than resourceful so far. Looking back, he could see that it was only logical that they would deceive him with the same talent they had shown in capturing the nukes.

Once onboard his yacht, he immediately spoke with General Martinez, who in turn ordered a rapid, extended search for submarines; the only probable explanation for their guests' disappearance. Castillo didn't hold out much hope. Most of the patrol boats looked as if they belonged in a World War II movie. He was sure none of them had any modern detection equipment. However, they did have a few depth charges which were quickly dispatched around the area where the catamaran had sunk. About half of them didn't go off and the other half simply blew up prematurely, before they had sunk nearly enough to have any effect on the survival pod; already a few hundred yards away at the bottom of the ocean.

The captain of the catamaran and his men had escaped just as planned, allowing the egg-shaped vessel to sink and drift away, when the first explosion's shockwave hit them. They all knew their escape had been discovered and all they could do was to wait for someone to recover them. It had been decided earlier that they would wait for the activity above to taper off, as long as a couple of days. Then they would activate their beacon for twenty-four hours. If no one came, their last resort would be to go back to the surface and launch their inflatable rescue raft. They hoped it wouldn't come to that. None of them wanted to end up in a Cuban jail, or worse.

Back in Gulfport, Mississippi, General Paten wasn't having a very good time. They had expended the search perimeters and his troops were now going from property to property, looking for signs or trails of anything that could have been used in the theft of the nukes. Paten knew by then that the thieves were long gone. No one had detected any signs of the stolen weapons anywhere in the entire country. Radiation detectors had been flown to all of the most likely targets and were being manufactured around the clock to be placed on roadways, rivers and railways.

When his phone rang, showing the phone number of one of his field officers, he quickly answered with a bark. "What?" No one could blame him though. He was more overtired and stressed than he's ever been in his life.

"I think I have good news General. We found a farm that looks like it might have been the launching point of the operation," said Captain Muras. Without waiting for Muras to finish, Paten immediately told the Captain he was on his way. When the General's helicopter landed on a concrete slab in the middle of a field, the General instantly knew they had the right place. A large tree mover was standing behind a barn, similar to the one they had found thirty miles away, and the location looked like it had seen some traffic recently. Large tire tracks and the remnants of burned materials littered the ground.

The warehouse was of great interest because it contained what looked to be some kind of fabrication plant. If they could figure out what these people had been making, it would certainly help them locate them. There were no direct neighbors around, but one resident, a mile or so down the road, provided them with some information. The guy was hard to understand. The presence of a large tobacco wad in his mouth contributed to that fact. But he was able to tell them that the people had been making some kind of concrete anchors or pier blocks. He told them his nephew had worked for them before the storm. Paten's mind raced. This was obviously how they had transported the warheads; encased in concrete. Immediately, he alerted his headquarters to initiate a search for trucks carrying large concrete forms and particularly, to make sure they checked any recording devices like interstate cameras, truck stations and even gas stations. Now that they knew what to look for, he was confident they would nail these guys quickly.

Back at his base in Gulfport, Paten waited for any results of the renewed investigation. The President had been in touch with him on a daily basis and he had finally been able to give him some hope of success. About twelve hours later, a clear picture of the events began to unravel itself. Cameras at a gas station had picked up nice shots of a tractor-trailer truck, carrying what looked like bulky material, covered with tarps. There wasn't much truck traffic that next day after the hurricane, so that became their best lead. Further snapshots from various locations confirmed the direction of the truck and also the fact that there had been several vehicles involved. Finally, they nailed the actual destination point of the convoy as Morgan City, Louisiana, at the home of a Mr. Landry: owner of the plant in Mississippi. Within a couple of hours, General Paten was landing at a shipyard close to Morgan City, where the captain of the tug boat had been located and detained by the local police.

From his story, it was quickly obvious that the man didn't have a clue of what he had helped transport. After giving a brief description to the General as to where he had taken the barge, he was allowed to go back to his business. General Paten looked around, deep in thought. They were four days behind them, plenty of time for them to be long gone once again. The only saving grace was that it seemed the warheads had been taken out to sea and weren't likely headed for any domestic location, at least not right away.

A Coast Guard report placed Landry and his ship off of the coast of Louisiana less than three days ago and Paten learned some video footage of the interception was available. He was looking forward to viewing it. In the meantime, all assets in the Gulf were put at his disposal and he immediately put some vessels on emergency alert to locate the catamaran. Paten was charged up. They had finally had a break and he was confident they would soon discover the exact location of the yacht.

Back at his headquarters, his people were trying to sort through the numerous satellite snapshots of the area taken during that time period. The large sailboat wasn't that difficult to locate. They were quickly able to put a trail together of where it had been heading. But that's when things became somewhat more confusing. The yacht had been seen drifting close to the western Cuban coast and then was seen even closer to some other vessels on the southwestern coast of Cuba; but then the next day...nothing. It was as if it had vanished.

Paten knew that his next call was going to be a hard one; informing the President of this possible international twist and its consequences. As a top priority, his call was routed directly to the President, aboard Air Force One at that very moment.

"Mr. President," began Paten. "We've located what I think are the perpetrators of the armory theft. However, we believe from the evidence we've gathered, that they are now under Cuban control and we presume that our weapons are as well."

President Russell was in disbelief. He had never, ever expected the Cubans to be involved in this affair. All along, this action had been perceived as a terrorist act from the usual suspects. This put a whole new twist on the situation. It made no sense to him. Why would the Cubans risk obliteration for a few warheads and with no one to back them up? The President would have to think hard and fast to figure out what his next move would be.

"General Paten, this is disturbing news to say the least." The President sighed and rubbed his temples. "We'll have to put all of our assets in that part of the world on high alert. This scenario hasn't even been rehearsed in decades and I'm not even sure we even have one that would apply to present conditions. Alright, good work General. I'll get the ball rolling on this. Let's just hope those Cubans have enough sanity left to back out of this without starting another war." On that note, the President hung up the phone and made contact with his immediate staff on hand.

Chapter 18

It had been over an hour in the cold, deep water when Heraldo and his group finally made it to the mother-sub. At an eighteen-hundred-foot depth, it was out of the question for the large submarine to open its belly and recover the small craft. They would have to rise to about three-hundred feet to safely pressurize the loading bay. So, with the mini-sub magnetically attached to the mother-sub, they ascended to the required depth. Slowly, the large bay doors opened and using its small joystick, Landry maneuvered the mini-sub into the large loading bay. Once inside, it became attached to a lifting crane, which gently picked it up and placed it into its storage area. The mother-sub's doors sealed shut once again, the compartment slowly depressurized and they were finally able to open the hatch of the mini-sub. Stretching out of the small space, Maria, Landry and Heraldo finally felt like they were back to the land of the living. It had been a grueling experience for them all. Heraldo wrapped the still shivering Maria into his arms, burying his face into her hair. He had his Maria back. Landry quickly retrieved a large, down blanket for her and she followed Heraldo into their private quarters.

The submarine's marble bathroom had all of the amenities of a five-star hotel, including a large tub; big enough to comfortably accommodate two people. Heraldo started filling it with hot water as Maria began to undress and rub her cold, wet skin with a towel, trying to warm up as the bath filled. After Heraldo had undressed, he gently grabbed her hand, threw her towel to the floor and led her to the tub. Within moments, they warmed up in the steamy water, wrapped up in each other. It wasn't long before their passion overtook them. They kissed and touched with a thirst, fueled by the eternity of their separation. Their aquatic love lasted a solid hour. Once they were both blissfully satisfied, they enveloped themselves in the thick bathrobes; warmed by the heated marble shelves adjacent to the tub.

Heraldo had recovered his love, but for better or worse, things would never be as they once were. He knew this was the beginning of a new life for them both, and as long as he had her by his side, there was little he felt he couldn't accomplish. With Maria sound asleep in their bed, he quickly put some clothes on and went to find Landry.

Back at the command center of the submersible, Landry had attempted to locate the catamaran, but from the absence of any signal, inferred that it had met its planned demise. This also meant that his men were still out there and needed to be recovered.

Landry glanced at Heraldo as he entered. "I'm afraid we've lost the catamaran," said Landry. "But don't worry. I'm sure it went down as we planned, with the men escaping in the salvage pod. I'm trying to locate them as we speak."

The small salvage pod had a transponder that, when activated by a set signal from the submarine, would transmit a low-frequency signal for a period of five minutes. Landry was trying to trigger the beacon. Onboard the egg-shaped capsule, the cat's captain and his crew were anxiously awaiting. With only minor instrumentation, the pod was more like a coffin than a salvage craft. There weren't even any windows; just a small monitor indicating depth, heading and beacon signal strength still on zero. They each felt like Apollo XIII astronauts, uncertain about their future and somewhat helpless in this hostile environment. All three of the men experienced immense relief when the indicator suddenly beeped, responding to the probing signal from the submarine. It had only been a few hours since they had scuttled their ship, and help was on the way, not a moment too soon for the men accustomed to the great expanse of the ocean and its fresh air.

Landry steered the submarine, still hugging the ocean floor, towards where the signal was emanating from; about ten miles north of them. The capsule had drifted far enough away, so he felt safe recovering it, considering there were no detectable vessels in that area. Apparently, the Cubans had given up after their earlier meager attempt at blowing them up.

About an hour later, the submarine was hovering close to the salvage pod. It magnetically hooked onto it and slowly ascended to load depth, while changing course to a southwesterly direction. At three-hundred feet, the mother-sub's bay doors opened and two divers retrieved the capsule with the help of the reeling winch system.

Both Landry and Heraldo greeted the three men, who looked relieved and extremely grateful. It had been a leap of faith indeed. Back in the control room, Landry and Heraldo pondered their next move. With five nukes onboard, there was no possible way to go back to the United States without terminal consequences. This would require some serious thinking.

"I think we should get rid of the warheads. It's not like we have any use for them. I'm sure the military will double up their efforts to get us as long as they think we have them."

"I agree," said Heraldo. "However, maybe we can kill two birds with five nukes, so to speak. That Castillo character needs them and I'd prefer a pile of cash, while at the same time passing the headache on to someone else. I'm sure you do too." Landry agreed.

Castillo had gone back to his yacht and was under no illusions as to his ability to recover neither the weapons nor his prisoners. So, having parted with the Cuban general, he ordered his ship back to sea towards Colombia. This was going to be problematic for him. His partners were expecting the goods and he couldn't deliver. As powerful as he was, these people had tentacles everywhere and could become a real nuisance. He was greatly relieved when his phone rang; Heraldo on the other end. Heraldo was in no mood for politeness. This guy had killed his brother and had almost killed his wife, so he spared the formalities and reverted to his most basic Spanish while addressing Castillo.

"I hope you're ready to live up to your end of the deal Castillo. I want my gold and here is how we're going to do this. I'm sure you've heard of the Cayman Islands," said Heraldo in a mocking tone. "Be there in two days and be prepared for some heavy lifting if you know what I mean." Castillo, hiding his excitement as best he could, replied simply.

"Okay, I'll be there." Heraldo hung up the phone without another word. He told Landry it had been easier than expected and Landry, having listened to the conversation, agreed.

"Yes, I'm sure this guy wants his nukes more than we do." This being said, the sub's heading was slightly adjusted towards the Cayman Islands. It was somewhat ironic that the Cayman Island were located so close to Cuba; being such a bastion for rampant Capitalism. But it was also highly convenient for them, as there was no doubt that Castillo possessed or had access to financial resources there. Although under great scrutiny from the

Americans, it would still provide a good platform for their exchange, better than Cuba anyway.

Landry, having served a short time in the military, had no doubt that by now, all their assets in the US had been discovered and he was probably on the top of the FBI's most wanted list. Their only ace was the submarine. It should have remained undetected and if they had any chance of survival, should remain so for the duration.

General Paten was rather angry at himself, angry because of the precious time that had been was wasted right after Hurricane Gordon. The lack of cooperation, slow response by the local authorities and the eventual escape of the perpetrators, was going to be the greatest mismanaged caper in the history of mankind. From what the evidence showed, this was now an international matter and he was slowly being pushed aside. The President and Congress would decide on what the next steps should be. Still, in his head, the Cubans just didn't fit the bill for this operation. They simply had too much to lose by provoking the biggest pit bull on the block. As insane as he thought the Castro regime was, this just wasn't their brand of dementia.

But all Paten could do, was to rewind the events and see if they had missed anything. The barge; what had happened to it? The Coast Guard never saw it and they hadn't detected any radiation on the catamaran at all. Of course it had only been a cursory search. They could have very well hidden the nukes underwater, below the hull. There were just too many unanswered questions in Paten's mind to so easily put the matter to rest.

On the submarine, cruising at five knots at a depth of a thousand feet, Heraldo and Maria were slowly getting reacquainted with each other. It had been a long separation and a lot had happened since her departure for California over a month before. She slowly told Heraldo all that had happened to her during the course of her kidnapping. Heraldo was particularly interested in where she had been held in Cartagena. He couldn't fathom the incredible brazenness of Castillo. He had to give the guy some credit. He certainly had a set of balls on him, coming up with this operation and being so confident that he could get away with it. It was almost unreal.

"Why do you think he took it upon himself to want to steal these warheads?" asked Heraldo.

"Well, from what Celina told me, he has some buyers willing to pay a huge amount of money for them," said Maria.

"A terrorist organization?" asked Heraldo.

"No, it's some Middle Eastern government; Iranian I think," she responded.

"Wow! That's not good," said Heraldo. "Those guys have been after that for a while now. I guess they figured it would be easier to buy it than to make it; might even be cheaper too." Heraldo thought about how he would love to know exactly how much those guys had offered Castillo for the weapons. Maybe one billion was low-balling it. His mind raced as to how he would structure his new deal with Castillo. The figure of one billion per nuke came to mind. It was certainly something to reflect on for the next couple of days.

Heraldo put his thoughts to rest for the time being and intended to make the trip to the Caymans a pleasurable one, filled with lovemaking and relaxation. The submarine proved to be very comfortable. Maria and Heraldo had quickly settled into a routine of exercise and long, relaxing times in the plant room, enjoying the artificial sunlight and fresh oxygen. Contrary to its conventional counterparts, the submarine was a complete recycled, self-sustaining environment. The plants onboard provided them with adequate filtering of potentially toxic gases, without having to rely on chemical scrubbers and fresh water was generated from the hydrogen fuel cells. Small quantities of nutrients controlled by computer and injected into the hybrid hydroponic system. All of the waste generated by food consumption was recycled and put back into the water circulation of that system.

Heraldo had a true love for gardening. Even as a child, it had provided him with an escape from daily hardships. It had been a time to collect his thoughts and plan his future.

Meals were held in the sub's dining room. Heraldo had hired a brilliant vegan chef and sushi master, so the meals were up to par with some of the best restaurants in the world. If someone had to spend time in the depths of the ocean, it was the simple pleasures, such as food, that became essential for one's sanity. The only thing they would have been lacking, if on a very long trip, would be a sufficient stock of fine wines. Equipped with a state-of-the-art cellar, the sub could hold just over one thousand bottles of wine. It was already somewhat stocked with wine from some of the best vineyards in the world. Landry and Heraldo had amassed them all over the years and there was certainly enough to carry them over for a year or two. But if the present situation were to extend into a more permanent one, they would have to find a way to restock their precious cargo.

As for fish, Landry was the consummate fisherman. He had created a system by which the sub would somehow attract fish by dragging an electronic, shiny bait system and some capture nets, all automated and retractable into the submarine without any human intervention necessary. This provided all onboard with a very interesting assortment of catches; from tuna to octopus. At the greatest of depths, they even caught some unusual creatures that Landry hadn't ever seen before; all of which, in the hands of their master sushi chef, always made for a special treat. One of the requirements that Heraldo had put forth when hiring the culinary staff, was that some of them also be proficient in chemistry and biology. Testing for toxins and heavy metals in their food would become second nature to them, and it was a must for the kind of sustenance they would be living off of.

Unfortunately, mankind had managed to contaminate most of the earth and showed no willingness to do much about it; always trading the health of its minions for the profits of a few. Although health concerns of the masses never really preoccupied the thoughts of Landry or Heraldo, they were, after all, drug purveyors. They did however feel some resentment towards "the establishment" for its manipulation of the many behaviors that were both detrimental to themselves and the world at large. They also resented its great hypocrisy when it came to dealing with "illegal" drugs.

Like Landry always said, McDonalds alone was responsible for more heart attacks and strokes than all of the *other* drug dealers in the world combined. It almost single-handedly putting a large portion of minorities into an early grave; all legally and with a clown's smile. But it, by far, wasn't the only one to do so.

By the time the sub was within thirty miles or so off Grand Cayman, all of its occupants had enjoyed some much-needed rest and were eager and ready for the challenges to come. Landry and Heraldo had further discussed how to go about negotiating with Castillo, and a more lucrative plan had been concocted. The submarine was equipped with a communication drone; a small automated saucer-like device that could move quickly through the ocean to the surface, even from considerable depths. It provided the necessary link between the low-frequency water communication and whatever airborne broadcasting needed. It was time to contact Castillo, so while resting on the bottom of the ocean at about nine-hundred feet deep, the sub released its drone, which quickly ascended and went into full relay mode.

"Mr. Castillo, I hope this day finds you well," said Heraldo in Spanish. "We are ready to do business. I hope you are too."

Castillo had anchored his yacht the day before, off George Town and its harbor, giving him enough time to consult with his local banker. The tables had been turned on him. He no longer had the advantage and had no choice but to meet the monetary demands Heraldo had made on him. He was going to have to give up a billion dollars, but with forty-nine billion left for him, that was a small price to pay in his mind. Plus, by delivering the nukes as promised, he could avoid what could have become a nasty and permanent headache.

The money wasn't a problem for him. He could transfer that amount from any of the various accounts he held in most major banks around the world. However, Heraldo had been specific about wanting gold, so Castillo had been forced to purchase it from his Cayman banker friends. It had proven to be one of the toughest and lousiest business deals for him ever. The going rate for the yellow metal was forgotten. The quantities involved demanded a premium price and even with his considerable financial cloud, Castillo wasn't able to do any better than a thirty-percent premium. They had him by the balls and they knew it. It was the quickest three-hundred million dollars Castillo had ever lost. But as a good businessman, he knew it was a small price to pay for the riches to come. The gold had been gathered from several local banks willing to make a quick buck. All of it had been stored in a private vault; an odd assortment of Swiss, South African and other provenances, along with some plain bars which were the product of "recycling" from who knew where.

The bottom line was, gold was gold and as long as it was the standard "pure gold": twenty-four karat grade, it would do just fine. Roughly fifteen metric tons of gold didn't take up that much space. It was only a small pile of about two to three feet at the base and wasn't taller than three feet in height. However, transporting the bounty was an all-together different matter. Due to the weight, over two hundred crates had been required. Each one was made to look non-descript, like an old-fashioned ammunition box, with ropes on each side. Each contained a reasonable one hundred and fifty pounds and could be carried by two strong men. The boxes had been made large enough, so as not to cause suspicion as to their contents. They had required several trips from the harbor to the yacht, and the crates had been marked with engine parts' insignias, so as not to appear out of place. Thank goodness, the whole process had been as efficient as Swiss banking and had gone without incident. Castillo, gathering his thoughts, answered Heraldo:

"We are ready indeed. How do you propose we do this?" Heraldo had already planned the event several times in his mind. He wasn't going to take any more chances with Castillo.

"I am going to give you coordinates at sea, to a depth of about one-hundred feet, so your divers have easy access. You will find what you are looking for there, one of them at least and provided you leave our share of the arrangement, you will be allowed to remove it. The rest of the goods will be provided to you at a later date for the same amount each. We obviously changed the arrangement, but considering you changed the original arrangement, so be it."

Castillo didn't like what he was hearing one bit; from one billion to five. This was definitely proving to be a bad week.

"You drive a hard bargain Mr. Heraldo, but for now I will go along with it."

Heraldo replied quickly. "I will call you when everything is in place. Be ready to depart shortly. Goodbye Mr. Castillo." As soon as he hung up the phone, Heraldo had his men place one of the nukes in a sealed, heavy-gauge Mylar bag and load it onto the mini-sub. The distance to the drop point was only about ten miles away, and the submarine was directed to go full speed in that direction. About a mile away from the higher seabed shelf, where they planned to do the drop, they launched the mini-sub and bottomed the submarine at the considerable depth of five-hundred feet, deep enough not to be visible to passing aircrafts. Heraldo quickly sent the coordinates to Castillo. All they had to do was wait for the yacht to show up and drop its cargo. Castillo was on his way, full speed ahead at over twenty knots. It would only take him twenty minutes to reach the spot.

Onboard the mini-sub, Landry had chosen to place the nuke on the belly of the sub, harnessed by straps that would require release from the outside. When they arrived at the drop location, Landry entered the pressurization chamber and shut the hatch to the control room, leaving Heraldo to man the sub. Once suited up, with the chamber pressurized to outside conditions, the final hatch was opened and Landry, equipped with his re-breather underwater gear, slowly emerged from the mini-sub and looked up. In the twilight, he could clearly see the top of the ocean and some fish that appeared to be floating in the air. In other circumstances, he would have truly enjoyed his magnificent surroundings. Diving was the closest a man could come to a flying bird and he would have enjoyed spending time exploring. However, time was running out. He could already hear the sounds of the engines of the fast-approaching yacht. Quickly, he moved to the underbelly of the sub and slowly released the two nylon straps holding the warhead. Gently, he held it, guiding it as it fell to the bottom, being careful not to stir up too much sand.

Once it was resting, he reached for a small package he was carrying in a mesh bag. Heraldo called it insurance. It was a small, explosive suction device, strong enough to destroy the nuke and render it completely unusable. Equipped with a keypad, it needed a set sequence of numbers to deactivate it. If not deactivated, it would blow up in twenty minutes. Landry quickly affixed the device to the nuke. It was time to hightail it out of there. The large yacht was within view and even at high noon, was casting a shadow of complete darkness on the bottom of the ocean. Not wasting a second, Landry quickly made it back to the mini-sub and after closing the hatch, gave Heraldo the signal to go. At the same time the mini-sub jetted away, five divers plunged into the crystalline waters and rapidly headed for the solid object, while a small inflatable boat started trailing the mini-sub. Heraldo noticed the action from his bulbous top window. A couple of divers had jumped from the speedboat, and using torpedo-like, handheld propulsion devices, were tailing them and gaining ground. Heraldo needed some time to reach the drop-off where they would be safe and could disappear into the ocean's darkness. Finally, Landry made it back inside the mini-sub's cabin. He spoke first.

"I don't like this one bit. These guys are up to no good." Before he could utter another word, small projectiles headed in their direction, but due to a last-minute evasive maneuver from Heraldo, they missed their intended targets and ended up in the sand, with small puffs of powdery clouds. Not wasting a second, Landry reached for an explosive device and armed it for thirty seconds. Sliding back into the pressurized chamber and slamming the hatch closed, he instantly released the water intake valves and flooded the compartment. It was going to be a close call...only fifteen seconds left. Struggling to open the outside hatch, he finally threw the small explosive outside, with only five seconds to spare. His heart raced. He knew he had to get the hatch closed. Otherwise, the shockwave from the explosion would most likely kill him. With only about two seconds to spare, the hatch finally sealed shut. Heraldo had been continuing his evasive maneuvers, which were getting harder and harder to accomplish, considering the two divers were less than thirty feet away and gaining ground. Landry looked back through the window of the closed hatch, just in time to see the expressions of the divers on their tail. They had no doubt seen his little package. From the looks on their faces and the whites of their eyes, they knew what was in the pipeline. A second later, a violent explosion rocked the mini-sub. A few alarms started beeping, but other than the severe jolt and a cracked window, Landry and Heraldo would live to tell the tale. But the divers weren't so lucky; floating like dummies in the water. Heraldo picked up his phone, patched through the systems onboard the mother-sub and connected to Castillo.

"Up to your old tricks my friend? I tell you what. You have less than fifteen minutes to drop the gold and be on your way before I blow up your package. As you've probably noticed by now, it came with a little extra gift.

Once I can confirm you've lived up to our arrangement, I will give you the code to disarm. I'll either call you in twelve minutes or not. Goodbye."

Castillo was once again livid, but could he really blame Heraldo for living up to the challenge? After all, he had hired him because of his skills and resourcefulness. Now the proverbial snake was turning against him, doing his snake thing. Castillo's men had brought the warhead and its attachment onboard the Yacht. He could clearly see the clock ticking and the time running out. With little choice in the matter, Castillo ordered the gold crates dropped overboard. Ten minutes was going to be tight. The crates had been placed on a steel pallet and were being picked up by the ship's crane and slowly lowered towards the ocean. Once each one touched the waters, the quick disconnect on the clevis was triggered and down went the load; a treasure that would surpass the richest Spanish galleons.

Heraldo, back in control of the situation, gave the mini-sub a one-hundred and eighty degree turn and traced his path back to where they had left the nuke. He heard a buffered sound as the massive weight of the boxes of gold hit the sandy bottom of the ocean floor, followed by large plumes of silt. They had succeeded. Now all they needed to do was retrieve the gold. Heraldo didn't feel comfortable bringing the mother-sub into such shallow waters. Its shadow would be visible, plus they would be vulnerable to whatever other surprises Castillo had in store for them. Instead, the plan was to use a large, inflatable blimp-like structure to compensate for the weight of the gold and drag the massive thing to about a three-hundred-foot depth, where the mother-sub would simply winch in the precious cargo.

Not wasting any time, Landry had gone back out and had quickly fastened the heavy nylon net, around the boxes of gold, which had landed onto a flattened, airless flotation device. He released the pressure of two large tanks into the device. Landry's calculations had been right on the money. The whole contraption slowly lifted itself from the ground and hovered, ready to be pulled. At this depth and pressure, it took just about all the air stored in the tanks. With the net bag of gold in tow, the mini-sub was moving again. It covered the mile back to the mother-sub in about twenty minutes. Once back in its vicinity, the mother-sub slowly ascended to about three-hundred feet as its giant bay doors opened. From its belly, came a couple of divers holding the winching cable. They quickly fastened it to their precious cargo. Slowly, Heraldo maneuvered the mini-sub into the loading bay and he and Landry quickly debarked. It was going to be a somewhat tricky operation to bring this much weight in without sending the mother-sub to the bottom of the ocean. The large submarine was equipped with four vertical thrusters which would come in handy in this maneuver. A small amount of gas was let out of the flotation device, just enough to straighten the line to the sub. Once the cable was taut, the thrusters would take over and compensate for the progressive weight gain, as the divers had opened a small valve on the float. It took them about ten minutes to get all the air out. Once that was accomplished, the divers unhooked the deflated balloon and carried it back to the submarine.

With the full load being reeled into its belly, the thrusters began to decrease their activity as the water was expelled from the submarine's ballasts to compensate for the weight gain. Heraldo and Landry oversaw the operation from the control room.

"Man," said Landry. "Looks like we're rapidly approaching maximum load capacity. I never thought too much gold could become a bad thing." Heraldo smiled and replied.

"I'll deal with that kind of problem any day my friend. Trading a hundred and fifty pound nuke for fifteen tons of gold could justify some minor inconveniences indeed."

Once in its belly and properly stored on top of the black gold rods, Heraldo and Landry could finally focus on what to do next. Heraldo spoke in his careful and measured way.

"Let's get on our way now. The farther we get from the United States, the better I'll sleep. Landry quickly agreed and they both decided to head straight for the island of Tobago, off the coast of South America, at cruising speed, an eight-hundred-foot depth and over a thousand miles away.

Chapter 19

Castillo was licking his wounds even though they weren't physical. For the first time in his life, someone had beaten him at his own game and robbed him of the ultimate glory of complete and utmost victory. Yes, he had indeed acquired one of the nukes. That would help keep his Middle Eastern friends at bay, at least for the time being, but deep down, he knew that as long as Heraldo and his crew were out there, it would remain a touch-and-go situation. Not wanting to take any more chances, he quickly arranged for transport back to Bogota via one of his private jets. He, Celina and the nuke would travel by Lear to his private airport. The quick helicopter ride to Grand Cayman was uneventful and with some time to spare, both he and Celina opted for a nice meal overlooking the ten-mile beach and the beautiful sunset to come. Having feasted on fresh lobster and grilled fish, Castillo couldn't help but think that if anything positive had come from the whole operation, it had certainly been Celina. They were definitely made for each other.

Back in Washington, the President was having an emergency meeting with the Secretary of State. The agenda was the "acquisition" of nuclear weapons from the United States by the Cubans. The whole scenario appeared bizarre but it had to be dealt with nevertheless. Through the Canadian embassy, the Cuban government had been contacted and had vehemently denied the entire operation; stating that the accusation was just a ploy, another excuse for American Imperialism and its long-coming plans for a Cuban invasion. Cuba also stated that they knew the US had sent heavy reinforcements to its air bases in southern Florida. They divulged that through numerous Castro spies, the movement of the US military had been easy for them to confirm. Raul Castro made speeches all over Cuba, warning his people of the impending conflict. Hard-core Cubans in Miami jumped on the opportunity and called for an invasion of Cuba to restore justice to the island and get rid of the communist scourge.

The President didn't like to have his hand forced into a decision, especially one that would involve the lives of American combat personnel. He had fought hard to get the country out of the conflicts initiated by his predecessor, and he had run on an anti-war platform during his campaign, pointing to the facts that the previous conflicts had been initiated as an excuse for stimulating a sick economy and a lackluster stock market at the beginning of the first decade of the millennium. He wasn't about to start a new war with his closest island neighbor to the south; not if he could help it.

The fact that the Cubans could once again, currently be in possession of nuclear weapons was made into a major crisis by the media. Comparisons to the missile crisis and the Kennedy administration were all over television. Anyone listening to what the media reported would have thought Armageddon was coming. Of course, little attention was being paid to the fact that the nukes in question only possessed a minute portion of the megapower of the old Soviet Union arsenal. It was by no means a species-threatening event.

Congress was no help either. They kept going for the sound bites and pandering to armchair worriers, which constituted a majority of the so-called "heart land of America". Congress called for swift military retaliation, making it painfully apparent that nothing much had been learned from the recent past. The President cringed at the thought of even more soldiers having to put their lives on the line. The Secretary of State, at the President's request, had insisted on meeting with Castro to attempt to diffuse the situation, even on neutral territory somewhere in the Caribbean. But Castro had responded that he didn't trust the Americans not to dispose of him as they had done so in the past with many of their enemies, he stated publicly that he wasn't looking for to be assassinated. So, a meeting was obviously out of the question.

Chavez joined the party as well, stating that he would put the might of the Venezuelan army at Castro's disposal. He said he was always willing to help a brother in distress against the evil empire. After having parted with Castillo back in Cuba, General Rodriguez, in view of the latest events, couldn't help but think that the interception of the Catamaran and the capture of the gringos had been more than just the usual drug operation Castillo had involved him in, in the past. It made sense that what Castillo had been after was the nukes, and having the nukes brought into Cuban waters had brought a shitload of problems for Cuba. The General wondered if he should come clean with his bosses or keep his mouth shut and risk a war. Either way, he was probably doomed. So, for the time being, he decided to keep quiet. Over the previous five years, he had amassed a good bit of money through his facilitating of the drug trade; enough to retire abroad. He decided that right then was probably as good a time as any, and he decided to leave, just as soon as he could figure out how and quickly.

General Paten was back in Washington, his prior assignment having been completed, at least in the eyes of his superiors. He knew he had left a lot of loose ends and the latest threat of war with Cuba had prompted him to insist on a meeting with the President and his staff.

"Mr. President," said Paten. "I implore you to consider the facts here. Yes, it looks like the Cubans were involved by the presence of their patrol boats around the catamaran. However, there was another ship there that belonged to some Colombian concrete company. I beg you to let me investigate this further before we get involved in another conflict."

The President stopped him. "I'm in full agreement with you, General Paten. It's not the intention of this administration to start a new war. But with so little to go on, we may not have a choice. I will authorize you to pursue your hunch, but I'm afraid things are unraveling faster than you or I can control. All I can do at this point is wish you luck General."

Paten was grateful. He thanked the President and his staff and quickly headed back to his office at the Pentagon. The President's next meeting was with General Brighton: commander of all the armed forces to be involved in this conflict. On the agenda was the invasion of Cuba. The plan set forth was as expected: the usual two-face operation. They would knock out communications, radar, air force, ground defenses and navy. The General assured the President that this would be, in his words, "a cake walk". Cuba's measly defenses made Libya look like a super-power. In other words, this was going to be an easy operation; so much so, that the General brought up the point that this should have been done a long time ago. If anything, this was the perfect opportunity to correct a half-century of wrong. The second phase: a two-front invasion, concentrated on Castro's guard and the capturing or killing of the Cuban dictator and his brother. A five-thousand man ground force would be sufficient, as he was not expecting much resistance from the local population. Present at the meeting were also several anti-Castro Cuban scholars, who offered their ideas of plans for the best way to transition the island.

A consensus was reached that would, in essence, make Cuba a territory of the United States, just like Puerto Rico. After five years, an election would be held, to choose between complete independence and the possibility to become the fifty-first state of the United States. Throughout this meeting, the President couldn't help but think about the nukes. Was

Castro planning to go out in flames with Havana? Or worse, did he have a way to deliver the bombs to cities like Miami? These were serious concerns and he addressed them to General Brighton.

"We can pretty much guarantee you sir, that no missiles from Cuba will reach the United States. We have several battleships in position around the island with the capacity to intercept anything leaving the ground. In fact, we don't even believe they have the capability to launch one from the ground. As for the scorched Havana scenario, our attack will be so brutal and quick that their reaction capacity will be, for all practical purpose, null. The Castros are planned as the first casualties of this war, Mr. President."

Not feeling particularly reassured by the General's statement, the President thanked them all and led them out the door of the oval office. Speaking to his Secretary of State, the President voiced his concern.

"I don't think we have a choice in this matter. Waiting would only allow the Cubans more preparation time if they are indeed planning a nuclear strike. I think we have to do this now." Even as he said it, he almost couldn't believe it. This day was definitely not a day this President had ever thought he would have to prepare for. Especially since he had been elected based upon a non-militaristic agenda, having to pull the trigger on a conflict with Cuba was probably the most difficult thing he would ever do. But, with a blank check from Congress and their approval of this war, he ordered a "go" for the operation named: "Cuba Libre". He hoped to God the nukes didn't detonate and also hoped to God they would find those nukes. He certainly didn't want to be the second president in history to start a war based on bad intelligence. The President placed a courtesy call to General Paten and gave him the bad news.

"I'm sorry to hear that Mr. President. Do you want me to continue my investigation?"

"Yes," replied the President. "Just in case, I don't want to leave any loose ends."

Back onboard the submarine, Heraldo kept track of the latest events in the United States. It seemed the Cubans were getting the blame for the theft of the nukes; a lucky break and a much-needed opportunity to put some distance between them and their last confirmed location. Their destination, the island of Tobago, was just off the coast of Venezuela and would provide a relatively safe, if not temporary refueling point. The immediate intention was to remain within range of Castillo, as there was little doubt they would be trading with him again. Heraldo would certainly be happy to oblige, as long as the relationship remained mutually beneficial.

The submarine had been functioning without an itch; the dual fuel cell system converting the stored hydrogen into water and electricity, which supplied the needs of the vessel. At only a five mile per hour speed, the large submersible was highly efficient and used relatively little energy for propulsion. With the ability to replenish its hydrogen only when anchored in a current, the concern for fuel generation was always on Heraldo's mind. Currents simply weren't present everywhere and if a long stay underwater were required, another form of energy gathering would come in handy. While building the sub, Landry and Heraldo had discussed the issue with their engineers and an alternative had been considered and then created, in the form of a heat exchange system. A couple of them had been constructed for the purpose at hand. Volcanic areas were plentiful in the ocean and if one could tap one of the numerous high-temperature vents, present on the ocean floor, one would have the ability to secure a plentiful and simple source of energy by generating steam. Through the use of turbines, one could convert that steam energy into electricity.

A lot of the islands in the Antilles actually consisted of volcanoes in various stages of activity. So, Heraldo knew that finding a proper, superheated water vent would be doable without even having to search much at all. Both Landry and Heraldo understood that once the Americans realized their mistake regarding Cuba's involvement, they would once again become the prime target. There wouldn't be a safe place anywhere in the world for them to hide and spending the rest of their lives in this submarine, although extremely well-appointed, would probably drive them mad.

Back in his office at the Pentagon, Paten was busy following his hunches; gathering intelligence from all satellite sources on the last area where the catamaran had been sighted. The only additional data he had acquired had shown a burning ship which he presumed was the catamaran. It seemed to have been destroyed by the numerous Cuban patrol boats in the area. It seemed Landry had stolen the nukes and made some kind of deal with the Cubans. But, the deal had gone sour and Landry was either captured or killed. So, did the Cubans have the nukes or not? Paten knew he needed a serious break if he was going to crack the case. With the invasion of Cuba currently in the works, he hoped it would even be possible for him to go there and question witnesses or even participants.

General Martinez knew time was running out. The Americans would be there soon and he needed to get out before the fireworks began. He was still on the western part of the island, having spent several days in vain trying to locate any survivors or items of interest from the few remains of the catamaran. He didn't see any point in going back to Havana, even though he had been requested to do so. Apparently, he wasn't the only high-ranking military man who had gone AWOL recently, so he wasn't too worried about repercussions. He had ordered his men to scatter under the pretense of regrouping later, once the invasion was underway. But most of his men had read between the lines and had thanked him and wished him luck.

Still enjoying some authority, he commandeered a fishing vessel in the port of La Coloma and having taken as much fuel from his patrol boats as he could store on the small vessel, he and a couple of his men prepared to leave the island. He knew he could probably make it to the Cayman Islands easily. If not permitted to stay, he decided he would sail to Venezuela. As the first US missiles reached specific targets in and around La Havana, Cuba, General Martinez was slowly steering his very old wood plank boat out of the harbor. The smell of fish was overwhelming; ingrained in every inch of the vessel. But Martinez didn't mind at all. In fact, the aroma reminded him of his father and the long days he had spent at sea with him, fishing in their small rowboat. He hoped destiny would take him back to a simpler worry-free life.

He hadn't yet traveled even ten nautical miles when a bright searchlight was aimed in his direction; lighting up the small boat and the sea around them. A voice came over a loud speaker and spoke in Spanish, asking him to stop and prepare to be boarded. It was an American vessel; a fast, large, inflatable Coast Guard speedboat. Two men, armed with automatic rifles, jumped onboard and asked the General and his men for identification papers, while two other men boarded and started searching the old fishing boat. Martinez, while handing his papers to one of the guardsmen, told them he was a defector of the Cuban army. The guardsman spoke Spanish fluently; a second-generation Miami Cuban. He immediately realized they had caught themselves a mighty big fish: a Cuban general.

General Paten had instructed those under his command to be on the lookout for Cuban military officers escaping the island, especially on the south-eastern part. So, a couple of Coast Guard cutters had been dispatched to the area for that very purpose, with orders to immediately inform him if they were successful. General Martinez was swiftly taken into custody and back to the Coast Guard vessel, where a call was immediately placed to Paten.

Back at the White House, General Brighton, the President and several of his advisers were monitoring the progression of the Cuban invasion. There had been no real resistance from the Cuban military and as planned, the Castros had been the first casualties of war. Immediately, Cuban state television and radio stations had been knocked out and replaced quickly with new, informative programming, broadcasting out of powerful transmitters on one of the support flotilla ships; all relaying signals from a Miami Univision studio. Armed forces were asked to surrender and they did, fading into the general population. A serious transition plan had been put forth, reassuring the island's inhabitants that they would be safe and cared for in the immediate aftermath of the invasion. The propaganda machine was working this time and it helped that the United States had over a million Cuban expatriates. The President drew upon this pool of Americans to make Cuba's transition to democracy as smooth as possible.

However, it wasn't completely smooth by any means. Huge legal issues popped their ugly heads up among the expatriate Cuban community in Miami and elsewhere. Who would get the spoils of war? Would the country revert to pre-revolution ownership, the same way East Germany had after the fall of the Berlin Wall, or would there be a new division of land ownership? Those issues were already being vehemently debated on every Hispanic television station. The President had put together a panel of experts to look into the legal implications and come up with a general proposal for reparation. Reverting to pre-revolution land ownership was considered by many to be inequitable. After all, land ownership had been the root of the original revolution and would leave many of the current island's residents expropriated and homeless, perpetuating the cycle and a recipe for future trouble.

A plan was conceived to give original owners back a small percentage of their land. In essence, a war tax would be applied on the land and each original owner would have the first chance to re-purchase their original land, in its entirety, for current market value. The proceeds, or "war chest" as some opponents of the idea called it, would be used to provide basic welfare and education for the majority of non-land owning Cubans and would allow them to be reintegrated into a capitalistic society.

In essence, the island would be put up for sale to the highest bidders. President Russell had very little doubt that if all of this could be made legal, and that was a big "if", the island would quickly undergo a huge economic boom; stimulated by the large influx of wealthy Cubans from all around the world, particularly from Miami. President Russell knew that this war could actually turn out to be the first profitable war the United States had experienced since World War II, if a six-hour invasion could even be considered a war. *One can only dream*, thought President Russell.

Still at his office, General Paten took the phone call from the Coast Guard vessel and after some quick questions, translated by one of the officers onboard, quickly determined that this guy was worth talking to in person. He immediately secured a flight to that part of the island. But since it was so unpopulated, it hadn't been secured yet and wouldn't be until a formal police force was reinstated. He knew that could take several weeks, so he decided to make the Havana airport his destination. From there, he would take a helicopter ride to the western part of the island and then out to the Coast Guard's ship.

He was thankful to catch a little sleep on the four-hour flight from DC to Cuba. He couldn't seem to sleep lately, considering he was smack dab in the middle of one of the most stressful times of his entire life. When he finally arrived in Havana, he witnessed a beautiful sunrise over the island. Paten couldn't help noticing on his final approach, how interesting the architecture of the city was, as if frozen in time. He made a note to himself to come back and spend some time there, when time allowed.

Once on the ground and in possession of his small amount of luggage, General Paten headed for his next mode of transport. But apparently, everyone was short of helicopters and he had been assigned to wait for some troop transport carrier. He wondered if it was simply fog of war or plain incompetence? Nonetheless, he decided the next best thing was to move the prisoner from the Coast Guard ship to Havana, using one of the Coast Guard's own helicopters.

In the meantime, he needed a place to stay and opted to go to one of the several resorts catering to Canadian and European tourists; all of whom were leaving the island en masse, as was apparent by all of the buses and old taxis lined up in front of the airport, dropping off their passengers, who all seemed more than ready to leave. Not in the habit of taking too many risks, but deeming the situation safer than most wars he had ever been involved in, the General opted for a taxi ride to a beach resort only twenty minutes or so from the airport. He saw that the public relations stunt had worked for most of the inhabitants of the island. The receptionists at the hotel greeted him as if nothing had happened, like he was just an ordinary tourist. After booking a suite that was large enough to conduct the business at hand, he decided he would seek out some well-deserved breakfast after a quick shower in his room.

Within just a little while, after a nice, hot shower and some good food, he was relaxing on the large patio overlooking the ocean, listening to the sound of the crashing waves. Closing his eyes, feeling the millage of his years and the lack of sleep, he could almost imagine he was on vacation. Five cups of coffee later, as he made his way back into his room, his satellite phone rang. The Coast Guard was approaching Havana. He quickly gave them his location and ordered them to land the helicopter at the hotel, on the beach. Within five minutes, he heard the characteristic beat of the approaching Coast Guard helicopter. The small craft quickly landed on an old lime patch; crushed sea shells from a long gone era.

The Cuban general was escorted to Paten's suite. The guards stayed on the small porch as the two Generals shook hands and entered the sitting room of the hotel suite.

"General Martinez, would you like something to drink or eat? I can call for room service."

Martinez responded in broken English. "I love to use your bathrooms if that is alright. It has been a long ride." After taking care of his business, Martinez rejoined Paten, who was sitting in a comfortable rattan chair, drinking more coffee.

"Have a seat," said Paten, offering him some of the fresh brew. Not wasting any time, Paten dove right into the meat of the subject.

"On August 15th, there was an incident on the water that we would like to know a little more about. We're aware that you were present in the area at the time," said Paten, bluffing. "Specifically, we would like for you to tell us about a catamaran you intercepted on that date."

Martinez wasn't particularly surprised by the question. He knew the Americans had been keeping close tabs on drug-related activity and currently, without the protection of his government, he would simply be considered a common criminal. He knew he needed to use this opportunity to keep himself out of jail. He considered the possibility that the gringos would trade information for his freedom.

Martinez answered after a few moments, in much better English. "I am willing to cooperate General, but I want assurances that I will not be prosecuted if I do so."

General Paten raised his eyebrows in surprise. "Well, you certainly speak better English than you led me to believe," he said. "If you give me what I want, I'll personally make sure you are free to go. No one is interested in your past activities General Martinez; unless of course, you are somehow involved politically."

Martinez relaxed a bit. He had never been involved in politics and had really never even believed in the Revolution. That was why he had always gone with the money, avoiding confrontation, obeying but not volunteering for anything compromising; like a lot of his peers, he just made sure to stay out of trouble.

Paten continued, pleased that the Cuban general seemed so ready to cooperate. "What do you know about Landry, the boat captain of that catamaran that burned up?"

Martinez didn't really have any information on the subject. He told Paten that he recognized the name from Castillo talking about the interception, but that was it. The only thing he knew was that Landry had been onboard that boat with another man who had been brought to Mr. Castillo's yacht.

Paten was intrigued. This was new information. "What other guy?"

"A Mexican I think," answered Martinez. Martinez was glad Castillo's name had come up. He knew the Americans always liked to go after the big fish, so this had been a good opportunity to deflect. As if reading his thoughts, Paten continued.

"How close were you to Mr. Castillo?"

"He and I have done some business together," answered Martinez without delay. "He is a big partner of the Cuban government. He invests a lot of money on the island."

"What was on that sailboat that both you and Castillo wanted so badly?" Paten asked pointedly. He knew there had to be more. His gut told him Martinez knew a lot more than he was letting on.

"I don't know. He didn't say. I presume it was either money or drugs," answered Martinez.

"Was Castillo involved in the drug trade on the island?" asked Paten. Martinez paused for a brief moment, not sure what to say. He decided to keep it simple.

"It's possible. I was only asked to support his operations by providing security, but I wasn't actually involved in his transactions."

"What happened to the sailboat's cargo?" asked Paten. Suddenly Martinez realized that drugs weren't the target of Paten's search at all. He should have caught on earlier but it immediately made sense to him. This was all about those stolen nukes. It seemed like Castillo's handiwork after all. Obviously, that's why the Americans had brought him here.

"You're looking for the nukes, aren't you?" asked Martinez pointedly. "You actually think we took them?! I'm telling you we never had them. Castillo must have been after them and maybe those people on the catamaran had them, but we didn't sink their boat, I assure you. They burned it themselves and we weren't able to find one trace of them at all. In fact, Castillo thought they must have had a submarine or something. We didn't see any other boats at all. The Mexican and his wife escaped into the water that night and were never seen again."

Shit thought Paten. He believed every word the Cuban general said. He had been concerned that this damn war was a rush job. Now he was going to have to call the President with bad news once again. He spoke to the Cuban general.

"Well Mr. Martinez, I appreciate the information. You're free to go. Just stay where we can find you in case we need to speak with you again."

Quick to seize the opportunity, Martinez responded by thanking Paten and posed one last question. "General, sir, can you make it possible for me to go to Miami?"

Paten didn't hesitate. That wasn't such a bad idea. "Yes, fine. Just stay in this hotel and I'll make the arrangements for you to be transported there with the appropriate paperwork." Martinez was immensely grateful and shook the general's hand heartily before he left to go check into the hotel.

Paten made a mental note to make sure he gave orders for Martinez to be tracked in Miami. He wanted to make sure he stayed on their radar for a while, maybe even indefinitely. Twenty minutes later, after another shower to help wash the exhaustion-induced cobwebs out of his mind, Paten was on the phone with the President of the United States.

"Mr. President, as much as I hate that I was correct, I've confirmed that the Cubans do not have the nukes. I have a witness that is now going to be sent to Miami at his request. He is a general in the Cuban army and in my opinion, an extremely credible witness." Paten closed his eyes as he waited for the President to respond. There was dead silence for several moments. Then...

"Let's keep this information confidential for now General, understood?" said the President quietly.

"Yes, of course Mr. President. You have my word."

"Thank you, and once again, thank you for your diligence General Paten."

"Thank you, Mr. President." The line went dead as the President ended the call. Paten actually felt sorry for him. But, this story was now the President's to spin, for better or for worse. It was times like these that Paten thanked his lucky stars he wasn't a politician. *Now what?* he wondered. He knew Castillo was probably his best lead. That made more sense since he was the main party to this operation. He didn't think it was Landry. Paten had a gut feeling that Landry was just small-time; ex-military who didn't fit the profile of a terrorist at all. He was probably just a gun for hire. But Castillo? From the intelligence Paten had gathered, from the not-so-cooperative CIA, Castillo had his hands buried into many ventures and had long been suspected of being involved in the drug trade. But no one could tell if he had ever been or had become an arms dealer. That was what he had to figure out, and pronto.

Chapter 20

Castillo had returned to Bogota, anxious to unload his new cargo. At ten billion a pop, the incentive was certainly there to call his Iranian friends. What worried him was his inability at the moment to make good on the rest of the nukes, at least for the time being. But Castillo left word through the proper channels and expected a quick reply. So when his Persian contact, known only as "Mr. Smith", came to Castillo's building once again, the man was quickly escorted to the large patio area overlooking the indoor tropical gardens.

Having seated himself on one of the oversized Italian leather sofas, the small-statured Mr. Smith seemed to disappear into the folds of the vast full-grain cowhide, his complexion adding to the camouflaging effect. Castillo entered and upon seeing the man, rapidly covered the distance between his personal elevator and the seating area, like a cheetah after its prey. The Iranian's body stiffened in surprise as Castillo spoke.

"Mr. Smith, how nice to see you," said Castillo confidently.

"Same here," responded the spry man in his heavily-accented Spanish. Castillo's brain was in overtime mode. He knew it was imperative that he not appear weak and out of control. So, he immediately took command of the conversation.

"Mr. Smith, I have a fully functional warhead for you, ready for delivery." He said it as if he were talking about delivery of an ordinary piece of furniture.

"Well done," said Mr. Smith, visibly relaxing a little, but very much in control. "My superiors will be delighted. They were beginning to worry that you would not come through for them."

Castillo, pretending to ignore the veiled threat, continued. "I trust that you've been following the international news regarding these warheads?" Mr. Smith nodded grimly, never taking his eyes from Castillo. Castillo continued. "The latest events regarding the invasion of Cuba by the Americans and what it means for our business here, makes it imperative that I remain extremely vigilant. I have no doubt that by now, the Americans have figured out the nuclear warheads are not on the island of Cuba. We can only assume that they probably already know of my involvement in this transaction. Because of this, I have taken many extra precautions and have scattered our bounty to various, secret locations. As long as our business, with this first weapon, is completed to our mutual satisfaction, then the others will be released when appropriate to do so. I assure you this doesn't change the terms of our agreement Mr. Smith. My decision to do it this way simply insures the safety of it."

Mr. Smith didn't seem particularly preoccupied with the whereabouts of the warheads, so he responded simply. "We have a submarine off of the west coast of Colombia as we speak, ready for pick up. All you will have to do is drop it into the water, with adequate protection and flotation, at the location I will give you. As for our monetary arrangement, you've already received one billion dollars in compensation as an advance. A nine billion dollar oil contract will be sold to the Chinese, with your mining joint venture as a beneficiary, as soon as we receive the weapon. We will let you know when we're ready for the next one."

Castillo, although relieved at the outcome of the meeting, remained a bit edgy regarding the remainder of the nukes. The thought crossed his mind that maybe the Iranians only needed a single nuke. He worried that he might have cut himself out of the deal, or worse. He tried to push the thoughts away. Maybe he was just being paranoid. With this in mind, Castillo replied.

"I will have my attorneys in Beijing ready to take possession of those oil contracts. Once all is in order with the contracts, the warhead will be dropped at the location of your choice. Castillo stood up quickly, not waiting for the Iranian to reply. He reached out to shake the man's hand and continued. "Let's make this happen."

The man stood quickly and shook Castillo's hand. The meeting was over. "Will you be leaving us Señor Smith; leaving Colombia?" Smith didn't respond to the question. He simply muttered 'goodbye' in Spanish, which was enough. Castillo smirked to himself. He had retained the upper hand, he was sure of it. He was also sure he had managed to put some sense of urgency into the Iranian's mind. He wanted to convey fear which, coming from a man of his stature, would hit the mark. Castillo made some quick phone calls to set up the transport and put one of his helicopters on standby for the voyage to the Iranian submarine.

Iran had purchased several Russian submersibles not too long before and had been anxious to put them to good use. Although non-nuclear, they were quite modern in other aspects and had remained undetected and a low priority for military intelligence, due to their assumed lack of potential threat. Castillo also woke his attorneys in China and brought them up to speed on the deal. It all needed to take place in real time and under his verbal authorization only.

This deal could be a winner after all, thought Castillo. *We're just going to have to watch the Americans carefully*. Castillo, contrary to your run of the mill drug pin, enjoyed substantial political clout. Well-greased, high-end movers and shakers of the Colombian government were at his beck and call. Although Americans were given the red carpet treatment when the fight involved the FARC: the leftist jungle armies who had tormented Colombia's establishment for over half a century, they weren't usually welcome otherwise. That was what Castillo was counting on; a turn against the Americans, if they made any attempt at all to extradite him. Of course, right now, Americans weren't really worrying about the intricacies of the law when it came to foreigners; especially anyone they considered to be a terrorist. Still, he didn't see an elite American force landing on his building and taking him out; not now and not ever, without starting a war with every Latin American country in the world. This certainly wasn't Pakistan; at least he hoped not. Later that day, Castillo received the exact location of the drop, through his military-grade, encrypted communication system. It had been scheduled for ten o'clock at night; to facilitate the overseas transaction.

The Chinese had been as cooperative as anyone would expect when it came to the money. They would benefit greatly from this deal; getting cheap oil on credit and a partner in the exploitation and sale of their minerals. Listening to political concerns about buying Iranian oil, regarding international western relations, was like being forced to listen to a barking dog. It was highly annoying, but once you shut your door, you really couldn't hear it anymore and China was a very large house indeed.

The low-flying helicopter made good time in the drop zone, helped by a tail wind from the mountains. The warhead had been placed in a fiberglass container, with flotation devices attached all around. It looked like a giant orange donut. The seas were calm and dark. As expected, the submarine was on schedule. It had emerged just a moment before the helicopter started its descent, slowly lowering its large package towards the ocean. Within seconds, the helicopter pilot was able to lower the donut shape contraption directly onto the bridge of the submarine. The deal was done.

Castillo had confirmed all documents were in order in Beijing and had authorized the final drop. This had been easier than your run of the mill drug delivery and certainly more profitable. Once onboard the submarine, the warhead would be taken back to Iran, across the Pacific, headed straight for Papua and thereafter, the Gulf of Oman and its final destination, with several mid-ocean fuel stops.

Castillo was grateful that at least one of the nukes wasn't his problem anymore. In a way, the latest twist of events had worked in Castillo's favor. By keeping the rest of the nukes from him, Heraldo had spared Castillo the headache of having to hide them all. Still, he needed to make sure he could get to them whenever he needed to.

Heraldo and Landry had plenty of time to think on their long journey to South America. They had found wealth beyond, what would have been a year before, their wildest expectations, but by the same token, they were now isolated and condemned to a life in the shadows. Landry knew that he could never go back to the place of his birth, but somehow that didn't faze him too much. He had always felt that he had lived there on borrowed time. They still had four nukes to sell and at this point, more gold just seemed rather superfluous. Plus, the fact that they were rapidly approaching the sub's physical limitations in that department. There was something else they could get from Castillo and they brainstormed on defining the new task at hand with just about every waking hour. When they were finally satisfied with their plans, it was time to phone Castillo to propose their new agreement.

Castillo was rather surprised to hear from Heraldo, although part of him felt relieved. He had feared that once they had their billion in gold, they would simply disappear and never be heard from again.

"Mr. Castillo, I think we have a proposition for you that you'll find of great interest." Castillo was all ears. He hadn't expected them to take the initiative in that department. "We would like your company in Brazil to build us something in exchange for possibly the rest of our merchandise." Heraldo's old habits of watching his choice of words whenever on the telephone wouldn't die so quickly when referring to contraband. I'm sending you a blueprint of what we want, as we speak. You can open those files to review, but the bottom line is: we need you to build us a number of prefabricated structures out of concrete and steel."

Castillo quickly opened the PDF file, leaving the CAD file until later. A series of what could best be described as giant boxes appeared before him on the screen; all different sizes but quite large by prefabrication standards. There was also a list of parts and machinery to go along with them. Castillo had a civil engineering degree and quickly figured out what Heraldo was up to.

"Looks like you're building an underwater city, aren't you Mr. Rodriguez?" said Castillo.

Heraldo responded immediately. "Yes, indeed we are; and we intend for you to keep this quiet. I'm sure you can piece this out in your Brazilian plants, as structural components for oil wells. As you can see, some of these are very large and you will probably need to purchase some barges to fit these requirements. We figured out, for three of our packages, you are getting quite a break on the money side of things. We estimated your cost to build these for us will be in the vicinity of about two billion dollars. If you can build these and deliver them to us, at a location of our determination and keep it quiet, we have a deal. Oh, by the way, we can arrange pick-up within five-hundred miles of your plants."

Castillo quickly ran the figures in his mind. The man was right regarding the cost. He knew he could make it happen too. His only problem was time. What if the Iranians demanded the rest of their warheads? He knew he would have to expedite this job. So when Heraldo told him it all needed to be done within one month, his was relieved and he responded quickly.

"Okay, we have a deal." Castillo suddenly realized they were talking about three nukes, not the presumed four that remained from the original five. "What about the delivery of the fourth? Castillo asked.

"Well, we'll keep that one as security. If you double-cross us or try any funny business like before, I promise you'll get a one way ticket to the sun's inner core," Heraldo said sternly. "Don't think for a minute that we wouldn't be able to deliver this to you in Cartagena, or wherever you would choose to hide. You should know by now that we are resourceful individuals; capable of more than you could ever imagine. I'll be calling you back in seven days and hope that by then, you have some serious activity going on regarding building our structures." On that note, Heraldo terminated the connection.

Back at the Pentagon, Paten was hitting a bunch of dead ends. What he really needed was to "interview" Castillo. But all requests with the Colombian government had gone nowhere. The reciprocity game wasn't working with this guy. He knew that until the US had more proof of Castillo's involvement in the theft of the nukes, no judicial action would be undertaken and no investigation initiated. If anything was going to progress there, it would have to be a strictly covert operation. That in itself was not impossible. A relatively large contingency of US military and intelligence personnel remained present in Colombia; courtesy of the 'war on drugs' funding, initiated back in the days of President Reagan.

Paten mulled over the idea, trying to figure out how to make it work. A trip to Colombia was in order, but he would need some serious support there; behind his ranking and status of General. Only the President could empower him with the kind of authority he needed to get this job done. Paten didn't hesitate to call him this time. After all, the President owed him a favor.

"Mr. President, Paten here. I'm not getting anywhere with my investigation. The suspects have all left the country, with my primary one, that Castillo character, in Colombia. The only way I can make any real progress is to go to Colombia and actively pursue him. I'll need our local support down there and this is why I need your help."

President Russell didn't have to think too much about it. He knew that soon, he would have to explain why no nukes had been found in Cuba, and knew that he better have some very good explanations when that time came. As the holder of the truth, Paten would be better off abroad anyway; not that the President didn't trust him to keep his mouth shut, but you just never knew what turn of events could precipitate some serious diarrhea of the mouth.

"Just keep a low profile over there General. I don't want another CONTRA scenario. I have enough to deal with right now with this Cuban invasion. I'll get the Secretary of State in the loop along with all of the other necessary agencies. Good luck to you General. The country is counting on you."

Later that day, General Paten flew to Miami from Ronald Reagan Washington National Airport. From Miami, he boarded a plane to Cartagena, Colombia; all flights via civilian airlines and coach class. He was exhausted when he finally arrived in Colombia and immediately got a cab to his hotel. The Hotel Caribe was a well-appointed inn that had gained fame as the site of some Secret Service hanky-panky not too long before. Paten couldn't help but smile at the thought. He decided that's what they got for hiring jocks, obsessed with their bulges, and turning them loose in Candy Land. The entire, very public escapade had just reinforced the image of Americans so widespread around the world, as self-entitled, violent and sexually repressed.

It was his first time in Colombia and Paten was surprised by the pleasant climate. For some reason, he had expected some serious heat; similar to what he had endured in Mississippi. Mission aside, he realized this could be a pleasant stay. He also wanted to try some of the local cuisine if time allowed.

The next morning at nine o'clock, after a well-deserved and restful night of sleep, a car from the American embassy arrived at the hotel to pick him up. The embassy, as most were these days, was looking more like a fort than an embassy. It had plenty of obstacles for bombs, considering the bomb-throwing idiots were everywhere. He immediately met with the security people, a term used rather loosely for the ragtag group of intelligence and army personnel. He didn't go into any specifics as to why he wanted to interrogate Castillo, but he knew they would all assume it was drug and money-related. Before he revealed specifics, he wanted to surround the guy with massive surveillance, including the monitoring of all communications in and out of his building. He explained to them that money was no object and that the most up to date equipment should be used. "Get it if you don't have it," were his instructions.

With their marching orders in hand, the men and women went on their way and Paten scheduled a meeting two days in the future, to inspect the work in progress. After his get-together, Paten decided to take a ride around in a taxi, to get a better feel of the city. In his very basic Spanish, he instructed the driver to ride around the tall building where he knew Castillo resided. The structure was truly massive, the tallest in the city by far. But it wasn't possible to drive right up to it. It was in the middle of a tropical garden, surrounded by a large concrete wall with red roof tiles along the top. The main entrance was guarded by a small army of men with stubby, automatic weapons; as well as retractable metal pylons, each one foot in diameter, which disappeared into the ground when vehicles were granted access. Paten had to admit, no one was going to force their way into that armory, not even with a tank.

From the look of the whole set-up, he wouldn't have been surprised if the guards even had some sort of armor piercing armament inside their concrete bunker-looking guard house. He was disappointed and knew that no one uninvited would be able to penetrate it. The White House itself didn't even have that kind of blatant security. Paten certainly hoped the boys back at the embassy had some serious equipment, or at least some inside sources. Otherwise, this was going to be an impossible nut to crack.

Back at his hotel, while eating lunch in the patio area overlooking the pool, Paten contemplated giving Castillo a call. Sometimes the direct approach was the better one. In this case, he really didn't have many alternatives and he was doubtful that all the technology in the world would deliver much useful information when it came to this guy. Of course, once contacted, the cat would be out of the bag. Paten didn't want to risk a dead end, depending upon the outcome.

Chapter 21

To presume that Castillo didn't already know General Paten's presence in Bogota, was a mistake. As soon as the minute inquiries were made with the Colombian government, Castillo's ears started ringing; long before Paten finally got up the nerve to call him. Key officials had been bribed long before for this very type of information and Castillo, confident of the outcome, was already expecting Paten's inquiry. Castillo needed less than a month of free reign to complete his deal, and he wasn't about to let a United States general mess with his bottom line. With this in mind, he arranged for a limo to pick the General up and sent one of his secretaries to meet Paten at his hotel.

Paten was in his hotel room, catching up on some work via his laptop, when the phone call came in from the front desk. His curiosity was piqued when he was told a lady was there to meet him. He quickly put on his jacket and made his way downstairs. A very attractive woman, in a short dress, was standing next to the reception office. She smiled at him as soon as he made eye contact.

"Mr. Paten, I presume," she said in a very sexy voice that didn't go unnoticed by the General. "Mr. Castillo has requested me to invite you to his place for a meeting. I believe you were expecting this?" Paten was taken aback but didn't show it. He smiled and took a moment to reflect. Should he walk into the tiger's den? He was somewhat divided, but what would be the risk? If he disappeared, his people would know where to find him. That would give them the necessary excuse to get rough too. Plus, refusing the invite would make him look weak. For some reason, he didn't want to look weak in front of her. Men really hadn't evolved much since the Neanderthals walked the earth.

"It would be my pleasure," was his contrived answer.

Sitting in the backseat of the large Mercedes, with the girl that looked like Miss Universe, they made quick time to the entrance of Castillo's compound. The limousine, once on the grounds, entered a tunnel that led it to an area which could only be described as a car elevator.

"It won't take long," his companion assured him, as if answering the question in his mind. The car finally emerged into a large, immaculate garage, boasting a collection of racing and luxury automobiles from the pre-World War Two era. Paten had always admired the incredible variety of automakers, back in the days where cars could be made by a few individuals in a small garage. He had always said that if he had the money, he would have been a car collector.

They both stepped out of the Mercedes and Paten was immediately mesmerized by a 1935 Le Baron Convertible Roadster Lincoln parked close by.

Castillo had walked into the area unnoticed and spoke. "You can sit in it if you like General," said Castillo. Paten jumped at the sound of the unexpected voice and turned around. Castillo stood right in front of him, dressed in an Armani suit and a smile. Both men sized each other up and Paten replied in an aloof tone.

"That would be nice. Maybe later."

Castillo shook his head as he glanced at the car. "You Americans; always all business." He shrugged. "Okay, let's go somewhere more comfortable to talk. I trust you have had a pleasant stay so far in our city?"

"Yes, it is quite nice," replied Paten. Castillo led Paten to the area where he had met with the Iranian only a few days earlier and motioned for Paten to sit right where the Iranian had been seated. Castillo smirked a little; the humor not lost on him. Paten looked like the typical middle-aged American general; short graying hair and a slim and athletic build: not overly muscular, but certainly in shape. His appearance was in contrast to the somewhat potbellied look of the self-indulgent Castillo.

After offering the General a drink, the two men turned to the business at hand. Wasting time and playing games wasn't Castillo's style, so he started in right away. "I know you are looking for the nukes General and I can tell you right off the bat; I do not have them. I was hoping to get them when I was in Cuba, but that turned out to be a dead end as you probably already know. It's a shame your country had to start another war over it though," he said with a smile on his face.

"Then who has them?" asked Paten.

"Someone named Landry; a countryman of yours. And if you must know, I haven't seen him since I was in Cuba." Paten's mind raced. He was recording his conversation with Castillo for later review, but he didn't perceive him as lying.

"Let me ask you something if I may, Mr. Castillo. Would you tell me if you found out where these weapons were?"

"Of course," said Castillo. "And to prove to you that I'm sincere, if I ever get them, I'll sell them back to you, for a considerable sum of money of course." Paten was incredulous. This guy had some serious cohunes. But after thinking about it, Paten realized this might be the best course of action for all involved; a way out of this mess with no costly war or embarrassing recovery mission. It was going to be a tough sell back home though.

"That is a decision you must understand that I cannot make," said Paten. "But, I will relay your offer to my superiors. Now, if that's all we need to discuss, let's wrap this meeting up and look at that car." Paten smiled and Castillo nodded in agreement, returning his smile. They certainly had something in common.

After indulging his curiosity and spending another hour with Castillo chatting about his incredible automobile collection, Paten couldn't help but understand why this man was so successful. He really had a way with people. Here he was making deals that anyone else would completely shun. Back at his hotel, Paten immediately contacted the embassy and downloaded and encrypted the recording of his conversation. He marked it for maximum security clearance individuals only and sent it to be analyzed for deception.

As expected, the in-depth analysis revealed that it had appeared Castillo hadn't lied to him. Castillo's headquarters were now under constant surveillance. No communications or individuals could leave or enter the building without being thoroughly examined. Castillo however, was not going to give them much to play with. That same day, he somehow exited his compound by helicopter and his whereabouts became unknown.

Castillo thought the meeting with the Yankee general had gone well. It was somewhat of a relief that threats and posturing had not been part of the conversation. Maybe he could go full circle on the deal; sell the nukes to the Americans and blame the Iranians in the process. He would be killing two birds with one stone. Castillo had opted to go to Brazil and directly supervise the construction of the structures for Heraldo and Landry. The quicker that was done, the quicker he could put all of this behind him. Plus, he knew the Americans were on his back now. It was just as well that he was leaving Colombia promptly and without their knowledge. He didn't need them breathing down his neck at the moment.

The quick helicopter ride to his private airport, where his leer jet waited to take him to Recife, went without incident. He had decided to take Celina with him. She would enjoy his place over there: a beautiful Mediterranean-style castle overlooking the ocean. She and Castillo had grown fond of each other in more ways than just sexually. Deep down, she was glad that she hadn't opted to go with Maria, not that she was really given a choice. Celina was mesmerized by Castillo, especially his mental ability to manipulate the people around him. He was better at it than she could ever be and until now, she thought she had been at the top of that food chain. She had found in him, her true soul mate, and even if he didn't admit to it, she knew he felt the same way about her. He was exactly what she had always wanted: the ultimate alpha male.

Heraldo and Landry, still cruising around at about a thousand feet of depth, were just about to reach the island of Tobago. They opted for a quick land party. They hadn't seen the sun in over a week and cabin fever was starting to set in. The area would be relatively safe for them and if stopped, they could produce Canadian passports with aliases. In these parts, they wouldn't raise suspicion of any kind. By local law, they had twenty-four hours to report to customs and they most likely wouldn't be there that long.

The submarine was bottomed at a one hundred and fifty-foot depth. Maria, Landry and Heraldo all took the mini-sub to about one hundred yards off of a small beach where they anchored it. The small submarine had one apron-like structure all around it that could be inflated. From a distance, it made it appear as a run of the mill zodiac. All of their clothes had been placed in separate, large zip-lock bags, which they each towed behind them as they swam towards the shore. From their maps, there were a couple of resorts in the area with restaurants. They relished the thought of a good meal in the open air. Once on the beach, they quickly put on sandals and light clothes and started up a hill to the first hotel they saw. It was a luxury hotel and by the looks of it, quite empty. They booked rooms immediately. Heraldo and Maria enjoyed their shower in the large marble bathroom, once again making love with a passion awakened by the warmth of the sun.

Landry went for a swim in his private pool overlooking the bay and its tropical paradise. The sun started to set and the view was breathtaking; all shades of orange and gold enveloping the horizon. It was time to eat, so the three of them met on the terrace of the hotel for a feast of a meal. All of them opted for tropical drinks, even though both Landry and Heraldo mostly drank wine. But something about the freshness of the fruit juices and the local liquors made tropical drinks a must for anyone with any semblance of a palate. They feasted on fresh spiny lobsters, grilled to perfection on an outside charcoal fire, accompanied by fresh cut baby greens from a local garden, tossed in delicious vinaigrette.

Afterwards, with a taste for something meatier, they opted for a local goat stew; rich in exotic flavors and natural taste, with some definite Indian influence in its preparation. By the end of the meal, they all felt quite content and almost in unison, came to the decision that they wouldn't go back to the sub until morning. Maria was quite relieved. She wasn't looking forward to swimming back in the dark. She had been fearful of sharks since early childhood.

The next morning, Maria woke to a sumptuous breakfast in bed. Heraldo had been up early to check on their small sub. He ordered a feast to be delivered to the room and woke Maria up with a gentle kiss to her forehead. She opened her eyes and smiled at him. The last several weeks had been trying on all of them, and this was the first time she had really felt normal again. She was ready to enjoy life once more, just as they had back in New Orleans.

"It's going to be hard to leave this place," said Heraldo, as he finished his coffee. "I wish we could stay longer."

But they all knew that it wasn't an option. After all, they were still fugitives and needed to be extremely careful. If they remained undetected, more times like these could be enjoyed. By mid-morning, they left and swam to the mini-sub. They left on the surface at first, but once they were a fair distance away, they slowly submerged back to the mother-sub.

Some of the staff at the hotel, curious and with plenty of time on their hands due to the absence of guests, couldn't help checking out Heraldo's small group as they made their way to the water and the little inflatable. What became really interesting to them was the fact that the little boat, rather than rounding the sea coast to another small bay where their ship presumably was, simply motored at a right angle from the shore and then simply vanished within the surf, creating a story that would be talked about for many days.

Once onboard the large submarine, they resumed the last leg of the trip, which would take them close to Recife in Brazil, where Heraldo hoped Castillo was working diligently to prepare their structures.

Paten had accomplished what he could in Colombia and with the boys keeping an eye on Castillo's operation, his presence was no longer necessary, especially since Castillo had apparently given them the slip. On his way back to the States, Paten was running over in his mind, how he would present this new twist of events, with Castillo as their agent for the recovery of the nukes. The press had dropped the nuke stories a while back when the invasion of Cuba had started; one story silencing an older one. Somehow, everyone had assumed that the United States had recovered the weapons in Cuba. Although it was never officially confirmed, this information had been allowed to propagate and soon, the topic had died down. It was certainly a lucky break for the President.

The next day, back in his Washington office, Paten called the President and scheduled a face-to-face meeting. On the call, Paten noticed the President's tone seemed bittersweet, as if intuitive to the future development of this ordeal. Once in the oval office, facing the President and the Secretary of State, Paten unraveled the events of the last few days.

"So we still have nukes out there, unaccounted for and in the hands of whom?" The President was incredulous.

"Presumably, they're in the hands of a Landry and a Sanchez, both from New Orleans. We have a little information on them. The wife of Sanchez was the victim of a kidnapping in California and was never found. The FBI thought it was somehow related to the other kidnapped individual, a Celina Cordona. But, in view of these events, I think they're mistaken. I have a strong suspicion that the kidnapping was the motive for the theft of the nukes; a form of payment or a ransom demand."

"In your opinion, who's behind this operation?" The Secretary of State interjected.

"Well, it's hard to say at this point. We can assume the usual suspects like the terrorists we know of: the "Axis of Evil", etc.

"I thought we were finished hearing that stupid phrase already," scoffed the President, referring to the flare for the dramatics of his predecessor.

"Well, you know what they say Mr. President...if the shoe fits."

The President looked at Paten carefully. "Now, what you're proposing General; is for us to buy back our own nukes? Is that what you're really asking?"

"As much as I hate to say it Mr. President...yes," replied Paten. "This is the only option that doesn't involve starting a new war Mr. President. And without even counting the potential loss of life that any alternative scenario would encompass. This solution would, by far, be the least costly one."

"What's the role of this Castillo character? Is he involved?" asked the President.

"Yes, most definitely," answered Paten. "I believe he's the one brokering this deal. And as unsavory as this may sound, dealing with him directly in this matter will help us control the situation, simply because he's as motivated to recover the nukes as we are; provided we can come to some kind of monetary agreement."

"I hate to think what the going price for nuclear warheads is on the open market these days," rumbled the Secretary of State.

The President sighed. "Okay General. I trust you have this situation under control. I'll get you the money when needed, but not through the usual channels. I insist we keep this under the utmost secrecy for now. This will remain a top secret and strictly military operation."

Somewhere in the middle of the Pacific Ocean, Captain Hassani was surfacing his submarine for the necessary midway refueling. It was nighttime, but the half-moon cast enough light to clearly see the ocean. A freighter flying a Panama flag was bobbing about one hundred meters away from them and a small craft was toting a fuel line to the submarine. Being out in the open made Hassani nervous. He knew his mission was of the utmost importance and he didn't want to take any unnecessary chances. His journey was going to be a long one; covering tens of thousands of miles to his final destination: the eastern Mediterranean Sea to the coast of Israel. But first, he had to make a brief stop in the undercover submarine port in Iran, for a quick refit and calibration of the nuclear warhead, into a submarine-based Russian short-range missile.

The Nation of Iran had been pushed to political unrest by the latest sanctions, so the Ayatollahs, in their great wisdom, had conceived a plan to exchange the welfare of their country for the survival of the nation of Israel. They simply wanted to be free from all sanctions and free to pursue their nuclear ambitions. In exchange, they wouldn't destroy Israel. That was their latest apocalyptic scheme. In their opinion, the West and the Americans would surely comply with their demands, as the life of their precious nation of Israel depended on it. It was irrelevant to them that it would also eradicate a majority of the Palestinians, once again expendable and insignificant to the issue at hand. They believed that when God's work was being done, small issues like these were a small price to pay. Sacrifice was holy.

However, before their new demands were made upon the world, some dissension had arisen in the government, with the President of Iran himself opposing the latest scheme for a new, more twisted version.

Castillo had settled into his palatial home on the water, close to Recife. With the Americans under control for now, he could concentrate on how he would negotiate his next deal with the Iranians, or more appropriately; how he would cancel it all together. The Americans would most likely be willing to pay to get the warheads back. If he could somehow find out what the Iranians had planned for their first nuke; that information would go a long way in securing the best possible deal with the Americans, and would keep the Iranians too busy to effectively plot any revenge against him.

Heraldo and Landry's project had started construction, both in Recife and abroad. The list of items was considerable and some required fabrication in Germany and China. With money being no object, Castillo had been able to put a rush on most of the items and wasn't going to have any problem meeting the deadline. Some supplies would have to be flown in, but that was a small price to pay considering Castillo was going to receive at least forty billion dollars for his efforts.

The collection of 5 fifty-thousand-square-foot, giant dome-shaped containers; all Kevlar and epoxy-reinforced concrete, would weigh a massive amount. They would easily exceed the capacity of any marine platforms Castillo had at his disposal. The contraptions would simply have to float without any help. In essence, the giant containers would need enough buoyancy to stay on the surface. Each one of them was equipped with ballasts on the bottom, so they could be sunk later on when at their final destination. Some smaller, relatively short tunnels; made of flexible and articulated material, would connect these forms once they were in place. Each container served a particular purpose and per the contract, had to be preloaded with all of its equipment. It was Heraldo and Landry's intention to come as close to a fully-functioning ecosystem as possible. So, a great deal of the preparation involved procuring a collection of trees; particularly productive in oxygen generation, and a large collection of edible plants and farm animals. All living organisms and their surroundings had to be decontaminated of any possible diseases and pests.

Each structure came with its own power, heating and air-conditioning systems, with enough reserves to operate for a period of thirty days without refueling. The temperature inside most of the enclosures would cycle between seventy-two degrees during what constituted the sixteen hours of light time, and sixty degrees during the eight hours of dark time. Having developed some adequate hydrogen-storage technology for the submarine, Heraldo and Landry had opted for a hydrogen fuel-based system as energy storage. This hydrogen would be stored on the bottom of each pod by molecular-bounding, derived from advanced nuclear technology. It was rendered extremely safe that way. So rather than using electrical cabling between each structure, hydrogen provided the fuel and was converted into electricity by a fuel cell system, to drive all of the equipment at a local level.

The main underwater energy source was going to be some subterranean steam vents, present in many of the earth's oceans. This heat and chemical energy would be converted into hydrogen and sent to each pod. Several bell-shaped caps, to capture the gases, had also been part of the long wish list submitted to Castillo. One of the largest habitats was going to be a fully-producing vineyard, with a small Tuscan-style abode within it. This was going to be the home of Heraldo and his wife. They would be able to produce good wine and for that purpose, some burgundy vine cuttings had been purchased, with the hope of grafting them on the already-planted vines. They could control the soil, the light and all other climatic conditions, to mimic the ideal conditions of the best vineyards in the world; even if that involved a somewhat harsher climate from the temperature norms they had established in the other enclosures.

One thing that helped produce exceptional wine was the struggle of the grapes. If there was too much sun, like in most places where vineyards were grown, it made for an overabundance of sugar in the grapes and therefore lesser character and depth in the wine itself. The climate in the northeast of France, a Burgundy region, wasn't nearly as pleasant for humans as the climate in Tuscany. But for their intended purposes, it would do just fine. They could always visit another pod for another more clement climate, like the one Landry planned to reside in.

Landry had opted for more aquatic surroundings, mimicking his native Louisiana. He would live in a wood cabin on stilts, on top of a lake, which would include alligators and a collection of fresh-water fish that he had always enjoyed catching and eating. He would be surrounded by cypress and wild sugar cane. One request from Maria had been to exclude bugs, including mosquitoes, which had made Landry somewhat skeptical as to the feasibility of his eco-system. But he would have time to debate her environmental bullying later.

Another pod had been dedicated to the raising of farm animals; chickens, sheep, goats and cows. None of them were vegetarians and although they all enjoyed a large variety of plants in their diet, they also enjoyed good cheese and other dairy as well as good cuts of beef and other meats. As for the rest of the crew, to deprive them of meat would probably lead to a mutiny down the road, so a vegetarian diet was out of the question. Chickens weren't the only birds present. There was a vast assortment of guineas, emus, quails, pheasants and wild pigeons; all part of the selection of meats that would be offered in the sub-oceanic colony. With Heraldo and Landry in charge, the bar was set high when it came to the quality and variety of food offered. This was by no means your typical expedition-type culinary setup; no dehydrated crap…only the best and freshest.

Castillo remained unfazed by the vast project. At two billion dollars' worth of expenditures, he still stood to make quite a bundle; regardless of who bought his warheads. So his focus remained on getting things done quickly and very well; something he was good at. He would deal with the question later of who to sell the nukes to. His gut told him that the Iranians would probably pay more. But the Americans were unlikely to accept his refusal. So, in the end, he would most likely choose the most self-preserving road and give General Paten a call.

Chapter 22

A few days later, having had time to digest the pros and cons of the situation and careful to keep his location untraceable, Castillo used his relay system to make a call to Paten; a call that appeared to originate from Colombia.

"Good morning General Paten," said Castillo. "I trust your meeting with your superiors went well. I myself have had the opportunity to consider my options and have arrived at a price for our little transaction."

Paten was all ears. He hadn't expected Castillo to be so eager to transact and made himself ready for what he assumed would probably be a rough beginning.

"Yes indeed," said Paten. "How much?" He had no intention of wasting any time.

"Well, considering my other offers, ten billion dollars per weapon seems like a fair proposition. This price is non-negotiable and if it's any consolation, I've had better offers money-wise. But, in addition to this money, I want immunity for myself and my companies in relation to this deal."

Paten was a little taken aback. He hadn't expected such large figures. But then again, the alternative could cost just as much, if not more, and would be fraught with risks. After all, the latest two useless wars the US had been involved in had run into the trillions of dollars.

"You must understand that once again, I have to run these figures with my superiors," said Paten. "But, I do feel confident that we can accommodate you in both aspects; your monetary request and the legal aspect. Neither should be an issue. Also, we don't have any proof of your involvement in any illegal activities at this time."

Castillo was satisfied and informed General Paten that he would call him back in a day to get his final answer and work out the specifics of the trade. *Time to get in touch with our submarine friends*, thought Castillo. Castillo couldn't get an immediate communication to Heraldo, but left a message for him to call in to the dedicated mailbox. Heraldo usually made surface checks with the drone, to download news and messages, once a day. He promptly reached Castillo a few hours later. Heraldo was eager to find out how well the construction was progressing, especially since they were about ten days away from the final deadline.

"The structures are all completed and are curing," Castillo explained. "Testing so far shows pressure capacities of over fifty-thousand pounds per square inch. This should get even better with time. I wouldn't be surprised if we reached sixty-thousand pounds by floating time.

Landry and Heraldo had specified a considerable amount of extra capacity in their designs. Their intended depth was about two thousand meters, still reachable by their sub, but not even close to the maximum water pressure the structures could sustain.

"This isn't the reason why I'm calling you though. I've made a deal with the Americans as to the remainder of the nukes. Not that this concerns you, but this might take some of the pressure off of you once you deliver all of my goods to me. So you know; the first warhead was taken by the Iranians a week ago." The little jab from Castillo had not gone unnoticed by Heraldo. Castillo was obviously applying additional pressure to obtain the fourth nuke. Castillo continued.

"If you cooperate with me, I will tell the Americans that the Iranians were involved in this deal from the beginning and that you were just an unwilling participant." Heraldo didn't have any illusions as to their position with the Americans and was quick to respond.

"We shall see, Castillo. If any deals are to be made with the Americans, we will be the ones doing it. That fourth nuke remains with us for the time being. Just finish our stuff. Goodbye." Heraldo was surprised at the last bit of information Castillo had revealed to him about the Iranians. He hadn't expected that and communicated that new piece of information to Landry.

"We're getting deeper and deeper into this mess. I love how Castillo, the initiator of the whole thing, managed to once again extricate himself from it all; penalty free and with a profit. This guy is good," said Landry.

"And dangerous," responded Heraldo, who hadn't forgotten about his brother and his family.

For the next few days, Heraldo's submarine remained parked at the mouth of the Amazon River, recharging its fuel storage using its outside gills and turbine system within the mighty force of the largest river in the world. This was a good spot to be waiting for their project to be completed, concealed in the murky waters of the powerful stream. However, they always had eyes on their surroundings. They kept track of the ever-increasing boat traffic in the area. One never knew if some fool would drop anchor or cast a net. But, men were on standby to deal with the situation if necessary.

Landry and Heraldo reviewed their plans as to how they would take control of the large convoy of building blocks for their underwater world and take it to their final destination: off of the coast of Africa, a few thousand miles away. The plan was to drag the entire convoy underwater, to remain undetected by all eyes on the surface. It was important for them to remain hidden from possible satellite or surveillance planes that would, without a doubt, be sent to spy on them. Castillo wasn't to be trusted and they had no doubt that he would turn them over to the Americans once he had the opportunity to do so.

About twenty-four hours before the completion date, the submarine's anchors were lifted and the sub was on its way to the meeting point on the coast of Natal, close to the most eastern part of Brazil. Heraldo had specified a delivery of up to one thousand kilometers from Recife and this was considerably closer. He didn't want to give Castillo too much time to plan for something. Heraldo called Castillo to confirm all was ready and loaded, shipshape for the sea. Castillo confirmed that all was good to go.

"Good," replied Heraldo. Here's what you need to do now." Heraldo gave Castillo the coordinates of where he wanted the convoy to go.

"When do I get my goods?" Castillo asked firmly.

"You will get one package when we take possession of the convoy," began Heraldo. "…and are able to submerge it. Thereafter, every twelve hours, you will receive another package at coordinates which will be given to you at that time. If you make any attempt to locate us or if your American friends give us any trouble, you can forget about the rest of your packages and know that, as promised, we will come after you." The plan was for Landry to be on the mini-sub with a couple of his best men and one of the nukes fastened to the outside.

Much later that evening, the convoy met at the designated point; about fifty miles off of the coast, with Landry and the mini-sub. Castillo had chosen to go along with the convoy in a very fast, one-hundred-twenty-foot yacht: a latest model of Italian design, powered by two jet engines and standard diesel propulsion. Built of composite materials, to lessen its weight, it was capable of speeds upwards of fifty knots. Signaling the yacht with the mini-sub's powerful searchlight, Landry quickly approached the large ship and boarded it. Castillo stood on deck, dressed in his smoking jacket. The two men shook hands, sizing each other up. Landry didn't want to waste any time. They needed to get on their way as soon as possible.

Part of the delivery was an external control unit which worked underwater. It was about the size of an ordinary laptop with a suction cup-type antenna. This device regulated the buoyancy of the five large habitat pods; enabling them to be sunk on command and controlled their depth of submersion. Landry, anxious to leave the ship, spoke first.

"I'm sure you're anxious to get your warhead; just as I am anxious to get the hell out of here. So let's not waste any time with unnecessary protocol. I'll tell my men to free the nuke and get it ready for hoisting onto your ship. However, there's one thing. We've equipped it with a little safety device. It will deactivate on my command, but only if everything turns out okay." Landry's men had already detached the nuke and were lifting it up onto Castillo's ship. Castillo didn't object and handed the laptop to Landry, who immediately engaged the buoyancy systems on the pods. All seemed to function adequately, but he needed to run a pressure test, so he quickly set diving depths of one thousand meters. It would take about twenty minutes or so for the habitats to reach the depth.

In the meantime, Landry and Castillo walked over to the first nuke. "It's amazing how something this small can cause so much damage," said Castillo.

"Let's not find out how much, Mr. Castillo. I hope our specifications were rigorously followed," said Landry.

"Without a doubt," Castillo said confidently. The time it took for the pods to reach their final designated depth seemed like an eternity. Landry wasn't the social-type and remained mostly silent, listening to Castillo attempt to strike up idle chit-chat. Landry was relieved when the terminal beeped, signaling stabilization at one-thousand meters. Pressure sensors throughout the containers remained constant, showing surface pressure or close enough in tune with what would be expected from general contracting of all the forms. No leaks or breaches were present, as they would have been detected. It was time for Landry to leave.

"Well Mr. Castillo, I can't say it was a pleasure to have finally met you, but it's now time for me to go. Once underwater, I will activate the release on the bomb and it will be free and clear; ready for you to transport it." Landry stepped into his submersible. "Don't try anything or it will blow up."

Underwater, Heraldo had dispatched a drone to find the leading submerged pod, with the mission to hook up to the dangling cable that the tugboats had used to bring the convoy from Recife. Within moments, the sought after cable was seized by the robot and fastened to the mother-sub for its final voyage. Landry felt confident that Castillo wasn't going to try anything new, so he deactivated the bomb, even though he would have liked nothing better than to see the creep vaporized. The mini-sub's angle pitched to forty-five degrees and once it reached a thousand-foot depth, Landry signaled to Heraldo that all was okay. He coordinated the lifting of the pods to his depth while slowly moving east.

Once back onboard, they quickly released two of the remaining three nukes, after placing them in torpedo-like structures. The torpedoes were programmed to sail underwater; one for twelve hours and the other for twenty-four hours. Each would travel in different directions at about twenty miles per hour, before surfacing with the signal for Castillo to recover them. That's why Castillo had been so adamant about using such a speedy yacht. For him too, time was of the essence. Heraldo was anxious to take a look at his new acquisition, but there was no need for him to physically enter them. The laptop that Landry had received from Castillo, allowed for viewing of all areas within the structures. Heraldo jumped from frame to frame, making sure that all of the components he had ordered were accounted for. So far, everything looked good. He didn't think Castillo would shortchange them, no one could really be trusted completely, so he would eventually inspect every inch of the structures with a fine-tooth comb.

With the huge voluminous masses in tow, the submarine was crawling at two to three knots of speed. At that rate, it would take them forever to reach their final destination off the coast of West Africa. Landry and Heraldo wracked their brains, trying to figure out how to speed up. Each structure was equipped with four small thrusters, to allow for precise final placement. Somehow, they needed to coordinate these motors to see if they could boost their speed. Thankfully, one of the men onboard was a software designer and was familiar with the program that had been used for the pods. Within about eight hours of tinkering, he was able to make all twenty thrusters work in unison. It boosted their speed to six knots per hour. At that rate, they would reach their destination in about two weeks, not bad at all.

Heraldo's main concern was to remain undetected for the journey, so they sunk back down to three-thousand feet, below several layers of currents, rendering detection much more difficult. Due to the large mass of the objects in motion, they knew that it might still be possible for some satellite to pick them up, simply because of the water displacement they generated and its effect on the surface. The latest satellites could indeed detect minute rises in the ocean, and given the proper inquiry software, could theoretically detect them. As always, luck would play a part.

It had been several days since Paten had spoken with Castillo and he didn't want his only grasp of the situation to go weak. Recovery plans in the form of a nuclear submarine and a couple of battleships, now free from the Cuban invasion, had been sent about fifty miles from Cartagena off the coast of Colombia. Paten had lost track of Castillo in Colombia and despite all effort, had been unable to locate him so far. All conventional means of surveillance had failed, including the monitoring of all satellite communication in that part of the world. The sheer volume of communication that the internet had brought to the airwaves, compensated greatly for the increased storage and information-processing software capacity that they now possessed to monitor all communications. It was hard to find something if you didn't know how to find it; even if you knew where it was. Castillo was obviously using some kind of algorithm, integrated into the standard background communication, which made it very difficult to detect. Even if noticed, it would only appear as the random errors embedded in any signal. Warfare supremacy was no longer superior armament brought on by superior intellect. It was simply superior intellect.

Castillo had been playing the game of chasing nukes all over the southern Atlantic Ocean, having traveled over a thousand miles in the last twenty-four hours. His yacht was beautifully appointed as always. But at speeds of fifty miles an hour, it wasn't exactly motionless. He cursed almost continuously, trying to keep down the little food he had been able to eat within the last twenty-four hours.

"Damn that son of a bitch," said Castillo, referring to Heraldo. Once he had recovered both of the nukes, Castillo couldn't wait any longer. He took off in the onboard helicopter for the trip back to Recife. He landed directly beside his home, jumped out of the chopper and never looked back, as he headed towards the house. He had never been so happy to once again be on terra firma. Celina, waiting for him, noticed his wobbly walk.

"What's the matter with you? Are you drunk?"

"You don't want to know," Castillo responded, steadying himself. "We're going back to Cartagena. Pack your bags and get the dogs ready," he said, referring to the army of poodles that had come along with them. "We're leaving in one hour."

The jet was waiting for them at the airport and they landed the helicopter right next to it. The dogs always seemed to enjoy flying in the plane. Castillo had an entire room dedicated to them, with pillows and toys. Their excitement was apparent by the way they pulled and strained on their leashes towards the plane. Once onboard they darted for their private cabin. Castillo was finally feeling normal again and while helping Celina climb up the jet's staircase, even gently patted her on the behind.

"I'm glad you didn't come with me on the boat," said Castillo. "The seas were so rough. You definitely wouldn't have enjoyed it. Did you have a good time while I was gone?"

Celina smiled at him. "I just stayed by the pool most of the time. It was quite relaxing."

"I promise you," cooed Castillo. "Once this deal is over, we'll go to Europe, Paris, Monaco and we'll have a great time. But now, if you'll excuse me, I have to rest some. Please wake me up in three hours or so. I have to make a few phone calls. The quicker I take care of this business, the better for us."

As they approached Colombia, Castillo was woken up. With two more nukes on hand, it was time for Castillo to contact the Americans.

"General Paten, I have good news for you. I have what you want," said Castillo simply.

"That is very good news Mr. Castillo," said Paten. He instantly thought of how they would proceed with the exchange.

Castillo continued. "Now, once you release the money into my account, I will give you the location of the nukes. They should be available to you in about a day or so." Castillo wanted to make sure that his yacht was close to Colombia before proceeding with the exchange.

"How many are we talking about now? asked Paten.

"Two General; ten billion a piece is our agreement, so twenty billion total," Replied Castillo.

"What about the other two, Mr. Castillo?" Castillo, having recovered from the previous day's ordeal, was quick on his feet.

"I will give you that information as soon as I receive the funds for the first two; my security, do you understand?"

The General ignored the question. "You must also understand, Mr. Castillo that unless I recover all of them, this deal is of little value to us."

"It's in my best interest to keep you happy General. Get me my twenty billion and you won't be disappointed, I promise you. Let's talk again tomorrow at the same time and make sure you have your money ready." Castillo hung up the phone and immediately called his lawyers in Beijing to arrange for a new temporary bank account in Hong Kong to be opened.

Twenty billion was a large sum of money, even by Chinese standards, and he didn't want the Americans to play tricks on him by using their influence with the usual banking suspects, to endanger his ransom in any way. He would rather take his chances with the Chinese, rather than risk legal quack mire with the Swiss or some other over-the-hill banking sanctuary. Castillo couldn't help reflecting the irony of China, which had become the new tax haven for the capitalist West. The world truly had changed drastically in the last twenty years.

Chapter 23

Deep underwater, the convoy slowly progressed towards its destination. Heraldo and Landry were deeply engrossed in surveying areas that could potentially provide them with the ideal characteristics they were looking for. Deep enough so they wouldn't be bothered by humans, hidden enough by rocky surroundings so they would easily blend into any deep water scan and most importantly; an area that was volcanic in nature, with open vents, but stable enough so as not to endanger them. The mid-Atlantic area and its surroundings fit that bill quite nicely. Many volcanic submerged ridges, mountains and canyon would provide the ideal ground for what they had in mind. Already, only about six hundred kilometers on their way, they were passing beautiful rock formations and large crevices that made the grand canyon look like a small creek. Several areas had already shown some promise, but they wanted to be closer to Africa for logistical concerns. Going to the shore would still be necessary from time to time.

At their current rate of speed, they would reach their projected destination in about four days. Their actual velocity had proven to be somewhat greater, due to an unforeseen, deep water current. Nevertheless, they were using a great deal of energy to move the large volumes in tow and their hydrogen storage had not been full when they left. At the present rate of consumption, they projected they would run out of fuel in about ten days, if they kept all of the thrusters going. This was somewhat worrisome to Heraldo, who understood their vulnerability to detection while still in motion, but also knew that some time would be required before they could extract energy from the smoker vents they were going to tap. It would be a close call.

Given the twenty-four hour dead time, Paten opted to immediately go back to Colombia. He wanted to be on hand for the exchange. The twenty billion dollars had been appropriated from a war reserve fund. This was actual cash to be used in the event of an invasion; part of a contingency plan initiated during the Iraq war and kept in a secured location. The money would be dropped to a third-party foreign bank which would, for a substantial commission, wire it to the required account. It was so far so good as to the secrecy of the whole operation. The nukes were still presumed to be in Cuba. The media had lost interest; now focused, as expected, on the tremendous legal issues of property ownership of Expat Cubans. Even descendants of major, organized-crime families would own some considerable stake in the pre-Castro tourism and gaming industry in Cuba. It was the kind of circus the American media was best at and they would milk it for all it was worth over the days to come. Paten fully intended to recover the nukes, "find" them somewhere in Cuba and hopefully end what had become known as the Nuevo Cuban Missile Crisis.

Back at the US embassy, Paten went over the latest intelligence on Castillo. Not much of any interest. They had been able to pick up the origin of his latest communication with Paten, as being from a plane over Colombia. That in itself was of little interest, except that it demonstrated their inability to account for his whereabouts up to that point. Paten was insistent on keeping very close tabs on Castillo, and made the drones from the naval task force off the coast of Colombia at the disposal of his men. All they could do was wait.

Castillo and Celina landed on his building as the sun was setting on the ocean. They had made the quick trip from his airfield by helicopter, as usual. Castillo felt good to be home as he helped Celina herd the dogs into their suite. Castillo's mind was on the Americans. He knew they wouldn't rest until they had recovered the other two nukes. The Iranians wouldn't be a problem, but knowing Heraldo and Landry's whereabouts would be somewhat more challenging. He no longer had a hold on them and except knowing they were somewhere in the ocean at extreme depths, he certainly didn't expect that information to appease the General. He would definitely have to come up with something better by their phone meeting the next day.

The submarine had passed about ten miles from St. Peter and St. Paul's rocks, a unique and battered site where the earth's crust protruded over the ocean like a pimple in the middle of its face. It was a storm-prone area of the Atlantic that had cost many mariners their lives and even recently, had precipitated a chain of events that would cost an Air France transatlantic flight all of its passenger's lives.

The bottom here had risen substantially, pushed up by the huge continental land masses bucking horns with each other. They had to be careful negotiating the various crevices and peaks, while hugging the ocean's floor. Mindful of possible earthquakes, they kept their distance from overhanging rock formations. If it wasn't for the frequent tremors, the area would have probably been a good candidate for what they had in mind. The complicated bottom provided ideal hiding places where they could blend in quite adequately. Indeed, the discovery of the crashed airliner had only become possible because it had fallen into a barren flat area where sonar was able to pick up its remains against the non-obtrusive background.

Castillo's fast yacht had made good time heading back to Colombia. At full throttle and at over sixty miles per hour, it was sailing about fifty miles off of the coast of Venezuela, passing the island of Curacao and about to enter the waters north of Colombia. On their radar, they had noticed the presence of some larger ships in somewhat of a holding pattern. They wondered what they were all about. They didn't expect the Colombian navy to bother them. After all, Castillo's assets were known as off-limits. A call was made and Castillo promptly answered. Once he was informed about the ships, Castillo immediately knew what it was all about. He notified his crew to slow the ship to cruising speed and stand by for further instructions. It was time to call General Paten before the US Navy got too curious about the odd ship speeding by; safely assuming the boats were military.

Paten had made it onboard the single aircraft carrier, he had sent along with the rest of the naval formation and routed the call from Castillo to his satellite phone. As always, Castillo took it upon himself to direct the conversation by asking Paten about the money.

"I trust you are ready to transfer the funds, General?" asked Castillo.

"I trust you have what I want, Mr. Castillo," Paten answered.

"Yes indeed, we have two of them for you located within the ship going by. I'm sure you already noticed it," answered Castillo.

"I was wondering about that. But what is to prevent me from boarding it now and taking what is mine, Mr. Castillo?"

"I can assure you that won't be possible, not without a severe loss of life. You're not the only ones who can operate these devices. I believe three-hundred thousand tons of TNT equivalent will go a long way as to wiping out your little flotilla, General." Paten had no doubt that Castillo knew what he was doing. Even though these were military ships and seriously reinforced, a thermonuclear device, at this distance, could at least inflict major damage, if not completely sinking them altogether.

"I get your point, Mr. Castillo," said Paten. "I'm having the wire transfer initiated with our bank in the Caymans right now." Castillo quickly gave him the beneficiary bank information. "China...hmmm. That's a surprise," said the General.

"The world is changing General," said Castillo. "You Americans don't control everything anymore and you're going to have to learn to live with it; just as the Romans once did."

Paten wasn't about to get into a debate with this man over the state of America's power, so he ignored him. "You should be receiving the money as we speak."

Castillo was monitoring the account balance on his computer terminal, in real time. Within moments, the balance took a sizable jump; his contribution to the Sino-American trade deficit for the week, even though America didn't really need his help in that department.

"Thank you very much General," said Castillo. "I'm instructing my ship to stop where it is. It has a helipad and they'll be expecting you."

Paten immediately ordered a chopper to take him to Castillo's yacht. Ten minutes later, he had landed. The crates were loaded onto the chopper and strapped onboard firmly. Within only a couple of minutes, the General and his helicopter were on their way back to the Coast Guard carrier.

Satisfied to have at least two of the nukes back, safe and sound, Paten called Castillo and asked about the others.

"General, one of the nukes is still in the possession of your two countrymen: Landry and Rodriguez. The other one made its way onboard a submarine, en route to Iran, about two weeks ago. Obviously, I can't do anything about that one. But regarding your New Orleans' friends, I can give you their phone number. You can exert more pressure on them than I can."

Paten was somewhat dumbfounded. He had known all along that someone was financing this operation, but he hadn't thought of the obvious. After all, the Iranians had been seeking out nukes for a long time, with plenty of money to spend. The fact that they had obtained one created a whole new set of implications. Most likely, the United States wouldn't be in danger, but Ahmadinejad's words regarding Israel replayed in his head. No doubt, the next few weeks would be tense.

"Alright, Mr. Castillo, I'll take that phone number. Also, I need you to do something for me; something that will require you to become an active participant in recovering these weapons."

Castillo cringed. He hadn't expected to walk away scot-free, but he certainly didn't like the turn this conversation was taking. "Yes, General?"

"I need you to find out from the Iranians what they intend to do with this warhead. That information will go a long way as far as keeping us from 'dropping in', if you know what I mean." Castillo didn't need a picture painted for him. He knew exactly what Paten meant and quickly replied.

"Will do, General."

"Best of luck to you, Mr. Castillo."

Castillo was playing with a double-edged sword. If he contacted the Iranians, there was no doubt that questions about the leftover bombs would arise. He would have to pretend that he was still in possession of them. When they discovered he had gotten rid of them, there would be hell to pay; of that he was sure. But, he knew they would inevitably find out. However, the Americans would pose a greater threat to him if he could manage to stay alive long enough. He finally chose the lesser of the two evils and called Mr. Smith at the Iranian embassy.

"Nice to hear from you," said Mr. Smith. "How can I be of help Señor Castillo?"

Castillo knew he needed to play it really smooth, so he decided to invite Mr. Smith to one of his sumptuous feasts. "I'm throwing a little get-together for some friends; some of whom you met the last time you attended."

Mr. Smith couldn't help remembering that event. Although he hadn't taken part in the post-dinner festivities; deep down, he wished he had. His answer was quick. "I would be delighted to attend, Señor Castillo. Also, it might be a good opportunity for us to discuss our unfinished business, perhaps?"

Castillo kept his cool and answered simply. "Of course, Mr. Smith. That's an excellent idea." The call ended and Castillo went to work. This dinner needed to be ultra-special. He had to overcome the man's inhibitions and that wouldn't be easy. The last event had been top-notch, but apparently not sexy enough to tip the Iranian's self-control in the lust department. This time, Castillo would have to outdo himself. From his intelligence on Mr. Smith, Castillo knew he was a gambler; known to spend some serious cash in some of the world's greatest casinos. Castillo also learned that Mr. Smith, like a lot of his countrymen, had a predilection for buxom, voluptuous blondes; not the Russian fit-model types. So, Castillo puts his best feelers out for the hottest, sexiest full-sized girls in the business.

The party was on short notice, but Castillo's resources, particularly his planes, were put to good use for the preparation; rounding up the proper types of call girls from Vegas and Amsterdam. An incoming bevy of Betty Page and Marilyn Monroe look-alikes descended on his building. To the outside observer, they were reminiscent of one of those Elvis conventions. Massive quantities of Beluga Iranian caviar and premium champagne were also flown in for the event. Castillo was going to ensure two things: that Mr. Smith got what he wanted and that he himself got the answers that the Americans were looking for. He had invited a smaller number of guests to this party than the last one, and had taken particular care to pick only those certain guests that Castillo knew would behave and not detract from the mood of the moment; no sleepers or drunks...just major sex addicts.

The party started at eight, which was quite early by Colombian standards. But Castillo had decided to start the festivities with a good old-fashioned burlesque show, just to get his guests in the mood; a teaser, so to speak. The fifties were back and the two women on stage, dressed as office girls in business-style blazers and short matching skirts, were slowly undressing each other. From the look on Mr. Smith's face, Castillo knew his plan was already working. The man was blushing furiously, which was quite an interesting sight. Hopefully, he could take this little show without 'blowing it', so to speak. After having undressed each other all the way down to their barely-there lace bras, tiny panties and sexy fishnet stockings, the girls slowly removed even those items and naked, proceeded to kiss each other in all of the right places. After climaxing loudly in unison, the girls disappeared behind the falling curtain; only to reappear, wrapped in skimpily short towels, for the guest's applause and some enthusiastic hoots and hollers.

Castillo, always the perfect host, invited his guests to join him at the dinner table for the feast. The waitresses were dressed as Viking maidens, wearing short natural-looking leather skirts and matching bras; all of them blonde and statuesque of course. By the look on Smith's face, Castillo was worried he may have pushed it a little too far. The guy was so smitten with the female staff that he looked like he was about to have a heart attack. Castillo hoped the Beluga and champagne would help calm him down.

In keeping with the theme; a variety of wild game, roasted and braised to perfection, followed the appetizers. Although Castillo ensured that Mr. Smith's caviar plate remained on the table and was continuously replenished. The teasing of their female companions lingered until the end of the meal; until Castillo decided it was time for his guests to vacate the dinner table for the more comfortable, private, oversized booths that overlooked a large fountain. After directing Mr. Smith to the most secluded booth, Castillo discreetly signaled for the final part of the entertainment to take place. By that point, Mr. Smith was ready for it. The voluptuous vixens appeared and paraded around, dressed in transparent, silk gowns that revealed their buxom assets.

Not wanting to appear rude, Mr. Smith couldn't refuse the advances of the Viking goddess who was slowly rewarding him for his patience. Castillo had taken great care to monitor the action in progress from various angles. He was no porn director, but he was confident that this was probably some of his better work; enough recorded lewd and lascivious behavior by the little man, to get him either an award in Vegas or his head chopped off in Tehran. Castillo wasn't going to be the one to burst Mr. Smith's bubble though; at least not right away. Castillo decided to allow him 'to finish', so to speak. Castillo walked away from the monitors, knowing he would deal with him later. A solid hour passed, during which Mr. Smith endured enough sexual pleasure that a man his age could bear. He was ultimately satisfied, as he had never been before actually, and he finally sent the vixens away so he could enjoy a well-deserved, refreshing drink; provided by one of the attentive waitresses with a horny hat.

Castillo made sure that Mr. Smith's thirst-quencher would put the little man to sleep. Given his level of exhaustion, it didn't take very long. Mr. Smith's body was taken to a windowless room and set on a Roman-style chair. A large television monitor that took up almost an entire wall of the room, played recaps of Mr. Smith's sexual exploits. Castillo sat behind a desk while two guards stood by the door. The moaning and grunting finally woke the little man, who was sure he was still dreaming. Castillo wanted to hit him hard, while he was still under the influence of the drugs and in complete shock from what met his eyes as he stared at the screen.

"I'm so glad you enjoyed yourself, Mr. Smith." The little man slowly recovered his senses and suddenly became fully aware of what was going on. He forgot any pretense of decorum as he looked at Castillo and yelled.

"What the fuck do you want?!"

Castillo held up one hand and smirked. "Easy now, Mr. Smith. I think you and I have known each other long enough, so that we can get right to the point of this discussion without getting our panties in a wad. Obviously, you're fully aware of the production value of my little movie. The only way you're going to walk out of here is if you tell me what I want to hear. I'm not going to waste your time or mine."

"You'll never get away with this Castillo," interjected Smith, hissing the words between his teeth. "My government has long arms and you'll be a hunted man until you die!"

Castillo chucked sarcastically. "Spare me the melodrama, Mr. Smith. You're not in any position to threaten me. All I want to know is what your government is planning to do with that warhead. You tell me that and you'll be free to go; you have my word. You won't ever have to worry about your short film ever being seen by anyone else but the people in this room."

Mr. Smith seemed to calm down, pondering his dilemma. He wondered how he could have been so stupid as to be lured into this situation. He had thought Castillo was just buttering him up for another sale. He was shocked at the realization that Castillo was attempting to blackmail him. But the little man sighed, his shoulders dropping, finally realizing he had no choice but to betray his country.

"Okay, Castillo. I'll give you what you want." Deep down, Smith had been leery of Iran's entire plan anyway. It was full of pitfalls and dangerous repercussions, so maybe this was for the best. It was certainly better than risking total annihilation of his country by either Israel or the United States; most likely both of them, even though the strategists in Teheran had predicted non-intervention due to the confusion of the origin of the warhead. Mr. Smith finally started to explain.

"The warhead has been refitted inside of a small missile, to be launched off of the coast of Israel and aimed at Palestinian settlements. Our scientists have been able to boost the explosive capacity of the bomb to one megaton."

Castillo was rendered speechless for a moment. His brain tried to take it all in. *What a fucking devious plan!* he thought. *Make it look like the Israelis did it.* They would certainly be blamed for it, in conjunction with the United States; as post-event analysis would easily reveal the bomb's origin as America. What little of Israel remaining after such a huge explosion, would no doubt be overtaken by its neighbors with the support of worldwide public opinion.

"Jesus, man," Castillo said shaking his head. "Your bosses are even crazier than I thought. Thank you, Mr. Smith. You're free to go. Maybe this is for the best, even for you."

On that note, Castillo got up from his seat and walked over to Mr. Smith who was slowly rising from the couch. With a pat on the back, Castillo sent him on his way, wishing him well and wishing him a quick recovery from his exploits.

Castillo pondered what to do next. The Americans would go insane when they found out about this. Castillo smiled at the thought; wishing he could be there to see the expression on Paten's face when he heard this news.

Paten had gone back to the States and was in his office when Castillo called. "That was quick, Mr. Castillo," he answered. "I take it you have news for me already?" Paten hadn't expected such quick action on Castillo's part. He knew when it came to the Iranians that everything was quite slow and could be ridiculously complicated.

Castillo answered quickly. "Yes, I certainly do have news General, but I'm afraid it's not good." Castillo quickly relayed what he had learned from his Iranian guest.

"Holy shit," the General mumbled, a chill shooting down his spine as he listened. "I didn't expect this scenario at all. Of all the screwy scenarios they've ever come up with...this is definitely not one of those." The General sighed as he rubbed his temples. Even he had to admit the Iranians plan would work. It was downright brilliant in fact, unfortunately. "Well Mr. Castillo, if this is true and we can stop them; I'll consider my beef with you to be over with. As long as you never come to the United States, you will remain unprosecuted."

Castillo was pleased with himself. He had made thirty billion dollars in just a few short weeks and had managed to appease his foes, with the exception of the Iranians of course. The fact that he could never walk on American soil again didn't bother him in the least. When it came to the best places in the world where the wealthiest people could enjoy themselves and spend their money, that wasn't America at all. In his view, America was just a giant crappy department store; filled with low-end stuff and certainly unworthy of his high-end lifestyle and exquisite taste in everything.

Chapter 24

The submarine approached the Cape Verde Islands as Heraldo and Landry actively scanned the bottom of the ocean for prospective home sites. Infrared detection devices picked up some hot spots; from small lava spurs to superheated water springs. One particular location looked promising and Landry decided to board the mini-sub to take a closer look. It looked like an old, submerged volcano; the crater of which was clearly visible in the powerful searchlights, about four-hundred meters in diameter. Superheated water was clearly visible as it came out of small vents on one side of the volcano's mouth. Landry took some temperatures and flow measurements and was pleased to see that they should be able to extract over one megawatt per hour of power from this smoker; more than enough for all of their stations and to also create plenty of hydrogen. The bottom of the crater stood about three-hundred meters from the ridge of the volcano and was rocky and relatively flat. It would provide the perfect substratum for the large concrete pods.

By the look of the lava field, Landry determined that no eruption had taken place in several thousand years; and if past history was any indication, it would certainly be safe for them. Regardless, they had enough seismic equipment onboard to monitor any harmful changes in this volcanic beast and would have plenty of time to react if it ever decided to wake up. Landry relayed the information to Heraldo and they quickly decided to make this place their new home. The large convoy of concrete forms had been stopped and they hovered over the mouth of the volcano. One by one, with the help of their thrusters and ballasts, each pod was lowered into its final position.

Thankfully, the onboard computer handled the operation without a hitch. The placement of each had to be exact, as the tolerances for variation were small when it came to attaching the flexible connecting tunnels that linked all of the pods. The large concrete structures disappeared nicely into the crater, making them invisible to any lateral scans. Once in place, they were buried in silt, pumped in from the surroundings; completing their stealth-like appearance. It took the team just over five hours to fully place and attach all of the pods. Once settled, pressure checks were completed and the results were perfect. The power bell was secured to the volcanic vents and it also functioned just as expected, instantly generating hydrogen for the entire habitat. It was finally time to land the submarine.

One of the structures was equipped with large bay doors to allow full entry of the large submersible: the mother-sub. The structure was also equipped to pump water out, enough to allow access to the large submarine from a dry dock and plank. The mother-sub and mini-sub, as they had been nicknamed, were both docked with the bay doors shut. The area settled to normal surface pressures quite fast and their occupants emerged, to their new underworld home. The excitement of Landry and Heraldo was palatable. Like little kids at Christmas, they were ridiculously impatient to see their new surroundings. It was one thing to plan it, but nothing would compare to the actual feeling of seeing and touching their new underwater world.

Landry couldn't wait to see his cabin and quickly made his way to his personal pod. The water in his very large pond had just covered the bottom, as it was being generated by the onboard plant. He guessed it would take about a week for the large volume to be filled. He made his way to the pier that led him to his new home on stilts. Castillo had delivered quite well on the aesthetics of their specifications. The house was a carbon copy of the picture he had included in his plans; even the porch benches were identical. All of the aquatic life forms were presently alive and well in storage tanks, waiting to be released when the water conditioning and plant life were properly established. Like Noah's ark, several specimens of breeding species awaited, including his favorite alligators.

Heraldo and Maria weren't disappointed either. Their home, surrounded by vineyards, was quite picturesque and the sounds, made by the small birds nesting in the greenery, brought them back to the reality of life and its beauty. They needed this after so many weeks spent in the confined space of the mother-sub.

Barely settled in their new home, Heraldo suddenly received an interesting message on the communication system. A General Paten seemed to want to speak with them urgently. The only way the American could have known about this communication venue was through Castillo. Heraldo's jaw tightened as he realized with near certainty that Castillo had spilled the beans and worked out some kind of deal with the General. The outside world was once again nodding at them and Heraldo knew it couldn't be ignored. Sooner or later, they would have to deal with it; the sooner the better.

For this purpose, they had left several drones along their way to their present location, to serve as relays for possible future electronic communications. This drones had the ability to dive and hide when not in use, making them very difficult to locate. They also recharged themselves. Landry called Paten within a matter of minutes. Paten quickly answered his cell phone from inside of his apartment located across the interstate from the Pentagon.

"Mr. Landry, we finally meet, so to speak," said Paten.

"Yes indeed, General. How can I help you?" replied Landry nonchalantly.

Paten got right to the point. "You have a nuke of ours and we want it back. However, we don't want to spend any more time or money chasing you around the world. Obviously, neither you nor I need the publicity either. So, I came up with an idea that I would like to run by you, Mr. Landry. As you may know, one of the nukes was delivered to the Iranians; as in the Iranian government. I have it on good intelligence that they plan to blow up half of Israel with it, by using a submarine to launch it at close range, right off of Israel's coast in fact. Now obviously they aren't going to use the Suez Canal to get there. They're going to go around Africa and take the long way through the straits of Gibraltar and I'm sure that if they're not already on their way, they will be very soon.

We've decided to try to intercept them as they enter the Mediterranean Sea and if not successful, we'll intercept them off of the coast of Israel. However, if you could manage to do this for us, before they leave the Atlantic, I could make sure that I, myself, would be able to confirm your demise and lift any and all search and arrest warrants we have on you and your companion; as long as you don't ever come back to the United States or make your presence conspicuous that is."

Landry stared at Heraldo, also listening to the General. Landry knew this request would be difficult. The Atlantic was a large sea. But considering what was at stake, both men understood this was an olive branch that they couldn't pass up. Heraldo gave Landry one quick and firm nod.

"Okay," said Landry. "I think we can accommodate you on that. Do you have any information on the location of the submarine at this time?"

Paten smiled, relief washing over him. There was hope after all. He needed to resolve this entire incident before it became a worldwide catastrophe.

"Yes Mr. Landry. One of our ships, off of the coast of Somalia, detected something about a week ago. It has a Russian signature which is what the Iranians use, and appeared to most likely be a submarine heading south. They didn't engage with us and considering we had no knowledge of this possible mission at the time, we ignored them. Our ships were busy with some pirate activity in the area anyway."

Landry did the math in his head and realized almost immediately that they still had some time to prepare before the submarine would come within their range.

"Oh, and one more thing," said Paten. "That nuke you have. Use it on them and be discreet about it." Landry was stunned and couldn't help but wonder how in the world they would be discreet about blowing up a nuclear bomb.

"I understand General," said Landry solemnly. The line went dead and both Landry and Heraldo felt mixed emotions. How in the hell would they accomplish this new task? Luck would definitely have to be on their side this time. They knew they couldn't fail if they wanted to continue existing as they had. There was little doubt as to the consequences of the Iranians vaporizing most of the population of Israel. They would become the ultimate scapegoats and dealt with as such. Heraldo and Landry didn't waste any time and immediately started planning the attack. After all, there really wasn't much else to do.

Over the next few days, they pondered the specifications of the submarine in question and gathered information regarding its propulsion performance and other characteristics. One interesting fact was its range, if they assumed no major modifications had been made in that department. They realized it would have to surface somewhere between the Cape Verde and Canary Islands to refuel if it was going to reach Israel without refueling in the Mediterranean Sea, so closely to their destination. It was doubtful that they would risk exposed time on the surface, next to a tanker ship, in the middle of the most highly scrutinized sea. After all, refueling would be the time they would be at their most vulnerable. Landry and Heraldo decided that's exactly where they would attack them; off of the coast of Mauritania. They hoped they would be far enough away from populated areas and below the horizon, far from any witnesses, so they could detonate their last nuke. It was time for action. To accomplish their plan, they would need at least one boat. If they were lucky, it would have a helicopter to go with it. The decision was made to go to Dakar in Senegal to see about acquiring the necessary equipment.

The next day, Landry and Heraldo boarded the mother-sub and left the underwater compound, headed for the Senegalese port. At full speed, it took them twenty-four hours to reach the outskirts of the harbor. Just as in Tobago, they had assumed new identities; Canadians sailing the coast of Africa who intended to go back to the Florida Keys for the winter season. They took the mini-sub to the surface and with one man standing guard over what looked to be an inflatable, Landry and Heraldo left the mini-sub and started scouring the harbor for any ship that could do the job.

The port was a collection of ragtag buckets of rust, mostly small cargo boats. They were loaded with everything from bicycles to clothing. But one in particular was sitting, empty of cargo, and looked plenty large enough, with no superstructure to block a helicopter landing either. As Landry and Heraldo approached, they saw a young man scrubbing the deck with a brush. It reeked of the smell of fish. In fluent French, Landry asked the young sailor if he was the captain. The young man quickly responded that his boss was down below, working on the cooling system. Nicely enough, the young man offered to go and get him.

When the older captain appeared from the belly of his ship, he looked strikingly similar to the young man; except with a scraggly gray beard and a worn, black leather cap. Landry quickly introduced himself and asked the man if he would consider selling his boat. The Captain looked surprised but not displeased; a sign that Heraldo was quick to notice. The older man offered to show them around, so they reluctantly endured the smell and entered the sweltering mass of rust. The Captain told them the boat was in good working order, except for the refrigeration system. The compressor had blown a seal and they were waiting for parts to come in. Fermenting fish juices, in the summer African heat, had the newcomers gasping for air. After a quick look around, they hurriedly made their way back up into the open. What followed was the fun part. The man was definitely interested in selling, so a price was thrown out. After about an hour of heavy bargaining, the men all finally agreed on a price and Heraldo and Landry became the proud new owners of a sixty-foot bucket of rust.

As for the helicopter, thanks to the Internet, they struck a deal at the local airport for an old French military craft that looked as if it had taken part in the battle of 'Dien Bien Fu'. But regardless of its age, it still ended up costing them substantially more than the boat. The five-hundred-thousand Euros that Heraldo had carried, in cash, had been cut in half in a matter of hours. The boat was refueled and kerosene drums for the chopper were delivered, under the supervision of one of their men, while Landry and Heraldo returned to port to enjoy a meal at one of the restaurants overseeing the docks' activity.

"I think we're going to have a hard time locating this submarine," said Heraldo. "Our only real shot is the supply vessel; probably coming out of Nouadhibou. It's probably something simple like we have; carrying fuel drums. I'll tell you how I would do it," Heraldo said, pointing his fork at Landry while he chewed. "A quick refueling off of the coast of Mauritania, at night...that's how."

"I agree," mumbled Landry, as he swallowed a mouthful of food. "They wouldn't risk following the submarine for a long period of time, for fear of detection from satellites. So we need to set up some kind of airborne surveillance out of that area, to detect any ships leaving and heading straight out west. Another thing we can do is use some of our aquatic drones to help detect the submarine."

Heraldo considered that for a moment. "Do you think we can outfit them with listening devices quickly enough?" he asked.

"Yes," said Landry. "That shouldn't be a problem. We can use the chopper to pick them up and drop them off, to speed up the operation and cover more ground."

"That's an excellent idea my friend," commended Heraldo. After finishing their interesting meal; an assortment of tasty, spicy seafood dishes and some local beer, Heraldo and Landry made the short trip to the pier where their new acquisition was located. One of their men had headed out to the airport via taxi to fly "the Relic", as they had nicknamed their chopper. He would fly the chopper out to the boat, once it was at sea and far enough away from prying eyes. Heraldo would take the mini-sub and Landry would captain the old, refrigerating boat; nicknamed "the rust bucket", which was fine with him. The last thing he wanted right then was to be in a confined space with digestive issues which, he knew from experience, would soon arise.

Landry cranked the large, ancient Fiat diesel and the rust bucket shuddered and rattled to life, filling the air with a plume of black smoke that billowed from its stack. Landry hoped the beast would actually be able to make the trip. He feared the engine had seen much better days. At full speed ahead, the boat traveled at a solid seven knots; better than Landry had expected, so he was relieved. It headed for the high seas and soon became surrounded by the large swells of the Atlantic, going up and down with the motion of the ocean. Landry had good sea legs, but it was pretty rough on him; the smell of dead fish, the waves and his spicy lunch all contributed to him regretting his decision to captain the boat.

The mini-sub trailed him, still above water. Soon, they were far enough away from land and the mini-sub dove down to rejoin the mother-sub. About ten miles out, they turned their heading to full north; the mother-sub underwater and the rust bucket on the surface, at least for the time being. It would take them a full day to get to the area where they assumed would be the most likely place where the Iranian submarine would refuel. During their day of travel, all four of the drones were outfitted with passive sonar systems and powerful listening devices, tuned into the noise signature of the Russian submarine. It ended up being a challenge to land the helicopter on the boat with all of the wave action. But after a couple of tries, the experienced pilot managed to do so without falling overboard. The chopper was quickly chained up to the deck and its engine air intake vents covered up from the spray. Landry, finally over his seasickness, was enjoying the trip. It reminded him once again of his childhood; going fishing for shrimp with his father at the mouth of the Mississippi river. Deep down, he had always been a sailor. It was obvious that his one true love was the sea.

Hugging the coast of Senegal and then Mauritania, just outside territorial waters, they didn't encounter much traffic. From time to time, some small fishing boats could be seen on the East horizon and every once in a while, a large cargo or tanker ship passed them on their west side. About every eight hours or so, they slowed down for supplies and a crew exchange. Landry remained onboard and finally decided to sleep. The night air was surprisingly chilly and rest came easy to him, as he was rocked by the currently gentle waves of the ocean.

Early the next morning, Heraldo boarded the boat again, bringing the rest of the drones and some fresh eggs and bread. He joined Landry for a good, hearty breakfast; cooked on some diesel fuel burners in the primitive galley of the old rust bucket. It was almost time for action. The chopper had already taken off on a lookout pattern, about twenty miles from the coast, to tag any suspicious vessels leaving Mauritanian harbors. Pictures were taken with the high-powered camera and relayed to the laptop computer onboard the rust bucket. The men scrutinized them for any telltale signs of fuel transport. Heraldo didn't expect their supply boat to leave this early for the meeting point. The most likely time would be during evening hours, with enough time to spare for the tedious refueling by the drums. However, it was all good practice.

By afternoon, they decided to release the drones over a two-hundred-mile stretch; perpendicular to the coast, creating a curtain that would certainly detect their target if it came within range. But, whether or not it would ever come into range remained the fundamental question. They had gambled on the fact that the submarine would hug the coast, where it would be harder to detect amidst the increased amount of noisy aquatic traffic. However, there was no guarantee; and only time would tell if their gamble would pay off.

As the day rapidly turned into night, as it always did at their current latitudes, one of the furthest drones picked up an interesting signal. It wasn't quite what one would have expected from the Russian-made sub. It was much fainter and seemed to be moving surprisingly fast; about thirty-five miles per hour. Plus, their direction was, by all accounts, completely wrong. South-southeast was supposed to be where the sub was coming from, not where they were going to. Landry immediately notified Heraldo of the drone's signal.

"I think we have company; another submarine, probably nuclear and probably American. I think it's safe to assume that it's looking for the same target we are and worse yet, it may even be looking for us," said a concerned Landry.

"Keep a close eye on it," said Heraldo. Also, let's make sure our submarine stays put. Find some deep crevice somewhere to hide in. The last thing we need is for the Gringos to detect it." Heraldo realized it had been somewhat naive on their part to not realize that the Americans would obviously come to the same conclusion as they had regarding the Iranian's possible refueling location. They carefully monitored the heading of the American submarine for the next hour. It remained unchanged. Heraldo and Landry guessed they were on a diagonal pattern search, going up and down the coast as they approached it, probably for the sake of security.

Another hour went by and the signal from the submarine was lost; out of range. The rest of the night was uneventful. It even reminded Landry of going fishing; sometimes you caught something and sometimes you didn't. The next morning, after a night full of only short catnaps, Heraldo and Landry sent out the helicopter to recover the various drones, scattered over what was by then, a three-hundred-mile area. They didn't have the capacity, in their present level of activity, to recharge sufficiently. So, they had decided to bring them in and charge them, just in case they couldn't do so later on. Within a few hours, the drones were refueled and back in place. As always, waiting was the hardest part of the hunt. The nervous energy spent doing so, was as draining as the active phase of it; even to professionals like Heraldo and Landry.

When the alarm sounded again for the nuclear sub, at around one o'clock in the afternoon, it brought some much-needed excitement and relief. As expected, it was heading north-northwest; confirming Landry's theory and marking the beginning of a welcomed pattern. Being able to predict the movement of their target, especially in the underwater world, was a considerable advantage.

Course corrections to the old rust bucket's heading were made as they didn't want to raise any curiosity from the American nuclear sub by sitting in one location. Detecting them would be a piece of cake for the state–of-the-art war machine, so blending in as a fisherman's support boat was the key to their survival. Thankfully, the nuclear sub proved to be dependable in its behavior and just like the day before, it simply disappeared once again from their detection devices only a couple of hours later.

Chapter 25

Upon speaking with the President about the latest events regarding the missing nukes, General Paten had been given strict instructions to make sure that the entire affair with the Iranians was dealt with promptly and kept extremely discreetly. His orders were to, at all costs, sink the Iranian submarine. Paten had also been directed to eliminate Heraldo and Landry if at all possible, especially if the two men were unable to terminate the Iranians and still had a warhead in their possession. Under no circumstances, would it be acceptable to have a nuke uncontrolled.

With full knowledge that Landry and Heraldo were going to try to stop the Iranian submarine before it entered the Mediterranean Sea, Paten had come to the same conclusion regarding its refueling and had therefore made the only logical choice. Heraldo and Landry would simply have to be casualties of this little war; discarded with prejudice if they even entered the nuclear submarine's range. The bottom of the ocean would be the final resting place of Paten's adversaries and would provide a discreet end to this unfortunate ordeal; at least that's what Paten was hoping for.

It was around eleven o'clock that night when Landry and Heraldo finally detected the Iranian submarine for the first time. It had been hugging the coast of Africa and was about twenty miles away. It appeared to be slowing down, as a small boat, not unlike the one they were piloting, made its way towards it from the shore. Landry immediately directed the aquatic drones to form a cone pattern towards the north, to try to detect the American submarine which would without a doubt come lurking. Heraldo knew luck was on their side, due to how close the Iranians were from the shore. The sub had come within five miles of one of their drones, having been hugging the ocean floor up to that point, obviously to avoid detection.

Landry and Heraldo turned their boat around and made a direct heading for the port of Nouadhibou; almost in the exact direction of where the submarine was surfacing. They were only fifteen miles away and knew they could cover the distance in about an hour. Unfortunately, they weren't the only ones. The American sub, as if on cue, had popped up fifty miles or so to their north-northwest and was heading straight for their present location. All of a sudden, things got very busy and very complicated. Decisions had to be made instantly. If the Americans had confirmed their identity, they would have probably already been blown to smithereens, courtesy of one of their onboard missiles, which Landry and Heraldo were positive they carried. The two men quickly decided that more than likely, the Americans were too focusing on the surfaced Iranian sub. But they were well-aware that wouldn't be the case for long.

Suddenly, Heraldo had a thought and quickly shared it with Landry. What if the Americans intended to sink the Iranian sub underwater and were simply coming closer to their prey, so they could more easily choose when and where to make their final blow? After all, it hadn't been too difficult for the CIA to locate the resupply vessel for the submarine in Mauritania. Any foreigner, buying a large amount of fuel in that part of the world, was bound to attract attention and indeed, they had. Two American agents had been dispatched to Nouadhibou and had kept close tabs on the loading of oil drums and the subsequent departure of the small cargo vessel. That information had been quickly relayed to Washington and transferred to the local asset; the nuclear submarine by the name of "The Barracuda". Heraldo signaled their helicopter to head for shore and land somewhere inconspicuous. He knew there was no need to attract attention from anyone at this point. The dice had been rolled.

Landry and Heraldo were stunned at the speed of the American submarine. At forty knots, it would soon overtake their position. The Barracuda's plans were relatively simple: get within ten miles of the Iranians, wait for them to dive and follow them until they reached the Canary Islands. Then, when they reached relatively shallow waters, they would sink them at close range with a torpedo, set on proximity detonation. They wanted just enough power to knock out the sub and sink it, not to destroy it completely, as they fully intended to salvage the nuke onboard.

Part of that strategy became apparent to Landry, when he noticed the nuclear submarine suddenly stop and stand idle, as if watching its prey and ready to pounce. Its name fit well. Landry had slowly changed their course, careful to avoid getting too close to the Iranian sub, which was less than eight miles from them at that very moment. An hour passed: tense and uncomfortable for all onboard. The thought of the American war machine lurking in the depths close by, made their situation rather precarious. Thankfully, the Barracuda's attention had only been focused on its Iranian prey so far. The Iranians appeared to have completed their refueling and were moving north again at about eight knots. Twenty minutes later, the Americans also resumed their pursuit at a distance of about ten miles, hugging the bottom of the ocean.

Heraldo and Landry had to make some decisions. Obviously, Paten had decided to take matters into his own hands by sending a sub. The question remained; did they still have a deal or had their agreement only been a plot to shake them out of hiding so they could finish them off? There was only one way to find out. The next hour was spent recovering one of the drones with the helicopter and rigging their old ship for the next phase of their plan. Time was of the essence, if they had any hope of catching up with the Iranians. The men worked feverishly to make the rust bucket remotely controlled. The servos were attached to the wheel and throttle and the sonar detector and guidance computer of a recovered drone were both installed quickly. The old boat was now completely able to steer itself with a small laptop onboard. It would be more than capable of directing itself towards the Iranian submarine.

In a couple of quick trips, Landry, Heraldo and all of their men evacuated the boat via the mini-sub and headed back towards the mother-submarine. The helicopter pilot was told to head for the islands of Cape Verde where he would be recovered later. The chase was on. At twelve knots, which was the top speed of the old rust bucket, it would take close to two hours to catch up. They followed the old boat; the mother-sub's equipment keeping close tabs. The Captains of both the Iranian and American submarines became quickly aware of the small, noisy vessel slowly approaching them. The Iranians were sailing at periscope depth and didn't resist the temptation to view their pursuer, once the rust bucket came within their range of sight, just a couple of miles behind them.

At that point, the old boat had already overshot the American submersible and its presence had created quite a stir onboard. The Captain of the ship was extremely aggravated by this occurrence. The small, noisy boat threatened to ruin their plans and action had to be taken. He knew it must be the other party he had been informed of; the ones that also needed to be eliminated. The easiest thing would have been to simply torpedo the motherfuckers and get it over with, but that wasn't an option. He didn't want to alert the Iranians of their presence. As soon as he thought of the more discrete scheme, he promptly gave orders to his second in command who, in turn, couldn't help but stare at his captain with raised eyebrows.

"I want to come behind that boat from underwater, and ram it from the back; hard enough to sink them," the Captain commanded. "Keep our exposed time to a minimum. This is the only shot we have to get rid of them and not alert the Iranians to our presence. The second in command had not been briefed on the details of the mission, so he was rather surprised at this new and very unorthodox way of discarding of an enemy. He wasn't so much worried about their sub, which could easily take the floating tin can out without any structural damage. But he was certainly concerned about the damage to some sensors and other controls; a few of which would very likely become incapacitated by this bumper-car action. However, he wasn't about to contradict his captain. He immediately gave the orders for the Captain's instructions to be carried out. At least it would be a good exercise for his men in maneuvering in tight quarters.

The unmanned rust bucket was merrily cruising along at full speed with heavy black smoke billowing from its stack when the large gray submarine slowly approached it from behind, from the depths of the sea, like a shark seeking its prey. In a state-of-the-art maneuver, the sub's nose rose above the water, just behind the transom of the small boat, overtaking and crushing it as the force of gravity pulled the massive submarine back into its element. The small ship never stood a chance. Damaged beyond repair and pushed under the ocean's water, it would never resurface.

Onboard the Iranian sub, its captain had been keeping a close eye on the approaching small vessel, when suddenly it disappeared right in front of his very eyes. He wasn't quite sure what had happened. All he knew was that it had vanished in mere seconds, without any plausible explanation whatsoever. Total silence replaced the heavy beats of the diesel engine's rotating propeller. No flash or explosion had taken place. It was, by all accounts, the oddest thing the Captain had ever witnessed.

Onboard the American submarine, orders were given to minimize all engine noises and quickly submerge below several thermal layers of water. They didn't want to be detected by sonar, if the Iranians decided to actively seek out what had happened. That was indeed the Iranian's next move.

The pinging sounds of the powerful sonar's sound waves could be heard all the way to Heraldo's submarine. However, all that came back to the Iranian sub was a sea of emptiness. The Iranian captain knew that apparently, the small boat had already reached the depths of the ocean and it seemed nothing else was out there. He ordered the acoustic device shut down and proceeded to resume their course at normal speed. The American sub remained undetected, due to its hull made of the special rubber-like coating and its latest evasive maneuver as well. Landry and Heraldo had witnessed the whole scene with their passive acoustic detectors. Landry couldn't help but admire the bold move from the Americans; a textbook ramming, reminiscent of ancient maritime warfare. The American sub had practically stopped moving, hovering a couple of miles ahead of them at about a fifteen-hundred-foot depth. It was very difficult to detect them without the use of their sonar, due to the American sub's flexible and sound-absorbing coating which made it extremely quiet; even with pressure-changing stress and other internal noises.

"They're waiting for the Iranian sub to be out of range," said Landry.

"I guess we know now that our deal with Paten was just a ploy to uncover us and finish us off," said Heraldo. Landry nodded his head slowly in response.

Suddenly, the noise signature of the American sub became greatly magnified. They were back on the prowl, but still holding at a fifteen-hundred-foot depth. Landry and Heraldo looked at each other and without the exchange of one word, knew what their next move was. The American support vessel; sure to come, would be looking for the nuke in the wreckage of the small ship. Once they were unable to find it, which could take a while considering the nine-thousand-foot depth of their present location, a renewed search would be initiated for them. What they needed was a final solution; a way to permanently erase all tracks of their activity.

Landry ordered the submarine to follow the Americans in a parallel course far below them, making sure to avoid a direct line of sight by hiding in the numerous canyons and valleys nestled on the floor of this part of the ocean. They played a game of hide and seek that the Americans hadn't actively engaged in since the cold war; at least not with a worthy opponent. Thankful for the slow-going Iranians, Landry and Heraldo were able to pass the Americans on their side. Once they overtook the Iranian's location as well, by a solid ten miles, they slowly placed themselves deep into the canyon, right below their expected course.

Their last remaining warhead was placed into the deep-water survival pod, the only thing they had that was capable of withstanding the tremendous pressure of their present location. The nuke was set to its maximum explosive capacity, one hundred and fifty kilotons, and a remote trigger device was installed against the glass of the pod, connected to the warhead itself. The set-up was rigged to explode when the American submarine came within about four miles of the bomb, with the Iranians about six miles away. Once all was set, they ejected the pod, which sank to the bottom. At first, they left the area slowly, hiding as best they could. By the time both the Iranian and American subs were nearly in position, Landry knew that they needed to increase their speed if they were going to escape the blast area. Risking detection, he ordered the mother-sub to speed up to twelve knots of speed, while still taking refuge the best they could, among the small peaks and valleys at the bottom of the ocean. They had about forty minutes to get away and reach a safer twenty miles distance from the epicenter of the explosion.

The minutes raced by and all onboard were very aware of the possible impending doom that was to come. With only twenty minutes to go, Landry made the decision to increase their speed to twenty-five knots, their maximum velocity. It became obvious to them that they wouldn't reach the safe zone. Their only hope was to take cover behind a large enough hill to deflect some of the effects of the tremendous shockwave.

Onboard the Barracuda, an alarm sounded. Something was moving very fast and diagonally away from them. The signals were intermittent and nothing like the signatures they had in their computer files. The Captain was tempted to light it up with sonar, but knew that doing so would announce his presence to the Iranians: the primary focus of his mission. But, it didn't make any sense. He knew nothing could operate at that depth, especially not manned and certainly not that big. The decision was made to release a drone torpedo, equipped with cameras and explosives and capable of self-guidance. Programmed to seek out the large moving mass, it was released and wouldn't become active for a solid fifteen minutes, giving it enough distance to avoid detection by the Iranian submarine.

With five minutes to go, Landry squeezed the maximum speed out of the large submarine. A small object had just been detected coming from the position where the Americans had been not long before. He had no doubt that they had been detected and were facing an imminent attack. With that in mind, Landry plunged the sub into a Canyon, changing course forty-five degrees, hoping that the maneuver would buy them some time. Heraldo tapped Landry on the shoulder and pointed at the clock; only ten seconds before the explosion. Landry made his last maneuver and bottomed the submarine in the silt, behind an underwater hill. He hoped it would protect them enough.

The shockwave came like a giant earthquake, buckling the earth underneath them and sending those onboard up off of their feet and sideways. Alarms sounded everywhere, but they were still alive. From a quick, sideways look at his monitors, Landry saw the ship's integrity was okay too.

Not so for the American submarine. At less than two mile from the center of the blast, it literally imploded; sending its occupants to their maker instantly. Subsequent explosions from the various weapons onboard disintegrated the enormous hull into sections so small, it was as if they were from an average large plane crash. The destruction of its nuclear weapons sent a rain of radioactive material all over the bottom of the ocean floor.

The Iranians fared somewhat better since they were further from the explosion, with a less-exposed area to the shockwave, their sub began to take on water immediately. None would survive to see another hour, let alone another day. They slowly sunk and would soon reach crushing depth. Landry and Heraldo had been lucky once again. The torpedo sent after them was completely incapable of withstanding the extreme pressures they were currently at and the additional nuclear chock wave and its guidance system, damaged by the blast, sent it to join the fate of the Iranian vessel, crushed by the jaws of the ocean's weight.

After a fast overall check of the mother-sub, Heraldo and Landry were painfully aware that the Americans would be looking for their submarine fairly quickly. They needed to get the hell out of there, but not before removing the Iranian submarine. They didn't want to leave any telltale signs of what had transpired. The Russian-made sub was in better condition than expected; crushed at the aft, but still structurally whole, even though it had been breached by water in its entirety due to the rapidity of the events. Neither Heraldo nor Landry wanted to leave the remaining nuke. They quickly decided rather than taking the time to remove it right there, they would tow the entire sub back to their underworld lair. It took about thirty minutes to hook up the cable with the robotic drone, to the Iranian vessel. They headed back to home base, slowly picking up speed with their cargo in tow.

Paten had been monitoring the events from his office in the Pentagon, up to the pursuit of the small boat and its destruction. Shortly thereafter, he had lost signal from their nuclear submarine. A satellite monitoring the area had been able to pinpoint the exact location where the events had taken place. It revealed the first images of an ever-expanding water vapor cloud rising from the ocean. It also detected a substantial rise in the water level, spreading in a wave-like fashion from an epicenter. Paten didn't need to see anymore to know what had happened. A nuke had gone off and by the looks of things, he was doubtful anyone in the area could have survived it. The blast was so strong that seismographs all around the world detected it and an assumption was made that it had been a small earthquake, off of the coast of the Canary Islands.

Paten immediately ordered the Navy's salvage boats, already within five hundred miles, to proceed to the location, recover their submarine and investigate the incident. Over the course of the next few days, multiple scans of the area located some of the remains of the nuclear submarine, but they quickly opted to scrap the recovery, as no bodies and nothing worth salvaging were found; not even what was the equivalent of the submarine's black box. A secondary explosion onboard had pulverized all of the sensitive computer equipment and the last seconds of the submarine's activity would forever remain unknown. Paten, in his report to the President, concluded that the Iranians, realizing they had been found out, had decided to end their lives and had taken the Navy's submarine with them by detonating their warhead. The case was officially closed, with all responsible parties presumed dead. The public was never made aware of the events, as the missing nukes shortly and suddenly appear to be found in Cuba, putting an end to Paten's inquiry. Paten however, wasn't entirely convinced that all of the players had been dispatched. But he was certainly in no position to resume his investigation. A few months later, he went into retirement, after receiving a new medal from the President and a second star.

Landry and Heraldo, after five days of smooth and quick sailing through the ocean's depths, finally made it back to their homestead in the crater of their volcano. The Iranian submarine was towed safely inside of their underwater docking pod and was stripped of any useful instrumentation and equipment. The bodies found onboard couldn't be released into the ocean, for fear of later discovery. So, they were processed in the anaerobic digester, fully recycled into energy and food for their underwater world. The warhead was removed and studied. Landry was highly interested in what the Iranians had done to it to boost its yield. He discovered they had added a third stage to its design. Heraldo and Landry weren't quite sure what to do with the bomb, but decided to keep it as it was. After all, it could prove to be useful in the future.

It was put into safe storage, buried in the vault behind the tons and tons of gold and pretty much forgotten. Over the next several months, Heraldo and Landry settled into their new homes, living as farmers and winemakers. From time to time, they took trips in their submarine, seeking out lost shipwrecks and their valuables. Sometimes they even ventured onto land, visiting the small, neighboring islands of Cape Verde, under the cover of being Canadian tourists sailing the oceans of the world. Those visits allowed them to replenish their supplies and enjoy real sunlight, a meal in the open air and the sight of other people before they always headed back to their underwater world. However, it wouldn't be too long before the need for revenge for his brother and his family's death ate at Heraldo's tormented conscience.

He had traded with the devil; and by doing so, had negated his brother's demise. He cringed to know he had even profited from it. True, his brother could never be brought back to life but his brother's killers: Ernesto Castillo and his men would one day pay for it, with more than just money. Of that, Heraldo was sure.